# FIRST LIGHT

## HEARTSVILLE #2

### CHRISTINA LEE
### FELICE STEVENS

Published by Christina Lee and Felice Stevens in The United States of America

Cover Art by Reese Dante

www.reesedante.com

Photography by Eric David Battershell

www.ericbattershellphotography.com

Edited by Keren Reed

www.kerenreed.com

Copyediting provided by Flat Earth Editing.

www.flatearthediting.com

Proofreading provided by Lyrical Lines.

www.lyricallines.net

# 1

## OLIVER

Oliver pulled into First Light, a produce farm in Heartsville, which was a quaint little town tucked away in the Pocono Mountains of Pennsylvania. His hands were trembling on the steering wheel, his pulse thumping in his throat. Would Aubrey Hendricks appreciate the reason for his visit, or would he turn him away?

The transplant coordinator from the hospital had assured Oliver the Hendricks family was open to meeting the donor recipients, but maybe that wasn't such a great idea after all. She hadn't mentioned the farm directly, and the number he'd been given must've been a landline, because it rang ceaselessly. Now it made sense that the man was rarely at home. Oliver had looked him up in the spirit of paying it forward, wanting the widowed man to know how grateful he was to be alive. Except...maybe it would be too painful for him to remember the car crash that took his wife two years prior.

As his Mercedes crunched over fallen leaves and twigs down the gravel driveway, he passed a wooden Help Wanted sign bolted to a post and noted the large farmhouse with the darkened windows. It might be too late for visitors. Maybe he should find a motel and wait until morning. But he was itching to get out of the vehicle and move his legs; he'd been driving for two hours straight.

According to the website, which was rudimentary at best, First Light was a year-round seasonal farm featuring fresh produce and flowers for sale as well as a small bakery. Photos displayed strawberries and blueberries in the summer, apples and pumpkins in the fall, and pine trees in the winter. And given the baskets of blooming tulips, hyacinths, and daffodils hanging from hooks around the property, along with the lingering scent of lilacs, he would guess they even stocked up in spring. Sliding out of the car, he breathed in the sweet scents and settled on taking a chance, no matter the outcome.

A successful mergers and acquisitions attorney in New York City, Oliver had always imagined retiring into a simpler life in a picturesque small town. Not that he was anywhere near retirement at age forty-five. But once his cardiomyopathy—which the doctor explained was a weakening of the heart muscle—was discovered, and he was told he might not last another year without a transplant, he knew he had to make some significant changes.

He was assured the odds were good once he was placed on the transplant list. Still, the idea of enjoying life again after such a devastating scare felt surreal.

"If you can afford it," Dr. Smith had said when Oliver was in recovery, "you should take the time to do some things on your bucket list."

"I hear you, Doc." The weeks following the transplant had been touch-and-go, the odds of his body rejecting the organ frightening him enough to follow medical instructions to the letter. "I always knew I'd walk away from that high-stress environment, so now might be the perfect time."

Once he was released from the hospital, the kind of life he'd led for the better part of twenty years just didn't feel like him anymore. Not after being so near death. His colleagues threw him a lavish farewell party and wished him well. Though he still kept in touch with a couple of them, they inevitably grew apart, and he didn't feel they had much in common anymore.

His last relationship had ended before he became ill, and he certainly wasn't in the right frame of mind to fold someone else into his life when he didn't even recognize himself anymore. So he traveled a bit and visited his family in Westchester more than usual. He'd taken culinary classes this past year, plugging into interests he'd forgotten he had until given a large enough chunk of time to consider them. He maintained a steady workout routine to keep his heart ticking, even if it was on borrowed time.

And though he appreciated being given a second chance at life, he was also getting pretty antsy, which was why he'd decided to get in his car and hit the road, this time with a specific destination in mind. Besides, how many more cookies could he bake and give away before he succumbed to temptation and ate entire batches himself? Or muffins and cakes, for that matter? He was terrible in general with idle time, and his sister, Jennifer, immediately guessed something was up when he'd spoken to her just an hour before.

"Do you think I'm making a mistake showing up like this?" he'd asked.

"Not sure," she'd replied in a hesitant voice. "You never know how people are going to respond to this type of thing. He knew his wife's organs were being donated, and he gave permission to be contacted, but be prepared to get the door slammed in your face. What was it the coordinator said about the husband?"

"To keep in mind that Aubrey Hendricks is a grieving spouse and to take that into consideration. She wasn't allowed to say more, but there was something in her tone...which I guess could've meant anything," Oliver had reiterated. "But it made me feel like he might not exactly be an open book."

His sister sighed. "Tread carefully, Oliver."

Oliver scaled the steps to the porch and knocked on the door, but there was no answer.

He tried again, and again nothing. Maybe it *was* too late.

Just as he was getting back into his car, the sound of a motor pierced the silence. A man appeared from over the hilltop, riding a four-wheeler. As he parked the vehicle on a patch of grass a short distance away, he narrowed his eyes suspiciously at the stranger on his property.

Oliver noted his large frame, the brown, wavy hair beneath his ball cap, and the hardened eyes looking him up and down. Damn, he did not look friendly. That frown on such a handsome face was totally disconcerting.

He cleared his parched throat. "Are you Aubrey Hendricks?"

Oliver lifted his hand in a wave as the man approached. A moment of wariness flitted through his gaze before he barked out a response. "That's right. You here for the job?" There was a hopeful lilt in the question—either that or Oliver was reading into it too much.

"Uh..." Oliver stuttered, and he couldn't fathom why the word "no" hadn't sprung from his mouth immediately. He certainly wasn't looking for work on a farm, but he couldn't help being curious—about so many things. "My name is Oliver Hansen. How come you've got an opening?"

"The bakery hasn't been in operation for some time now, and we wanted to make a go of it again. Folks around here been missing our fresh-baked goods," Aubrey grunted as his penetrating eyes inspected Oliver. He found he didn't enjoy the scrutiny, so he stood taller, wanting to prove something to him. Who the hell knew the reason why? Despite being nearly six feet tall, he only reached the height of the man's chin, and Aubrey probably had fifty pounds on him as well. Still, Oliver had always kept himself fit, even more so after the transplant.

"What exactly would I be doing?" The question rolled too easily off his tongue. It was unfair to feign interest, but his curiosity got the best of him, especially when he looked beyond Aubrey's shoulder at the picturesque countryside—or at least what he could make out in the dusk. He bet it was even prettier in the fall.

"*Baking*," the man snapped, staring at him suspiciously. "Running the kitchen."

"Of-of course," Oliver stammered, feeling the color bloom on his cheeks.

"Pies were my wife's specialty." Aubrey's voice hitched on that last word, and Oliver felt his heart thump in his throat. Holy shit, his wife. The man was definitely surly, but grief always had a way of sneaking inside any tough exterior. "We still have her recipes, but I'm sure you've got your own style."

"If the residents have been asking, her recipes might be a good starting point." What in the hell was he even saying? He definitely loved baking and had excelled at making all sorts of desserts in the culinary classes he'd signed up for, but to actually create pies and whatever else for a business was ludicrous at best. So why did the idea of it give Oliver a little thrill? He loved a challenge, and the words left his lips before he had the chance to consider what he was getting himself into. "I'll take the job. I mean, unless you have other candidates to consider."

*For Christ's sake.* Oliver was supposed to show up, thank the man for the heart now ticking in his chest and keeping him alive, and then be on his way. But something in the set of Aubrey's jaw told him there was a story there—way more than he was willing to share—and it piqued his curiosity. He was always able to read people pretty well, which probably helped in the courtroom. Aubrey Hendricks kept a protective barrier around himself, but there was also sadness in the slope of his shoulders, and the bags beneath his eyes indicated he barely slept. Was he haunted by grief or guilt? Or just exhausted from the sheer effort of running this farm?

Regardless, he needed help, and it was the least Oliver could do. He practically owed the man his life. And didn't it just figure that the woman who gave him her heart also loved to bake? There had to be some sort of blind luck in that.

Aubrey inhaled deeply as if in relief, then set his jaw firmly again. His gaze seemed to scrutinize Oliver's black Mercedes before snagging on his expensive white sneakers. He wished they were a bit more scuffed up. "I'll have to let you know."

Oliver got the impression Aubrey didn't want to appear too eager. Either that, or he didn't think someone like Oliver was up to the task. And that only made him want the job more.

"Okay, then. I'm staying at the Clover Motel," Oliver replied, opening his car door. He'd passed the travel lodge on his way to the farm and remembered the vacancy sign. "I'm, um, new in town, and I haven't found the right place yet. So...you'll know where to find me."

Oliver could feel Aubrey's gaze on him as he backed out of the dusty driveway. He suddenly wished he owned a more average vehicle. But damn it, he'd earned this luxury.

Once back on the road, his breathing finally returned to normal. He could always drive straight out of town and chalk the visit up to some aberration. In fact, he didn't have to lay eyes on Aubrey Hendricks ever again. So why didn't he seem to be able to shake the man from his thoughts?

By the time he turned into the parking lot of the Clover Motel, he'd made up his mind. He'd stay put in Heartsville for at least another day.

## 2

## AUBREY

Being out in the fields didn't help. Neither did tending to the flowers, making lists of what fruits to plant for the upcoming season, or any of the things he normally did to take his mind off the yawning black hole of emptiness his life consisted of now. Those had been things he and Lisa had shared. He'd pick the strawberries and bring them in a big bucket to the bakery, where she and Cassie, her assistant, would be elbow-deep in flour and sugar. He'd drop off the fruit, steal a kiss and a few berries, and leave, not heeding her threats of, "Don't think 'cause you're cute, you get the first taste." Knowing she would save him the first piece of whatever pie she'd baked for the day.

Grief overwhelmed him, and he stopped the four-wheeler, his vision blurry with the tears he didn't dare shed in public. Two years she'd been gone, and yet he still heard her voice singing in the shower or laughing with Cassie in the bakery over some silly joke.

He needed to move on, but his heart was frozen in time. He had no idea how to take that first step.

The farm was suffering too, and though it nearly brought him to his knees to reopen the bakery, he knew he had to start somewhere. Putting the Help Wanted ad in the local paper for a baker was the beginning. What he hadn't anticipated was such a quick response. And this guy showing up yesterday, unannounced? Well, it seemed awful strange, but what did he know? He'd seemed a little tongue-tied and confused. *Chances are*, Aubrey thought, staring off across the fields, *I'll never hear from him again.*

Twilight settled in, finding him in his usual spot on his front porch, feet up on the railing, and his mutt, Duke, roaming the yard, sniffing at God knows what in the bushes, when Carol from the general store a few miles down the road pulled into the driveway. He stood while Duke rushed up to greet her, his stubby tail wagging.

"Evening, Aubrey."

"How are you, Carol? Come on inside. I was just enjoying a little quiet time."

Her eyes sparkled with laughter. "Until I came by and ruined it for you?"

*Damn.* "I didn't mean it that way."

"Don't worry." She followed him up the creaking wooden steps, and he held the front door open for her. As she passed by, she said, "I was kidding you. I came to see how you were."

"Same as yesterday." *And the days and weeks and months before that.* "Have a seat. Do you want some coffee or an iced tea?"

She took the club chair, and Aubrey the sofa across from her. Over the past two years since Lisa died, he hadn't had many visitors. Maybe it was because he didn't know how to respond when people told him how sorry they were. He'd never been one for making friends. Lisa had been the social one, and if their house had been filled with people for card games or trivia night, they were her friends. Aubrey preferred to remain in the background, speaking when spoken to. Conversation came hard to him. That was why he preferred animals. They loved unconditionally and responded without a whole lot of verbal communication.

"I'm good, thanks. You had a visitor yesterday, right?"

Aubrey wasn't surprised in the least that Carol knew. In Heartsville, with its population of nosy to the thousands, nothing could remain quiet for long.

"Yeah. Someone came by about the bakery job. Drove up in a big fancy car, so I'm not sure he'd be a right fit."

"I spoke to him earlier. He'd stopped by to pick up a few things, and we had a chat."

And in spite of himself, Aubrey couldn't help being a bit intrigued. "Oh?" He tried to sound nonchalant, but he wanted to hear what Carol had to say. "You met Oliver? What'd he say?"

"That he was from New York City but was looking for a simpler way of life. Destressing, I think he said. He spent time as a child in the Poconos with his parents—they had a weekend house, and he and his family would go swimming, fishing, and hiking."

His memory of the man was that he didn't seem the type to ever have gotten down in the dirt. His tight, dark jeans had shown off a nice, trim body, and Aubrey imagined he spent time in one of those expensive gyms.

Uncomfortable with the recollection, Aubrey shifted in his seat. It had been years since he'd thought about a man sexually. Not since he and Lisa decided to get married. She'd known from the start he was bisexual and that he'd had a few dates with men but only one relationship, with Elliot, his first and only boyfriend. Not that he didn't admire a good-looking man every now and then, but when he fell in love with Lisa, everyone else ceased to exist.

"Well, we talked a bit about the job, but I couldn't get a handle on him. It almost seemed as though he wasn't sure he wanted it."

"Oh, really?" Carol's brows knitted together. "He seemed pretty interested when we spoke. We were sharing recipes for crusts earlier."

"I don't know," Aubrey said, once again recalling the momentary confusion in Oliver's eyes when he'd asked him about the job. "There's something about him. I can't put my finger on it, though."

"Aubrey, can I be blunt?"

Having an idea what Carol was about to say, Aubrey shrugged. "Go on. I'm listening."

"It's time. I know how much you loved Lisa. And believe me, she loved you with all her heart. That's why I know she would want you to do this. Start living again. It'll never be the same, but you can make it work as well in a different way. Baking was something she loved doing, and bringing the bakery back to life would not only be a great first step, but it would honor her memory."

"That's the problem. I don't know if I'm ready to take that step yet."

"I have to get back home, but you think about it. And call Oliver. Maybe let him do a test run for you."

Aubrey walked her out to her car. "Thank you. I appreciate you coming by. I wish I could say I know what I'm going to do next, but I can't. Not yet."

She gave him a brief hug. "Follow your heart."

With Duke by his side, Aubrey watched the taillights recede and fade into the darkness. "Come on, boy. Time to head inside." He hadn't had a decent night's sleep since Lisa passed, and the early morning dawn often found him back on the porch, staring out into the fields.

Aubrey puttered around the kitchen, cleaning up his one dish and fork. Microwaved food was quick but didn't inspire him to eat, and he'd lost a good ten pounds in the past two years. He hitched up his jeans, which kept slipping to his hips. A wave of exhaustion came over him, and shaking, he braced himself against the counter.

"I can't do this anymore. I can't."

He grabbed his phone and looked up the Clover Motel. The line rang only once before someone picked up.

"Clover Motel."

"Hey, Lucas. It's Aubrey over here at First Light." He swallowed hard, hesitating a moment, knowing that once he did this, things would never be the same. "Is there an Oliver Hansen registered?"

"Oh, yeah. He came in yesterday."

"Can you connect me, please?"

"Sure thing. Hold on."

A few clicks and then Aubrey heard the ringing in his ear. His hand was sweating so much, the phone slipped.

"Hello?"

"Uh, hello. Is this Oliver Hansen?"

"Yes?"

Aubrey sensed the man had no idea who he was. "It's Aubrey Hendricks. From the farm? We talked yesterday about you taking the bakery position?"

"Oh, um, yeah. Right."

"I was wondering if you'd like to maybe come by tomorrow. You could do a test run and see if you think it would work."

"Uh, yeah, sure. I guess. Do you need me to bring anything?"

"Just the ingredients of what you'd be making. I have all the equipment you'll be needing."

"Okay. What time?"

"I'm up at five a.m.—"

"Uh, okay, I suppose I can do that, except the general store probably doesn't open until—"

Aubrey couldn't help but chuckle at Oliver's panicked voice. "Anytime after nine works fine. The store opens at eight, just so you know. How's that sound?"

"Perfect. Thanks for calling, Aubrey."

"See you tomorrow."

*Follow your heart,* Carol had said earlier. Aubrey wasn't sure he could follow something he'd already lost.

## OLIVER

Aubrey Hendricks had actually called. Oliver could scarcely believe it. He'd been losing his mind in Heartsville without a solid plan. He should've just told the man about how his wife helped save his life and been done with it.

But then he'd tooled around the quaint streets and shops and found that they appealed to something deeper inside him. The slower rhythm of the small-town life brought him a sense of serenity, one he wasn't accustomed to, and it made him want more of it.

Unlike a large metropolis, where the pace was too fast for niceties, most everyone was friendly in Heartsville, if a bit nosy. Like the conversation with a woman named Carol at the general store. In five minutes flat, she had practically gotten Oliver to confess his whole life story. A few seconds more and he would've probably admitted everything about the heart condition and transplant. Thankfully, he was able to steer the conversation toward favorite recipes in anticipation of the phone call he figured would never come.

The relief was instant the moment he heard Aubrey's voice, but then guilt and anxiety set back in. What in the hell was he doing pretending not only that he could run a bakery, but that he had just wandered into town, looking to start a new life? At least Carol had given Oliver more insight into the kind of man Aubrey Hendricks was. Hardworking, stubbornly quiet as he grieved his wife's death, and didn't easily ask for help. That last bit might've been the clincher for him, because at least they had that in common. He hated to put anyone out, and that made him want to help the man more than anything. And maybe also prove something—not only to Aubrey, but to himself.

What exactly, he wasn't sure yet.

In the morning, he headed outside to where his shiny Mercedes was parked in the motel lot, and for the second time considered it a flashy eyesore against the backdrop of the quaint, older town. The car had been a gift to himself for his fortieth birthday, but after everything he'd been through, he realized how it paled in comparison to being given a second chance at life.

On the way to the general store, he passed a Victorian-style house for rent and imagined what it might be like to live there for a little while. When his cell buzzed, he shook away the ridiculous thought.

"Hey, sis," he said as he picked up the call. He'd avoided her call yesterday, needing time to think some things through, but now she'd be sure to set him straight. And that was exactly what he needed. Wasn't it?

"So how did it go?" she asked as he passed a bar named Last Call and absently wondered if he should stop for a cold one later.

"I didn't end up telling him," he admitted.

"Why not?" The confusion was clear in her voice.

Oliver winced. "He wasn't very forthcoming...or friendly."

"That's a bummer. At least your intuition was right. Are you back in the city?" she asked, and as embarrassment colored his cheeks, he nearly confessed about the mess he'd gotten himself into.

"Actually, no. I've decided to stay in town for a couple of days.

It's charming here," he replied as he pulled into the grocery-store parking lot. "Remember when we used to go camping in the mountains? How we had so much fun exploring, we didn't want to leave?"

She sighed wistfully as if lost in the memory. They had talked about returning as adults someday, but then life got away from them. He'd done plenty of fascinating things around the world with boyfriends—from Paris to Amsterdam to Hong Kong—but never something as simple as this. It had never felt as necessary or appealing as it did right now.

Their mother had passed away from cancer ten years earlier, and then seeing the grief in his father's eyes when he'd held his hand before the transplant operation had nearly done him in. He knew even then how important it was to step away from his fast-paced life and appreciate the little things. Spend time with his niece and nephew. Make good food from fresh ingredients with his own hands like his mom used to do. He loved sitting on a stool at the counter, watching her. The joy on her face when he got his smaller hands in there after she requested help. Oliver figured it was purposeful on her part.

"So...remember Mom's famous chocolate silk pie?" It was something that had occurred to him last night when Aubrey had mentioned Lisa's pies.

"How could I forget?" She chuckled. "I still have her tin can of recipes tucked away in a cupboard."

"And who's the one who ended up taking culinary classes?" he replied with a laugh. "Do me a favor and look up the ingredients?"

"What are you up to?" she asked, and he heard her digging through her cupboard.

"Not entirely sure." And wasn't that the truth. She'd think he'd lost his damn mind if he told her the real story. "Being here is making me feel nostalgic. Maybe I'll treat myself."

"I do remember her secret ingredient was a scoop of coffee," she said. "Ah, here it is. That mixed with the bittersweet chocolate, heavy cream, and whole butter made it melt in your mouth."

After he jotted down the ingredients on the back of an old receipt he found in his car, he thanked her and then begged off the phone. He didn't want to give her time to knock some sense into him. Not yet.

"Maybe whip up something mouthwatering for Aubrey Hendricks. Like your carrot-cake muffins. Might soften him a bit," she said with a laugh.

Oliver nearly choked on how close to the truth she was.

"You never know," he hummed into the phone.

"You're not serious?" she scoffed. "Oliver, it's probably best—"

"I'm only kidding. But again, you never know," he mused.

He walked up and down the aisles, searching for the ingredients he needed and wishing he wasn't holed up in a motel room. If by chance he was going to stay, he'd definitely consider some rental property. But he was getting ahead of himself. First things first. Baking for Aubrey Hendricks.

He found everything on his list and threw in a muffin recipe as well, figuring he could use the leftover chocolate pieces. Hands gripping the wheel, stomach jittery, he drove up to the farm for the second time in a week.

There was plenty more activity around the farm than two nights before. A guy in overalls and a straw hat was positioned behind a long folding table near a small greenhouse as customers waited in line three-deep to purchase potted plants and flats of daffodils or tulips.

A large scruffy dog came bounding up alongside a woman who looked to be in her thirties. She waved and smiled in his direction, which was a pleasant change from his last greeting at the farm.

"Hi, I'm Cassie," she said as he slid out of the car and the dog nudged at his fingers. "And this is Duke. Are you the baker Aubrey told me about?"

He looked around the property for the man but didn't see him anywhere.

She motioned over her shoulder with her thumb. "He's planting in the strawberry fields to prepare for summer harvest."

He followed her line of sight even though he couldn't quite make out anything over the hills besides what looked like apple and pine trees on the sprawling property. "Strawberries...you said?"

"Yep, it's the one harvest he makes sure to oversee himself. They were Lisa's favorite," she confessed, a wistfulness to her voice. His heart panged as if in response. "Anyway, I've probably said too much."

"No, it's okay," Oliver muttered as he awkwardly toed at a rock on the ground. Shit, this was a mistake. He should just get in his car and drive the hell out of town. He had no right to be here like this, intruding on their private lives. Not when he was alive and Aubrey's wife was dead. "I'll...just come back later or something..."

As he turned to leave, her voice rang out. "Nah, Aubrey told me to expect you. If you follow me to the bakery, I'll get you started."

Taking a deep breath, he turned and trailed behind on unsteady legs to a small, white building beside the greenhouse.

"Here you are."

Oliver stepped inside behind her as she flipped on the light.

It was a warm, inviting space decorated with plaid curtains, honey-colored wood, and mason-jar candles on practically every surface. There was a long counter with a cash register, a glass case with shelves below it that were meant to display baked goods, and a couple of tabletops near the windows.

Behind the counter was the kitchen, and Cassie pushed open the door as she beckoned him to follow. Over her shoulder, he could make out the appliances as well as storage shelves.

He noticed dust motes floating in the air as he stepped into the decent-sized kitchen.

"How long has it been?" he asked, even though he knew the answer. The exact date, in fact. Lisa had died on the day he was told he would live.

"A couple of years," she replied, opening one of the windows to draw out the musty air. "I used to help her run the bakery. It'll be nice to get back in here again."

He glanced around at the preserves on the pantry shelves and at the canisters of flour and sugar, both of which would need to be replaced. "Why haven't you taken on the job?"

"Me?" she asked with a chuckle. "I only work the farm part-time, wherever Aubrey needs me. I've got plenty on my plate with a husband and three kids at home."

"Sorry. I didn't mean to presume."

"Besides," she continued, dipping her head and breathing in the fresh air wafting in from the window, "Aubrey definitely needed...*time*."

Silence descended as she pulled a rag from a drawer and began cleaning the dust off the counter. The dust wasn't substantial, so he wondered if she'd been the one to keep the space tidy until it was time.

*Time. For what?*

His heartbeat rose like a crescendo inside his ears, pounding so hard, he gasped for air.

*Time to help Aubrey Hendricks move on.*

# 4

## AUBREY

He smelled it before anything. The unmistakable scent of vanilla and sugar that could only mean something delicious was baking in the oven. And though his mouth watered from the once-familiar aroma, his eyes stung and he had to stop and pinch the bridge of his nose to hold back the tears. Once he opened the back door to the bakery, he knew it wouldn't be his beloved Lisa at the worktable, with the early morning sunshine in her hair, singing under her breath as she rolled out the crusts.

*Do it already. If not now, when?*

Without allowing himself to dwell on the negative any further, Aubrey took the four steps two at a time, pushed open the bakery door, and stopped short. Despite his earlier misgivings, a smile tugged the corners of his mouth upward.

"Hi," Oliver said with a cheery grin. Flour dusted the bridge of Oliver's nose, and his white baker's hat sat askew on his dark waves. More flour stuck to his cheeks as he rubbed his face, and Aubrey had to suppress a grin. Oliver looked more approachable than the man who'd stood before him the other day in his buttoned-up shirt and shiny sports car.

"Smells good," Aubrey said and circled the long, marble-topped table to join Oliver. "What've you got in the oven?"

"Have a seat while I clean up, and I'll tell you." Oliver rinsed and dried his hands. "I know it looks a little messy, but I've got everything under control."

Aubrey did as asked, trying hard not to stare. Bowls and measuring cups cluttered one side of the worktable, and a layer of flour covered the marble top where Lisa had rolled out her piecrusts.

Cassie came up behind him and murmured in his ear. "He made a chocolate silk pie that I'm dying to taste. I think we have a winner here, Aubrey."

Spying a platter of chocolate muffins, Aubrey reached across the table and picked one up. "May I?" he asked, and at Oliver's nod, took a bite of the muffin top, which was the only part he cared about. Flavor burst on his tongue, and he closed his eyes.

It was like coming home, its sweetness warming his numbed soul. The deep richness of the chocolate melted in his mouth, and he thought he tasted a hint of mocha. It was dense without being chewy, and light without falling apart. Whoever said food was comfort knew what they were talking about. The tightness in his chest loosened, and he breathed easily.

"What do you think?" Oliver gazed at him with worried eyes. "Is it okay?" He caught his full lower lip between his teeth, and Aubrey's heart lurched.

*Damn.* He was supposed to be concentrating on the baked goods, not how soft Oliver's hair looked with the sunlight playing on it. His emotions were already a mess; he didn't need to be thinking about anything but business.

"It's fine," Aubrey huffed out and set down the rest of the muffin. "What else you got?"

"I've got a chocolate pie in the oven. It was my mother's specialty and my favorite as well."

"I've never had that kind. We usually specialize in fruit pies, to take advantage of the harvests." At the sight of Oliver's downcast face, Aubrey heard how grouchy he sounded. He didn't mean to take the wind out of the man's sails. "But, uh, I'm sure customers would love it."

"I can make a mean apple pie. And whatever else is in season."

Pain spread through Aubrey's chest. He heard how short he was in his answers and winced. It wasn't fair to Oliver that Aubrey took out his pain on him, and hiring him to restart the bakery would be a good first step in the letting-go process Carol had mentioned. So even though it hurt his heart, he knew the time had come.

"I think that would be a good idea. As long as I get to be the taste tester." He blinked rapidly, hoping Oliver didn't notice the tears in his eyes.

"Sounds like a challenge. And I accept."

"We'll keep that on the back burner for when the plants start bearing fruit."

"I saw some recipes in the drawer when I pulled out the pans."

He nodded briskly. "Yeah. Those would've been my wife's."

"Lisa?" Oliver blurted out.

Aubrey swayed, his eyes sliding shut for a moment, then reopening when Cassie touched his shoulder. "You okay?"

"Yeah, thanks." He focused on Oliver, who'd begun to clean up the bowls and utensils and place them in the dishwasher. "How did you know her name?"

A strange look passed over Oliver's face. "Um, it was scribbled on top of one of the recipes."

"Gotcha."

Oliver finished loading the dishwasher while Aubrey wandered around the kitchen. Memories assailed him from all sides: his pride when he unveiled the handmade worktable he'd worked on for months to surprise her, the antique stores she scoured to pick up the old-fashioned milk cans to decorate the shop, the strawberry pie she baked for the grand opening...

"Aubrey?" Oliver stood in front of him with a pie in his mitted hands. "It's got to set for a little while, but I can make us coffee, and then I can cut it."

Things were moving so fast. Only three days ago he didn't even know this man, and today they were sitting all cozy in the bakeshop while he pawed through Lisa's things and wanted to bake her pies. Was he expected to turn off the past twenty years of his life and forget?

"Don't think there's coffee here. I'll go back to the house and get some." He adjusted his baseball cap. "Be right back." Without waiting for Oliver to answer, Aubrey hurried out of the bakery and crossed the front yard. Duke bounded over, and the two of them entered the farmhouse. He busied himself in the cupboards, looking for the coffee, when he heard a knock on the door. Duke barked and raced to the front.

"Aubrey?"

He heard Oliver calling, so he traversed the kitchen to the center hall and opened the front door. "Yeah? What is it? I was gonna bring the coffee to you." But it would've been rude to leave Oliver—pie in hand—standing on the porch; he opened the door, and Oliver entered his home, still holding the pie. "You can come in, if you want." Aubrey didn't wait for Oliver to answer and walked away, but he heard footsteps behind him.

"I couldn't find any plates or cutlery to use. I looked but decided maybe you'd put them away after..." He blinked and bit his lip for a moment, and Aubrey's heart hurt.

The night after Lisa died, he went to the bakery, thinking it would give him peace. Instead, he saw her face and heard her voice everywhere. He went to pieces, smashing every plate on the floor, sweeping the glassware off the counter, crying to the wind at the unfairness of it all. Of course, Lisa had been an organ donor, and Aubrey knew it was the right thing to do, but the thought of her body no longer whole devastated him. He spent the rest of the night alternating between pounding his hands on the marble counter and crying inconsolably.

The next morning, he cleaned up the mess, locked the door behind him, and didn't walk back into the building until he decided to place a Help Wanted ad in the paper. He'd seen Cassie going inside occasionally but didn't begrudge her the time alone. She and Lisa were close, and she deserved her own private time and place to grieve as well.

"C'mon in and set it down in here." He led the way back to the kitchen.

"This is a beautiful place. And wow, a real gourmet kitchen. Bet you cook some great meals in here." Once he set the pie plate on a trivet, Oliver walked around. "I love the big farm sink and the beams."

Aubrey wondered if Oliver normally talked this much or if he was simply nervous. He must need the job pretty badly.

"I only use the microwave. Cooking for one's kinda silly, and I don't know how to make anything much 'sides eggs and toast."

"Do you mind?" Oliver held the package of coffee aloft. "I'll do the honors if you want."

"Have at it." He took a seat at the big butcher-block island and watched as Oliver measured out the water and coffee. Soon the rich aroma teased him. It should've seemed strange that Oliver felt at home enough to open the refrigerator and take out the milk. It didn't. It seemed almost comfortable. Like they were friends already. Oliver picked up the little cow Lisa liked to use for the milk.

"This is cute. Can I use it for the milk?"

"Sure."

Peace washed over him, and once again, like earlier, Aubrey breathed easier. It was nice to sit here and share small talk with another person who didn't want to talk about how lonely he must be and how he needed to move on with his life. His parched soul drank in Oliver's chatter about the kitchen.

"If you tell me where your plates are, I can cut us a piece of the pie now."

Pointing to the cabinet over the dishwasher, Aubrey took out some forks and a knife and watched Oliver take out the plates as he continued to talk.

"Okay, here you go. Tell me what you think."

He noticed Oliver didn't take one for himself. Aubrey cut into the pie and took a piece. Smooth and creamy, the chocolate melted in his mouth, and he couldn't help but hum with pleasure.

"Ohhh, damn. This is amazing." Without hesitation, he took another bite and then another until the entire piece was finished. Like he used to do anytime Lisa baked, Aubrey licked the fork clean. He glanced up and found Oliver's eyes on him, watching.

"Uh, how about that coffee?"

A slight blush tinged Oliver's cheeks as he scrambled to the coffeepot and poured a cup for each of them. When he took the chair next to Aubrey's, he asked, "You liked it? It was my mother's specialty."

Aubrey lifted his mug. "To your mom. And to you, the new baker at First Light Farm."

5
___

# OLIVER

Oliver blinked. Running a bakery? What in the hell had he done? He felt like a fraud in front of this grumpy man, who at least looked pleased with his pie. His heart had been beating so hard, it was sweet music to his ears when he heard him say he liked it.

He absolutely should tell Aubrey that he needed to think about the position, and then hightail it out of town. Or tell him the real reason he was there, for God's sake. That look in Aubrey's eyes when he asked how he knew his wife's name nearly did him in. *Fuck.*

He opened his mouth to say something—anything—when the door swung open and Cassie stepped inside. "Hey, no fair. I never got a taste," she said with a pout.

"Sorry about that," Oliver mumbled. "I had to walk over here for some plates, and I guess I sort of made myself at home."

He could see Aubrey swallow roughly as his eyes skirted away, and Oliver realized not only that the comment had unnerved him, but that he was not easily won over, even if he did just offer him a job. That sprang him into action, and he reached for another plate.

"If Cassie loves it," Aubrey mused, "you're a definite shoo-in."

Oliver's nerves jangled all over again as he offered her a slice and Aubrey poured her a cup of coffee. Part of him hoped she didn't like it—but only a very small part. The rest of him was too proud and too excited; somehow he needed to prove that he was worthy of such a job.

He considered the fact that Aubrey never asked for recommendations or even a résumé, which could've immediately sent him packing. Maybe Aubrey was the sort of simple man who relied on his gut instinct. Fine by Oliver—he'd been operating on his for the past twenty-four hours.

Besides, he'd taken countless pastry classes the past year and even bought himself a high-end mixer. Still, none of that proved he could run an entire bakery. He didn't even know how many customers he'd be serving per day. He needed to snap out of it and ask some concrete questions so he knew what he was dealing with.

He held his breath as he watched Cassie take a bite of his pie, and he could feel Aubrey's gaze on him.

"Oh goodness," she said around a mouthful. "I think we need this pie in our lives on a daily basis. Right, Aubrey?"

"Well, I don't think our waistlines will thank us, but it sure is delicious."

Oliver couldn't keep his eyes from darting to Aubrey's flat midsection. The man certainly kept himself fit, and Oliver wondered if it was purely farmwork that created those shoulders and forearms as well. Christ, he needed to cut it out. No way should he be ogling his new boss.

Cassie sighed. "You got that right."

When Aubrey snickered, Oliver's cheeks burned and he averted his eyes.

"I think we rendered the man speechless."

He glanced in Aubrey's direction; his eyebrow was raised, and a smirk lined his lips. It was the first smile he'd seen, and as small as it was, Oliver's new personal goal was to get a full one out of the brooding, handsome man.

"Anyway, gotta get back to work," Aubrey said as if sobering suddenly, the brusqueness back in his voice. "You want the job or not? Cassie can fill you in, but we're open Tuesday to Saturday, eight to four."

There was a moment's hesitation as Oliver considered his family's reaction to this sudden news, but he thrust the thought aside because an overwhelming feeling rose up inside him—he desperately wanted this for himself. And maybe for Aubrey too. Maybe it would help him move on with his life, and Oliver could be the catalyst.

He didn't believe in kismet and all that jazz, so he wouldn't say he had a connection to Aubrey's late wife, Lisa. He was just profoundly grateful to her, and maybe this was his way of repaying her...by helping her adoring husband.

Complete rationalization or not, he wanted this like he wanted his next breath.

"When do I start?"

Cassie clapped excitedly, and Aubrey reached out to shake his hand.

When their palms connected, a shiver raced through Oliver as Aubrey's large, rough fingers engulfed his own. *Nice hands.* He was being ridiculous.

"We should go over the menu, so we can stock up on supplies and do some practice runs," Cassie suggested, and Oliver blew out a breath, glad he'd have her to lead him on this venture. He certainly wouldn't confess that he didn't have the first clue what he was doing, but he was a fast learner, and besides, he'd already tempted fate once. How hard could this be?

*That is so not the point, Oliver.*

Aubrey, who'd left his seat and was already in the hall, turned suddenly, his fingers splayed on the front-door handle. "Only thing I ask is to make the bakery your own. I can...ah, pack up most of Lisa's things in the next couple of days."

Cassie froze as she stared at him, her eyes softening.

"No, I don't have to..."

Cassie placed her hand on Oliver's arm, stilling him as she shook her head in warning.

"All right, then...as long as you're sure," Oliver said, forcing himself not to consider how all the country-style knickknacks lining the shelves must've taken Lisa years to accumulate.

"I'm sure," Aubrey snapped and then strode out the door toward his four-wheeler.

Oliver couldn't help watching him as he climbed on the seat and took off toward the hillside. "Is he always so—"

"Gruff?" Cassie replied with a smirk. "Don't worry. He'll grow on you too. And you already won him over with that killer pie. So it's bound to be mutual. You'll see. He's a good boss. A good man."

"Yeah?" Oliver should've inquired about these things before he took the blasted job. He was doing this all backward. What if he hated the farm or Aubrey was a bear to work for? *What in the hell am I doing?* he asked himself for the millionth time. But it wasn't like he'd made any real plans for after this trip. The trip to meet the husband of his heart donor, for Christ's sake. Now he'd be working for the man.

He hadn't even asked about compensation. Not that it mattered—he was doing fine living off his savings. His career had paid him handsomely, and he had options to fall back on, including selling his stocks or his apartment in the city if it came to that.

Oliver lifted his chocolate silk pie from the counter and placed it in Aubrey's refrigerator. He figured the man might want to snack on it later. And given the bare contents of his shelves, he'd need sustenance.

What was that he said about cooking for one being silly?

Yeah, he got that right. Which was why the idea of feeding

multiple people with his creations was appealing. Feeding *anyone* besides himself was appealing.

"He cares about his employees," Cassie said, snapping him out of his thoughts, which had been sort of on spin cycle ever since he'd arrived in this town. "They're like family to him."

Oliver stared off into the fields, visualizing that compassionate part she was referring to. Obviously, he'd had a wife he missed and loved. And it definitely sounded mutual. Maybe the same sensitivity extended to his employees as well.

"C'mon, I'll show you around the farm."

"Sounds perfect," Oliver replied, following her through the house and out the back door.

# 6

# AUBREY

He drove. He drove and drove, without a destination in mind, yet somehow knew he'd end up here. Aubrey shut off the engine and walked over to the gravesite with its simple granite marker.

"Well, I did it. And I know you're probably thinking, *It's about time, you stubborn man*. But it didn't feel like the right thing to do until now." He touched the top of the stone, a simple brush of the fingertips that still gave him that connection. "Just wanted to tell you." As abruptly as he came, Aubrey turned, jumped back into his truck and left, the wheels spitting gravel.

It felt good to be outside with the wind in his face. Spending that time with Oliver yesterday had woken him up a bit. It had been a while since he'd talked to a man around his own age, and a new face at that. He hadn't made many friends in school, with his family needing him to work on the farm such long hours, and when he and Lisa married so young, her friends became his. The field hands were mostly young seasonal workers, while his manager, George, was older, almost fatherly. Lisa's death had been hard on him too.

Back at the house, he found himself again walking to the

bakery, and when he entered through the front door, he could see Oliver had taken his words to heart. Several large boxes lined the floor, and he'd begun to remove Lisa's knickknacks from the shelves.

"Need any help?"

Oliver jumped and gave him an almost guilty-looking smile. "Uh, sure. If you want."

"Wouldn'ta asked if I didn't mean it." He took off his jacket and tossed it onto a wooden chair. "You can wrap 'em up, and I'll put them in the boxes."

"Sounds good." Oliver handed over the wrapped item he held. "Here you go."

They worked in silence for a minute before Oliver spoke. "How long have you lived here? Did you grow up on the farm?"

"You got a lot of questions, don't you?" But he smirked as he said it, wanting to soften his words.

"Well, I figured if I was gonna work here, I might as well know something about the farm, and since you own it..." He shrugged and reached for the first of the tin milk cans Lisa had lining the second shelf.

"S'okay. My family has owned this farm for generations. I've been living here all my life and working the farm since I was a boy. Back then we also raised chickens, but I didn't want to deal with the mess and the smell, so I cut that out years ago." The memory of it made Aubrey wrinkle his nose, and Oliver chuckled.

"I can imagine. It's much easier working with plants and fruits."

"You got that right." The sun beat warm on his face through the windows, and he took off his baseball cap and tossed it on the chair with his jacket. "Anyway, Lisa and I got married, and we lived here after my parents passed away."

"You never had any children?"

Aubrey shook his head. "No. It never happened for us, and we decided we were fine as is." At one point he'd regretted not having a child, but he wasn't sure he was cut out to be a father. The thought of a tiny person relying on him was terrifying. Plus, his case of mumps in his late twenties had put an end to any thoughts of them having a child. No need to tell Oliver his whole medical history or how he'd always suspected Lisa's parents resented him for not giving them a grandchild. He got the impression they wanted more for her besides living on a farm with a quiet man who'd settled into a simple life. He figured his infertility was icing on the cake.

"Yeah. I get that. My sister has two, and while I love my nephew and niece to pieces, I'm thrilled to be Uncle Oliver who gets to give them back at the end of the day with no responsibilities."

"Where're you from? I realize I didn't ask you any questions about yourself. I know you're not from around here." Aubrey took the first of the milk tins Oliver had wrapped and placed it in the box.

"Nope. I'm from New York. Born and bred. Let's go, Mets."

Aubrey chuckled. "Don't be starting that around here. We got some rabid Phillies fans who might take you out if they heard you."

Oliver snorted, eyes bright with amusement. "Pfft. I can deal with them."

"You'll have to, considering how your guys have played the past few years."

Oliver threw a wadded-up paper towel at him, and Aubrey ducked, laughing. That warm feeling returned again, same as he'd had in the kitchen when he ate Oliver's pie.

Oliver took another paper towel to wipe the sweat off his face, then reached down and pulled off his sweater. His T-shirt rode up, revealing a broad chest with some hair and a flat stomach. But that wasn't what caught Aubrey's attention, although it was a damn nice-looking body. It was the scar. A long, thin gash that ran straight down his chest, starting at the collarbone and ending a couple of inches above his belly button.

*What the hell is that?*

Then Oliver's T-shirt slipped back down, covering the scar, leaving Aubrey wondering about its origin. Whatever it was, Oliver certainly didn't seem to be suffering any aftereffects from it. And Aubrey didn't feel like he had the right to ask.

"This is going a lot faster with your help. I appreciate it." Oliver started working on the third shelf.

"No problem. So how'd you end up in Heartsville, anyways? We don't get that many new people." The last person Aubrey recollected was Emery from Last Call, his favorite bar in town, who'd arrived the year before and seemed to have fit right in with Quinn and Gray and became their cook. Aubrey had stopped there for a beer and a burger one evening during winter and met him. In fact, Emery fit in so well, Aubrey often wondered about the relationship between the three men, but he decided it was none of his business. *Whatever floats their boat.*

Oliver had gone still, sitting on his heels and looking out the window. He had a nice profile: strong jaw, full lips, and a nose that might've been broken at one point but fit his face. Aubrey couldn't help but wonder what a guy who obviously had money was doing in this little backwater town, taking a bakery job at a local farm.

"You ever want to simply chuck it all? Walk away from what you've known all your life and start over?" Oliver's soft voice wove around Aubrey, and he answered without thinking.

"Every damn day."

Meeting Oliver's gaze, he saw understanding and sympathy. "Yeah. So that was me. I had some hard life choices to make, and moving away from a fast-paced work-all-day-every-day-never-take-a-break career was the easiest decision I've ever made." He paused and gave Aubrey a slight smile. "And now I'm thinking maybe one of the best."

The heat warming him wasn't only from the sun streaming in through the front windows. A little disconcerted, Aubrey cleared his throat. "You can hand me that can, and I'll wrap too. Might as well help all the way through. The quicker you clean up here, the quicker you can start and we can make some money. Every bit helps, and the bakery used to be a nice little monthly income stream."

"Sure."

They worked for the next several hours until all the shelves were cleared and dusted off. "You did a good job. I'm impressed." Despite looking like he came out of a fashion magazine that first day, Oliver had worked hard, and Aubrey had higher hopes for the bakery now.

"I appreciate your help. It went ten times faster because of it."

"No big deal. Just doing what needs to be done." He turned to go.

"Aubrey?" Oliver called to him from behind the counter.

"Yeah?" Aubrey said as he fitted the baseball cap on his head. "Something wrong?"

"No, nothing. Just...have a good night."

He gave Oliver a short nod and left.

7
_____

# OLIVER

O liver unlocked the bakery and stepped inside to the lingering smell of fresh paint mixed with chocolate. He could scarcely believe he was here—not only in Heartsville, but on this farm and in this bakery. His bakery. His to run, at least.

The last three weeks had been a whirlwind as Oliver renovated the space and tested out recipes—with Cassie's help, of course. He couldn't have done it without her. She was kind and patient with him, and whenever she noticed him faltering, a question seemed to dangle from her lips, perhaps to ask more details about his prior experience, but she held back. She knew he was in over his head but encouraged him nonetheless.

One of the first tasks he undertook was to paint the walls a steel blue, which gave the bakery a subtle modern flair. He wasn't exactly sure it fit the vibe of the farm, but Aubrey's encouragement about making the space his own helped him take the leap. Besides, he got the impression that the man wanted him to get rid of any reminders of its former glory, so that was exactly what he did. The only thing he kept were two vintage metal milk jugs that fit the streamlined decor very nicely.

When Aubrey had checked on the progress earlier in the

week, his eyes had misted when they landed on the jugs. Oliver immediately regretted the decision, even though Cassie had considered them a nice touch. Oliver had stood motionless, waiting for some sort of backlash from his broody boss, but all Aubrey did was grunt and wave his hand. "Coming along, I see."

And then he'd fled the space as if he had something more important to do. And he probably did; he ran an entire farm, after all. Oliver noticed he worked long hours—whether by choice or to fill up his time, he didn't know. He recognized the pattern because Oliver had done much the same when his career had been all he had. That was before the illness had taken hold, the shortness of breath and dizziness becoming more frequent. A fainting spell had concerned his family as much as his coworkers. But now...now he was finding meaning in his life again.

Wasn't he? Taking a leap of faith?

*Damn it.* No matter how he tried to spin things, he was beginning this new opportunity under false pretenses. He needed to set the record straight sooner rather than later. As it was, his chest constricted painfully every time he saw the man. Not because he was dangerously handsome, but because the guilt was overwhelming. And he didn't want to be the object of the man's wrath, that was for certain. But perhaps he was reading him all wrong? Perhaps if Oliver explained why he'd come to this town in the first place...only to become enchanted with it. Coupled with his love of baking, it felt impossible to turn down the proposition. Maybe Aubrey would understand all that. Or maybe he'd show his ass the door.

The idea of leaving this quaint place made his heart heavy for more reasons than he could explain.

"You okay?" Cassie asked, tapping his elbow and startling him.

"Yeah, sure. Just taking a moment," he replied with a smile as he strode to the bakery counter, for which he'd purchased new pie-display stands. More sleek and modern, they made the counter look contemporary, and Cassie agreed. He'd mentioned that they also matched the decor in his New York City apartment, and then promptly confessed he'd been a successful attorney in his former life. That he'd walked away from the high-stress environment to begin a brand-new venture, which had included a year of culinary classes.

She also knew he was gay, not only because he didn't hide the fact, but because when she inquired if he had a special lady in his life, he'd blurted out that his sister was important to him, but he hadn't had a decent boyfriend in a couple of years. Cassie had only blinked momentarily before smiling, never missing a beat.

"I think we're ready," Cassie said with excitement in her tone, and his stomach squeezed tight.

They were doing a dry run of what a day at the bakery would look like before the grand opening next week. Farm staff were instructed to stop throughout their shifts to sample the goods and even take leftovers home.

He and Cassie had worked on a menu of several pie and muffin offerings, incorporating one of Lisa's recipes as well, but he didn't want to overdo it straight out of the gate. And besides, he wanted to stamp it with his own flair, whatever the hell that was. He was still fumbling his way through it but would inevitably figure it out.

Beginning of the week he'd asked the boss himself what desserts he'd prefer him to focus on, and Aubrey reiterated using whatever was seasonal on the farm. To Oliver, it made the most sense to focus on pastry that would hold up well with fruits and sometimes vegetables, like carrots and zucchini. Chocolate was just an added bonus.

They preheated the ovens and got started on their first piecrusts, and the morning flew by. They whipped up chocolate silk and apricot pie—the fruit currently in season—as well as apple walnut and banana cream. The muffin selection included chocolate chip, banana nut, apple cinnamon, and carrot cake with cream-cheese filling.

The line at the door formed well before noon, with plenty of employees he hadn't laid eyes on yet. He supposed food was always a good icebreaker. As employees stepped to the counter for their samples, Cassie would introduce them, and most, he noted, were farmhands, some seasonal, others lifers, like the boss himself.

Speaking of which, Aubrey stood in the back of the crowded shop, taking it all in, his arms folded, his mouth turned down in the usual manner, like there was a lot on his mind. Except when Oliver got a rare smile out of him. That grin could light him up all day.

Oliver expected to have frayed nerves, but as the day wore on —rather smoothly, he might add—he couldn't help the glow that started in his gut and traveled to his chest. He was actually doing it—living a dream. A dream he didn't even realize he had until recently. He was creating things with his hands and feeding people. Cassie had said that the farm felt like a family, and he was beginning to see that she was right. There was a camaraderie here that hadn't existed at the firm, a shared sense of purpose rather than a need to excel on your own.

He imagined inviting his father, sister, brother-in-law, and his niece and nephew to the farm one day—ignoring the obvious possibility that everything might fall apart once he told them and Aubrey the truth.

During his most recent phone call with Jennifer, he'd blurted part of it out. He'd shared his fantasy about owning property and running a bakery someday—obviously not expounding on how quickly that was becoming a reality.

"Have you lost your damn mind?" she'd asked with a chuckle.

"Maybe—or maybe I found my dream."

"It does sound appealing," she'd admitted. "I don't know

what's come over you, but I like it. What about Aubrey Hendricks?"

He'd cringed. "I'll keep you posted."

He hated keeping secrets, even came out to his family pretty early in life and let the cards fall where they may. But if he ignored this one too long, it might just do him in.

It was late afternoon, and Cassie was long gone for the day. Nearly all the food had been eaten or taken home to families, but he had made sure to save half of a chocolate silk pie. Digging in the back of the industrial-sized fridge, he fished out the tin, along with another bag he'd tucked away from a grocery-store trip the previous day.

He locked up the bakery, then made his way to Aubrey's farmhouse. He let himself in like he'd done earlier in the week to leave him leftover muffins at Cassie's insistence. Oliver opened the refrigerator, which was pretty bare outside of what looked like takeout containers. *What does the man live on, air?* He'd venture a guess that he'd find frozen dinners if he snooped in the freezer.

He slid the silk pie onto a shelf along with the meat and vegetables he'd purchased, hoping to inspire Aubrey to eat healthier. Not that Oliver had any room to talk—he'd been subsisting on takeout as well. Renting a place was at the top of his list, after opening the bakery, of course.

"You're just trying to fatten me up," Aubrey said from behind him, and Oliver froze. That voice—deep and smooth yet rough around the edges—did things to him that he needed to continue to ignore.

"No chance of that. You work too hard for any fat to stick to your midsection." Oliver glanced back and tried not to stare. Aubrey's wide shoulders took up all the available space in the doorway. His dirt-stained jeans hugged his hips in all the right places, and the way his unruly hair curled over the edges of his baseball cap was appealing in ways Oliver would've never imagined. "Or anyplace else, apparently."

As a wash of crimson spread across the man's cheeks, Oliver blinked in shock. He'd actually made Aubrey Hendricks blush. *Dear Lord.* He gripped the counter before he said or did something he'd regret.

Lusting after a straight man. *Stupid.* After a straight, widowed man. *Even more stupid.*

Fuck, this was ridiculous. He needed to level with Aubrey, and maybe now was the time. He swallowed back the warm bile as a far-fetched idea took shape in his brain. Maybe if Aubrey got to know him better, he'd understand. Be able to relate.

"I was hoping you'd be inspired to cook yourself an actual meal. Not that I'm much better, living out of the motel," he rambled, his knees feeling weak as Aubrey cocked an eyebrow. "How would you feel about me whipping up something decent with the stuff I bought? Nothing fancy. A couple of chicken breasts and some vegetables."

He could see the gears turning in Aubrey's brain as he likely settled on an excuse. He figured the man wouldn't accept the offer, and he supposed he had his reasons. "I've got a thousand things to do around here. So I'm going to have to—"

"No worries," Oliver said, letting him off the hook. His feet nearly faltered as he worked his way around him toward the hallway. "Hope you have a good night."

His entire body flushed as he made his way outside. Why the hell had he even offered?

As he got to the middle of the stairs, he heard Aubrey's deep voice. "Guess a man's got to eat."

# 8

# AUBREY

The house was the first thing he needed to work on. Like finally cleaning out Lisa's closet and putting her stuff aside to be donated. Not to mention taking care of the farm's bookkeeping, which he had to get started on. Lisa had always done that chore. He hated all that business-related crap. All he wanted was to be outdoors with the wind in his face and his hands in the ground.

He should've said no to Oliver's invitation, and yet he didn't want to. He was tired, so damn tired of sitting alone in the dark, staring at the stars all night. Accepting Oliver's offer to share a meal was a start, and seeing the flush on Oliver's smiling face made him realize it didn't take much to make the man happy.

"I won't get in your way, promise," Oliver said, bounding back up the steps and into the house. "Any requests or things you don't like?"

"Nothing with any fancy sauces. I like plain food, not too spicy."

"How about a nice stir-fry with the chicken and all the veggies? I have onions, mushrooms, peppers—"

"Oliver?" Aubrey folded his arms and couldn't keep the smile off his lips. It was kind of nice to have someone to talk to, even if the man was a bit chatty.

"Yeah?" His face fell. "Oh. You don't like stir-fry. Okay, hmm... what about chicken marsala?" Oliver chewed on his lip, gazing at him with anxious eyes.

"What I was gonna say is, stir-fry is fine. So is chicken marsala. I'm not gonna kick either off my plate, if you get what I mean. Now I'm gonna go upstairs, take a shower, and start going through some closets. If you need something, give a holler."

"Okay. I'll surprise you."

Amused by his eagerness, Aubrey mounted the stairs, and after a nice, hot shower, for the next hour he busied himself in Lisa's closet. Grief threatened again, but it was softer now. Less painful. It no longer stabbed him in the heart like a fresh knife wound. He could touch her shirts and dresses, remembering with a smile how beautiful she looked on their anniversary when they'd dressed up to go out to dinner. With care, he folded her clothes and bagged them for Goodwill.

Delicious smells drifted up from the kitchen, and Aubrey could hear music playing and someone—Oliver—singing along. His knees creaked when he stood, and he rubbed the small of his back. Hitting forty-five this year really brought his life into focus. For sure, it wasn't going to get easier, especially being alone.

"Aubrey?" Oliver stood in the doorway, an apron around his waist and smudges of flour across his cheeks and nose.

"What is it?" Surprised Oliver had come upstairs, Aubrey shook himself out of his daydream and realized he might have sounded a bit gruff. "Sorry."

"It's okay. Dinner? It's, uh, ready."

Aubrey sniffed the air, and the rich aroma of tomato sauce hit his nose. To his embarrassment, his stomach let out a huge growl, and Oliver snickered.

"Guess I don't have to ask if you're hungry."

"I'm coming. Just gonna go wash my hands."

"Okay. I thought it would be nicer to sit in the dining room since the kitchen is a bit of a mess."

"Oh?" Aubrey quirked a brow. "A mess?" He recalled the bakery after Oliver's first time baking and wondered how bad it was down there.

"I'll clean it up, don't worry, but I decided on the marsala and fresh tomato sauce for the pasta. It got more complicated."

By now they'd reached downstairs, and Aubrey went to wash in the little half bath next to the kitchen. He peeked into the kitchen and saw that Oliver was correct about the mess. Pots and pans filled the sink, and the scraps of vegetables lay on the cutting boards.

"Don't look, I said," Oliver called out. "I'll clean it all up afterward. Right now let's concentrate on eating."

He'd obviously gone to a lot of trouble, and because Aubrey was starved and more than a little curious to discover what he could about this man who'd dropped into his life and changed it around, he listened. He silently dried his hands and followed Oliver into the dining room. The table had been set with his plain white dishes, but the real centerpiece was the food. A big bowl of steaming pasta with a fresh, rough-chopped tomato sauce sat on one side of the table. Chicken cutlets smothered in a brown sauce with mushrooms and onions sizzled in a baking dish. A leafy green salad with tomatoes and onions and mozzarella cheese filled the wooden salad bowl. A bouquet of lilacs and lavender sat tall in a glass vase, perfuming the air.

Aubrey gaped, first at the table, then at Oliver. "You made all this? For us?"

"Well, food is meant to be enjoyed and shared. I love cooking and can do more than bake."

"You sure can."

Touched by the obvious hard work Oliver had put into not

only the preparation of the food, but the presentation, Aubrey vowed to try and be nicer to the man. They sat down and handed the food around. The salad was crisp and fresh, and the combined taste of the garlic and tomatoes with the creamy richness of the marsala sauce exploded in Aubrey's mouth. If food were orgasmic, this would be world-class.

"How is it?" Oliver asked, his own plate untouched. "Good?" He rubbed his sternum, and Aubrey wondered about the scar he'd seen running down Oliver's chest.

"Better than good. Amazing."

Relief lit up Oliver's warm eyes, and a smile burst over his face. An awareness of Oliver as a man shot through Aubrey and he stiffened, then shoved another forkful of food in his mouth.

"Something wrong?"

"No, nothing." Aubrey ate a few bites more and set down his fork. "Tell me something else about yourself. I don't really know much more about you than when you first drove up last month."

Oliver chewed and swallowed. "Oh, do you want a beer or some wine or water?"

"If I want something, I think I can find it," Aubrey said, wondering why Oliver seemed so hesitant to talk. So nervous and jittery.

"Yeah, sure. That was stupid of me. Well, um, I got tired of the grinding rat race of the law firm—all the endless time spent researching and the trial work sucked the life out of me."

Aubrey shuddered. "Sounds awful. I couldn't imagine being locked in an office building all day."

"Yeah. I was exhausted every night. It ended up being the downfall of my last relationship."

He could only imagine. "Girlfriend couldn't put up with it, huh? Can't say I blame her."

Oliver's jaw tightened, and he met Aubrey's eyes with an almost defiant glare. "No. Him. Boyfriend. I'm gay."

"Oh," Aubrey said and cut into his chicken. "Well, it's hard for anyone, man or woman, to be in a relationship if one partner isn't there most of the time." Oliver seemed to be waiting for Aubrey to comment on him being gay, but he wasn't touching that right now.

Again, he noticed Oliver rubbing his chest.

"Yeah, well, so with all these circumstances out of my control, I decided to make a big life change. I left my job, took cooking and baking classes, and decided it was time to take a hard look at my life, what I really wanted and where I was going."

"And that brought you here? To Heartsville?"

Oliver propped his chin in his hands and stared out the window at the darkening sky. "Have you ever had something so profound happen to you that nothing will ever be the same again? And all you want is to go back to the safety of what was, but that can never happen, so you have no choice but to take that first step into the wild?"

Pain lanced through Aubrey, but he said nothing. Oliver, realizing what he'd said, clapped a hand over his mouth. "Oh, shit. Aubrey. I'm sorry. That was really thoughtless of me."

"It's fine. Everyone handles things in a different way. And yeah, when my wife died, I wished I'd died too 'cause I didn't think I'd make it without her. But I did. And every day is another step further into the reality of my new life. Getting back to work on the farm without her was one step. Opening the bakery and hiring you, another. Cleaning out her closet...all baby steps."

Sympathy creased Oliver's brow, and his brown eyes softened. "But they are steps, nonetheless. So we should feel proud, right?"

Aubrey agreed. "Yeah. And I want to thank you for this dinner. I didn't understand how alone I was until you'd all go home and I'd be sitting here with only Duke for company. And he ain't the best conversationalist."

They finished their meal in relative silence, and Aubrey insisted on helping Oliver clean the kitchen. "You're not the help here, Oliver. I mean, yeah, you work for me, but..." He took off his baseball cap and set it back on his head. "It's different. Know what I mean?"

He hoped Oliver did, because he didn't. Not really.

# 9

# OLIVER

Oliver gripped the steering wheel as he pulled out of the motel parking lot. He'd been tossing and turning all week, his guilt increasing each night. He should've told him. Right then in the middle of the *second* dinner with Aubrey or the evening of the *third* time alone with the man when they clinked beer bottles after-hours on the porch. But something about Aubrey pointing up at the sky once they shared their mutual love of all things sci-fi and fantasy—books and movies included—had further endeared the man to him. Now even more time had passed, and Oliver still hadn't confessed the real reason he'd come to the farm.

*Damn it all to hell.* He stabbed the horn a little too quickly at a slow-moving vehicle as he replayed that very first meeting with Aubrey in his head. The night he showed up at First Light unannounced after driving for hours. Aubrey had ridden up from the fields, looking equally bone-tired and exasperated, inquiring whether he was there for the bakery job. Had Oliver been honest back then, things would've gone in a dramatically different direction.

*No, Aubrey Hendricks. I'm here to say thank you for saving my life. For allowing your wife's organs to be donated upon her death.*

He imagined Aubrey's stunned appearance as he staggered back and his eventual reply.

*Thanks for driving all this way to tell me. I appreciate knowing.*

Oliver would've remembered the small satchel he kept in his back seat with some essentials he'd put aside for just such a meeting.

*Wait a minute. Got something I want to show you.*

The other, more likely option, now that he'd gotten to know his temperament better, was that Aubrey Hendricks would've fumed about him showing up in the first place. He was not one to open up or soften very easily. He proceeded with caution and took his time with things. He was a giving boss to people he cared about. And Oliver could only hope he was at least beginning to make some sort of an impression on him—not that it was his goal. He was naturally curious about the man, drawn to him for no logical reason besides one of the things they had in common: his late wife, Lisa. Yes, Aubrey Hendricks was pleasing to the eyes, but he was also straight and had suffered a tragic loss. The fact that he'd agreed to spend any time with Oliver outside of work might've been an indication of his visceral loneliness. And Oliver understood that emotion all too well.

He had started off on the wrong foot with Aubrey—and in the whirlwind of his new position at the farm, his heart transplant had fallen to the backdrop of his mind, the quaint setting and the intriguing widower moving to the forefront.

So this morning, the day before the grand opening of the bakery, he was going to make it right, no matter the outcome. His stomach tilted uncomfortably, but he ignored it. He planned to explain to Aubrey how as soon as he came upon the farm, he was compelled to turn into the driveway, transplant or not. It probably wouldn't make a bit of sense, and it certainly was no excuse, but he'd say it anyway, if he was given the chance. More than likely he'd be sent packing, having learned a few more life lessons along the way. Those never ceased, not even when you were creeping toward midlife.

His first stop, though, was at the general store to grab a steaming cup of coffee and to pick up his blood-thinner prescription.

"Tomorrow's the big day," Carol remarked as she rang him up. Once she heard he'd taken the job, she'd been nothing short of excited for him. For her friend Aubrey as well.

Oliver smiled absently, not wanting to give his mood away. He could already feel the tension creeping up on him.

"Any luck finding a house to rent?" she asked, and as if on cue, his cell rang in his pocket. He shook his head and waved as he answered the call from his sister. Not that he wanted to. But he awoke this morning determined to set it all straight. It was time. And he couldn't keep making excuses to his family about why he wanted to continue spending time in PA.

Once he slipped behind the wheel and she asked how things were going and when he'd be finally home from sightseeing in the mountains, he finally fessed up. "I got a job running a bakery in Heartsville."

"A bakery...two hours away, in Heartsville," his sister deadpanned. "So you were serious."

"Of course I was," he replied, and somehow hearing how shaky her certainty was made him want to flaunt his recent accomplishments. "The grand opening is tomorrow, and I've already got all my recipes lined up and did a run-through with my assistant."

"Tomorrow? An assistant?" The shock in her voice was evident and to be expected. "That's what you've been doing this entire time?"

"Yeah, I'm sorry, I just..." Oliver immediately regretted not being up-front. "Anyway, her name is Cassie, and she pretty much could run the place herself. But she claims she's strictly part-time because she's got three kids and—"

"You sound so excited," she remarked with a laugh. "I just wish you would've—"

"I feel energized, like I got a new chance at life," he blurted out because he did not want to be lectured by his sister. "And hey, I even included Mom's French silk recipe in the lineup."

"This is so hard to wrap my brain around." She sighed. "But I bet her pie will be a crowd-pleaser."

"Already is. Even Aubr—" He trailed off, kicking himself for saying too much. Except there he went again, trying to spin things his way to soften the blow. To hide the mess he'd gotten himself into.

"Aubrey?" she asked. "Aubrey Hendricks? What does this have to do with him?"

"That job I mentioned..." He winced. "It's at his farm."

"Oliver Gabriel Hansen!" she shrieked, sounding exactly like their mom, and though his shoulders stiffened, a pang of nostalgia hit him as well. "Does this mean you told him?"

"I...I definitely planned to. He's still grieving. You should've seen him when I repainted the—"

"Now you're just making excuses," she accused, and that stopped him cold.

He took a deep breath, that jittery feeling returning to his stomach. "You're right. I actually intend on telling him today."

At one time, he might've been a cutthroat lawyer who'd spun the truth in a favorable direction, but nobody was on trial in this situation. And the truth could indeed set you free. If he wanted to keep his blood pressure down and that new heart ticking in his chest, he needed to come clean. For everyone's sake.

"I'd wish you luck, but I'm not sure I can honestly—"

"Don't bother," he muttered. "I got myself into this mess. I'll keep you posted."

He pulled up to the farm with renewed purpose, his sweaty

palms making his grip slippery as he parked on a patch of dirt near the other employees' cars.

But when he stepped out of the car, he immediately noticed a different air to the farm, a sense of panic and commotion all around him as distracted farmhands rushed to and fro.

"What's happening?" he called to Cassie as she rushed by him from the bakery.

"There was an unexpected frost this morning, and the boss is afraid the crops will be ruined." She headed toward a free four-wheeler, and he followed behind. "So it's all hands on deck, trying to save them."

"How can I help?" he asked without giving it a second thought.

"Hop on," she replied, and as soon as he was seated, she took off toward the newly planted strawberry and blueberry fields as he clung to her shoulders for dear life. He remembered, at dinner the other night, Aubrey also mentioning the young apple and plum trees they'd planted.

The first thing Oliver noticed once they were far enough along were large industrial fans with long extension cords running down the hill, blowing toward the bases of several saplings—he supposed to get the warmer air circulating around the soil, but he couldn't be sure.

After they parked alongside another vehicle and hopped off, he followed Cassie up and down some of the other rows as she adjusted the sprinklers aimed toward newly planted crops.

"Won't the water freeze?" he asked, wondering how it could possibly be helping to save the plants from the frost.

"Groundwater from the well is warmer and can help thaw the plants," she replied over her shoulder as she moved farther down the rows.

He could see Aubrey and a couple of farmhands on the adjacent field adjusting plastic tents over the new growth and creating what looked like a heat shield of some sort. He supposed the idea was to produce a greenhouse-type effect when the sun shone down on the farm midday. It certainly gave him a new appreciation of how complicated and delicate farmwork could be.

As if he could sense he was being watched, Aubrey lifted his gaze in Oliver's direction. He inhaled sharply through his nose as if seeing him standing in the middle of the strawberry field was completely unexpected. Oliver felt a warm blush spread across his cheeks. He found that he liked surprising the man. It made him want to do more, work harder. And maybe that was his appeal.

The task of saving the crops took them all morning long until Aubrey placed two fingers between his lips and whistled to get everyone's attention. When he pointed at his watch and then up the hill, everyone apparently understood his meaning and began trudging in the direction of the house. Oliver felt as if he wanted to collapse in a heap once he reached level ground. He squatted on the grass next to George, the farm manager, while everyone else spread out wherever they could find a dry spot. Sodas and sandwiches were handed out by a couple of employees who had stayed behind to order lunch for the crew.

He noticed how Aubrey ate last, waiting until everyone else was fed before he found a perch on the porch steps and dived into his sandwich. He wiped the sweat from his forehead, and for the first time all morning, Oliver saw the man's shoulders relax.

Oliver's truth mission was reduced to merely an elusive thought as he listened to the small talk around him about preparing for the night ahead. He figured it was better to keep in the shadows and help wherever he was needed.

In the afternoon, he and Cassie made their way to the bakery and got started on the pies for the grand opening. He vaguely considered postponing it, but then he remembered all the fliers had been sent out.

Cassie looked just as whipped as she helped roll out the

crusts for the pies, and he felt guilty that she'd needed to put in additional hours today.

Still, she took as much pride in the work as everyone else on this farm, and the idea of being part of such a stellar group of people made him feel a renewed sense of fondness, if not wistfulness, about the farm. Too bad he might have to leave it.

"Has that ever happened before?" Oliver asked, motioning to the fields behind them.

"It's rare. Aubrey keeps close watch over the forecast. But sometimes they're way off course."

Once the pies were set and placed in the refrigerator for the night, they prepped the muffin ingredients for the morning. Bone-tired, he made his way to his vehicle. Glancing at the dark house, he wondered what time Aubrey would make it to bed that evening. Conflicting emotions swirled through his thoughts as he sank into the front seat, melancholy taking center stage.

As he drove toward the main road, he sent out a wish on the wind that the crops would be spared tonight.

# 10

## AUBREY

The line to get into the bakery snaked out through the front door from early morning, and each time Aubrey glanced over to the little wooden building, a curious sense of pride thumped in his chest. Pride for Oliver at how all his hard work was being rewarded, but also pride in himself that he was able to see the bakery up and running and for the first time without having second thoughts or feeling like he was moving on too fast.

A blond man carrying a pie box and a bag walked up to him, and Aubrey recognized him as Quinn, one of the owners of the bar and grill Last Call. It had been a while since he'd been over there for a beer, but now that the crops were settled in, Aubrey planned on getting out and rejoining life again.

"Aubrey. Glad I had a chance to see you."

Quinn, as Aubrey recalled, was always the smiling one of the three men who owned the bar.

"Nice to see you again too." He tipped his chin toward the parcels in Quinn's hands. "I see you've visited the new bakery. What'd you get?"

The man's eyes lit up. "I got one of those chocolate silk pies—

Emery loves chocolate—and then a bunch of different muffins for Gray and me. I may've gone a bit overboard." His wide grin indicated he wasn't too concerned.

"Did you talk to the baker? Oliver?" Aubrey was curious as to the townspeople's thoughts of his new employee.

"Yeah. Seems like a nice guy. We were chatting about settling in and finding your way around in a new place. I gave him some tips on who to call if he was interested in renting."

This was news to Aubrey. He hadn't heard Oliver mention that, but it made sense. If the man was staying, it had to be uncomfortable for him to be living in one room—not to mention, the Clover Motel was on the opposite side of town from the farm.

"Yeah, I think he fits in pretty good around here."

"Well, I'm gonna head back to Last Call. Emery's got waffles and corned-beef hash for breakfast, and if I'm not there, Gray'll eat my portion and his. Stop by for a beer sometime. We'd love to see you more."

"I will, thanks. Say hi to the guys for me."

"Will do."

Watching Quinn place the box carefully on the seat of his truck, Aubrey decided that after the almost-disaster of yesterday's frost and the backbreaking work, he could use a little pick-me-up and headed over to the bakery. He entered through the back and had a chance to see Oliver in action with the customers. Aubrey always believed the measure of a person was how they dealt with people they met in everyday life.

One of the ladies from the little thrift shop in town was having a hard time deciding if she wanted an apricot crumble or the chocolate pie. The line was long, and Aubrey could see several customers getting restless. Oliver, however, was having none of that.

"Okay, Mrs. Watson. How about I do this—I'll do a half pie of each, if you don't mind me using the pies I've already cut up to sell individual pieces. That way you can taste both." He dropped his voice into a conspiratorial whisper, and Aubrey couldn't help but grin. "I wouldn't do this for just anyone, you know."

The elderly lady's cheeks grew pink. "Oh, aren't you sweet. That would be lovely. I'm sorry to be such a bother. My late husband used to say he was surprised I ever said yes to his proposal right away, since I could never make up my mind."

While she spoke, Oliver quickly boxed up the pie halves and handed them to her. She fumbled in her purse and drew out her money. "Thank you kindly. And I want you to come back and tell me which one you liked best."

"Oh, I will." She twittered out of the shop, stopping to tell at least two people in line that Oliver was the sweetest man she'd ever met.

While Oliver took care of the customers, Aubrey helped himself to a banana muffin and poured himself some coffee. He was aware Oliver didn't know he was there and was glad to be able to study the man.

He liked the easy smile that always rested on his lips and the way he greeted each person as if they were an old friend. It was an enviable quality, one Aubrey knew he didn't possess. It reminded him of Elliot, the first guy he'd ever been with. Aubrey had been drawn to him for his laughing nature and sweet disposition, but their affair was never serious. It was a purely physical attraction for them both. Elliot had left Heartsville after high school, and Aubrey had never seen him again, but it was true what they said. You never forgot your first.

Oliver had those same qualities. Aubrey guessed he was drawn to people who possessed what he lacked. Lisa had always said he was her gruff softie. She understood it wasn't easy for him to show his affection, but when he loved, he did so fiercely.

"Thank you, and if you come by tomorrow, I'll make sure to save the carrot-cake muffins for you."

"I will, Oliver." Dan from the hardware store gave a wave, then cocked his head. "Aubrey? That you hiding out back there eating all the merchandise?" He snickered and left.

Oliver turned around, and their eyes met. "Oh, hi. I didn't know you were there. How come you didn't say hello?"

Aubrey's face warmed. "Oh, uh, you were busy, and I didn't want to interrupt."

"So you thought you'd eat the profits instead, huh?" Oliver's eyes twinkled as he laughed. "Looks like it's settled down now after the morning rush. I told Cassie to take a break for a bit since she was exhausted. She was up with one of her kids half the night. You can come out from your hiding place."

"Wasn't hiding," Aubrey huffed out, but he joined Oliver out front and sat at one of the little tables Oliver had placed about the store. He set his coffee in front of him and wrapped his hands around the thick white mug. "Been busy, I see. I'm, uh, I'm hearing good things."

Looking a bit taken aback, Oliver blinked and turned red. "Oh, thanks. Yeah, it was a rush today. I guess people want to see what the new place is like."

"I'm thinking people have heard what it's like already and that's why they're here. They're curious about you. You're doing a good job."

"Thanks, Aubrey. That means a lot."

He sipped his coffee. "So I also hear you might be looking for a place. Quinn told me he's pointed you to a couple of realtors."

Oliver poured himself some coffee and walked over. "Mind if I sit?"

" 'Course not."

A sigh escaped Oliver's lips as he stretched out his feet. "Damn, my feet hurt. But yeah, it seems silly to keep living out of a motel room now that I'm working here. Especially since the Clover is across town and Quinn said there're lots of houses for rent over here."

For a millisecond Aubrey thought about offering him a room at the farmhouse. After all, God knows he had the space and wouldn't mind the company, but something held him back. "If you'd like, you could make some appointments to see places, and I could go with you."

"Oh, thanks. That'd be really helpful since I don't know much about the town or anything. I can call this afternoon once I close and clean up the bakery and set up some appointments, but let me know when you have time."

"That's the good thing about owning the place. I can sorta set my own schedule. Tell the boss I'm taking the afternoon off and I don't get any pushback."

He and Oliver shared a laugh, and Aubrey realized he was enjoying the man's company more each day. His smile faded, and Oliver grew serious as well. Their eyes locked, and Aubrey's heart kicked up as their stare grew more intense. He stood abruptly and knocked back the rest of his coffee.

"Well, I gotta get back. Let me know about those appointments if you make them."

"I will." Oliver remained seated. "Talk to you later."

With too many disturbing thoughts spinning through his head, Aubrey left the bakery and stood outside for a moment, feeling foolish over his behavior. Seeing someone else besides Lisa running the bakery was bound to tie him up in knots and leave him feeling edgy and uncertain. It had nothing to do with Oliver. Anyone could work there and he'd feel the same. He passed by the side of the bakery and peered in. Oliver still sat at the table, sipping his coffee, and then Aubrey saw it—that touch to the chest he'd seen Oliver make several times. Not as if he was in pain, but rather a brush of fingertips trailing up, then down.

That fading pink slash of Oliver's scar came to mind, and once again, Aubrey wondered what could've happened to cause it. Oliver looked as fit as anyone, but there was something about the whole way he showed up out of the blue with a story about leaving his law practice that didn't quite ring true to Aubrey. What could Oliver be hiding in his past that he'd come to a little town in Pennsylvania to start a new life?

# 11

## OLIVER

Oliver swung open the bakery door and flicked on the light, creating a warm glow in the early dawn hours. He was usually alone at this time until Cassie appeared after dropping her kids off to school. He always put on a pot of coffee and started on the muffin mixes. Cassie would arrange the display cases with the pies baked the previous afternoon, then help with the morning rush.

The routine already seemed natural, though it had only been shy of five weeks since he first accepted the job. He was doing something that made him happy and doing it well, if he did say so himself, and having the time of his life. He loved baking and serving the people of Heartsville. He'd definitely encountered his share of residents, all because of the love of food.

Meeting a handsome blond man named Quinn had been one of the highlights. He apparently owned Last Call, the bar he passed by nearly every day on his way to the farm and had always been curious about. Quinn had mentioned his two *partners*, Gray and Emery, and the way he said it led Oliver to believe there was something more there. Was he in a relationship with one of them?

It was on the tip of his tongue to ask Aubrey when he'd stopped by the other day to check on him. Spy on him, might've been more like it. The man had just stood back and watched him work, and Oliver didn't know how to feel about it. Did he operate that way with all his employees—to see if their performance was on par? He wasn't sure, but it made him feel unsettled.

There was also that moment between them when they'd shared a look that sent prickles across his skin. It couldn't have been his imagination. He knew what interest looked like. Longing. Curiosity. Could Aubrey be closeted or bi? Or maybe just lonely for companionship? Why else would he have agreed to those couple of meals together? Regardless, it wasn't his place to inquire, and besides, Oliver was hiding things as well. Actually, one really huge thing. So why complicate the situation?

And now even more time had gone by, and he still hadn't told Aubrey. He had even avoided his sister's phone calls, what with the whirlwind of the grand opening and all. *Yeah right.*

Still, it consumed his mind. Or maybe just the man did. Cassie had caught him staring out the bakery window last night after closing time when Aubrey was on his porch with one of the farmhands.

"Everything okay?" she'd asked, startling him. After following his line of sight, she'd knocked shoulders with him playfully. "He *is* a very attractive man."

"What? No, I wasn't..." he spluttered.

"It's okay. You are human, after all," she replied with a chuckle. "Too bad he's straight."

*Maybe he isn't bi after all. Wouldn't Cassie or the farmhands know?*

"Actually, I was thinking of the offer he made to go property hunting with me," Oliver said, and Cassie's eyebrows rose in apparent surprise. "Quinn gave me the name of a realtor who shows rental places for lease."

"Quinn from Last Call?" Cassie asked.

He nodded. "He stopped in the other morning, remember? Seemed cool."

"He's great. They all are, in fact," she said. "Serve good food too."

"So they all run the business together?" he asked, his curiosity getting the best of him.

"Rumor is they *are* together, but not my place to say."

Imagine that. Heartsville had its own little poly relationship, but Cassie didn't act like it was some sort of scandalous thing. He might be even more enamored with the place.

After the coffee percolated and he poured himself a mug, he wondered if the boss man might show up for a cup like he did a couple of mornings that week during the preparation for the opening. That was usually his only interaction with the guy all day unless he saw him on the porch after-hours and was asked to share a beer or Oliver offered to make a meal. Though since the grand opening, there hadn't been much time for that.

And as if he'd conjured up the man, the bell over the back door jangled.

Aubrey wasn't much for small talk in the mornings, he'd noticed. He looked sleep-rumpled but still perfectly dressed for the day. He poured Aubrey a cup after a simple greeting, and then Oliver sipped at his own rich liquid gold.

"I've got a couple of appointments lined up tonight, starting at six," Oliver mentioned around a yawn. "Does the offer still stand?"

"Definitely. I'll meet you out front by my truck."

Oliver's pulse thrummed all day, but he was skating on thin ice. Securing a property meant that he would be even deeper over his head. Having a job and living out of a motel was one thing. Laying down more roots was quite another.

Still, as he closed up the bakery sans Cassie, whose shift

ended midafternoon when her kids were out of school, he cleaned with more speed than he intended and then had to loiter. Finally, he spotted Aubrey walking to his truck, and he locked up behind him, his pulse skittering.

"You ready?" he asked, and Oliver noted that he'd washed up from that morning and changed—not only into a different shirt, but clean boots as well.

When he slid into the passenger seat, he also couldn't help noticing the man's cologne more intensely than any of the nights before. It had a citrusy, woodsy scent, and he wanted to lean over and inhale right at the spot above his Adam's apple. *Not if I don't want to get punched in the face.*

The first property he toured was a set of duplexes that shared a small backyard on a pretty uneventful street halfway between the farm and the motel. "Let me think about it," he said to the realtor, then had Aubrey follow her to the next appointment, right down the road from the farm.

As soon as he spied the charming white house with the red shutters, porch, and garden, his heart began beating a steady staccato rhythm against his chest.

"Ah, I recognize this place," Aubrey said, pulling in front of the rental. "Lisa loved this house for some reason. Especially the wildflowers in the garden. Always said it was postcard perfect."

And it was as if by mentioning his late wife, he had brought the secret front and center again.

A lump formed in Oliver's throat, and he considered not going inside, but he did anyway and loved everything about the place just like he knew he would. *Thanks a lot, Lisa.*

"This seems perfect," Oliver told the realtor, but he must not have looked completely convinced.

"Sleep on it and let me know your decision tomorrow," the realtor said as she waved good-bye.

He got back in the truck, and as Aubrey drove them to the

farm, Oliver said, "The place is great. You must be a good-luck charm."

"Don't know about that," Aubrey replied roughly as he pulled up the long driveway. "How about we celebrate with a couple of beers?"

His heart thumped hard. "I'd like that."

Once Aubrey opened two bottles of Bud, they sat side by side on the porch and watched the sun disappear on the horizon. The pink and reds looked painted by hand against the backdrop of the hillside. "It's really pretty here."

"Yeah, I never grow tired of this view. Except sometimes..." Aubrey seemed to shake away his thoughts.

"What?" Oliver asked after another swallow.

He shrugged. "Sometimes I wish I'd traveled."

"It's never too late," Oliver suggested, then clinked their beer bottles together.

"Yeah, I hear you. Always so much to get done on the farm, and I don't know where time goes," he replied, looking into the distance. "I bet you've been around the world."

"Not exactly. But plenty of amazing places," Oliver admitted. He'd traveled quite frequently over the years, in fact. "There's still nothing quite like the feeling of coming home. At least a place that *feels* like home."

"Or a *person*," Aubrey added, melancholy momentarily flitting through his gaze. Aubrey Hendricks was a romantic at heart; imagine that. He damn near made Oliver swoon.

Aubrey, of course, was thinking about his wife, Lisa, and guilt stabbed at Oliver's gut.

"Yeah...I haven't felt that in a long while," he confessed. Probably not since his last long-term relationship in his early thirties with a man he'd hoped was forever. Until he cheated and all Oliver's dreams were dashed at once.

"Is that why you left your high-powered job? Why you..."

Aubrey asked in a hesitant voice, then shook his head. "None of my business."

"It's okay," he said, tapping his arm. "Go ahead and ask."

"I...I can't help wondering about that. I hope I'm not overstepping, but you rub at a spot on your chest a lot. And I...I saw some sort of scar a few days after you got here." His face flushed as Oliver's stomach bottomed out. "It was only a quick glance, but I wondered...never mind."

The opportunity had been served up to him on a silver platter, and he needed to take it. Except it would change everything. *Everything.* Still, it was a long time coming, and it wasn't fair to Aubrey.

His pulse was thundering in his ears. "I had a heart transplant."

"Christ, I'm sorry to hear that," Aubrey said in a concerned tone as his eyes darted to his chest as if imagining the scar. Oliver wondered when he would've noticed it. Maybe when he'd been cleaning a high shelf in the bakery or something. "That why you quit your job?"

"It was to step out of the rat race. Start a new life," Oliver replied, treading carefully toward what he knew was the goal line. "I traveled some, took culinary classes, exercised more. But I...I came to Heartsville for a different reason. And when I saw your Help Wanted sign, there was just something that clicked...something that..."

Oliver felt warm bile crawling up his throat, and he swallowed it down. There was no turning back now. He needed to get it out—for his own mental health and maybe Aubrey's too. He only hoped the man would want to have the information, regardless of the outcome.

"Something that...?" Aubrey's eyebrows scrunched together.

"Aubrey. *Fuck.*" He swallowed roughly. "I came here because the hospital told me that the family was open to being contacted."

Aubrey's mouth opened and closed as if trying to process the information. "What family?"

Oliver's throat grew dry as a desert. "The transplant donor family."

Aubrey's hands were shaking around the bottle of beer he clutched, so it had to have dawned on him, but still he pushed for confirmation. "I'm not sure I'm following..."

Oliver sprang up from his seat and began pacing the porch in front of Aubrey.

Why the hell was this so damned hard? Would it be this difficult if he hadn't gotten to know the man? If he didn't love this farm and wasn't attracted to him? Not that any of that fucking mattered. Christ, he needed this over with before he had a panic attack.

"Aubrey, my heart was donated by you...from your wife," he uttered in a weakened voice. He cleared his throat and found the strength to continue from some source inside him. "Lisa Hendricks saved my life."

For one drawn-out moment there was silence, and he could hear the sound of the crickets from the garden, which were only a decibel louder than his heart thumping in his ears.

"Holy fucking hell," Aubrey whispered then gripped the railing as he stood—as if he might topple over. "And you didn't think to tell me?"

"On the contrary. I wanted to tell you a thousand times but chickened out. You're a hard man to...to *approach*, and that first day..." He rambled, remembering the night he pulled into the driveway and Aubrey's brusque tone. "I know that's no excuse. I drove all the way here to tell you and then just...became intrigued by the job offer, then charmed by this farm."

Aubrey stared at him across the distance as his breaths shot out in harsh pants. So many emotions crossed his face. Sadness, wonder, astonishment, gratitude...until his features finally settled on anger.

The man clenched his fists. "And you let me hire you? Without saying a word? I knew...I just knew there was something off. Were you *ever* going to tell me?"

Oliver took a step back, thinking Aubrey might clean his clock, though he would've definitely deserved it.

"Yes. The day before the grand opening, I showed up determined to tell you. But then the frost happened and the crops..." He shook his head. "The next day was the grand opening, and I'm so fucking sorry I didn't tell you that first night."

Aubrey's shoulders slumped as his eyes became almost vacant. Like he had vacuumed up all his emotions and locked them away to protect himself. "I need you to leave."

Oliver's stomach dropped to the ground even though he'd known with every fiber of his being that this would be the outcome. "Yeah, okay. I figured this would happen..."

"Just get *out*."

"I only have one more thing I—"

"Oliver. Drive the fuck out of here and never come back."

Like a dog with his tail between his legs, Oliver lumbered down the steps to his car, feeling like he was wading through cement. He sat a moment, gathering his spinning thoughts before starting the engine.

He couldn't fucking believe it. It was over. All of it was over. And Aubrey didn't even want to hear him out.

Would it have been the same outcome had he told him the first day? Would he have still shut him out, asked him to leave? Now he'd never know. He had screwed everything up.

He watched as Aubrey bolted down the steps, slid onto the nearest four-wheeler, and took off down the hill toward the strawberry fields.

He let out a breath and glanced down at the key to the bakery hanging with the others on the key ring. Then he looked behind him to the small bag in his back seat. He should just leave it but couldn't. He was obviously a glutton for punishment.

After a solid twenty minutes of waiting, he opened the car door and slid out the front seat with the key and the bag. He walked to the porch steps and sat down, the bag beside him.

After another thirty minutes had passed, he finally heard the sound of the motor from the hillside, heading toward the house. Aubrey parked the all-terrain vehicle and started for the house. Oliver stood up so as not to startle him.

"What the fuck are you still doing here?" he asked, but there was less bite to his voice, more sorrow. When Oliver saw his red eyes and tearstained cheeks, he was consumed by a longing so great, he had to plant his feet so as not to reach out and comfort the man. He wanted to take away his pain, but it was an impossible situation.

"I wanted to make sure you were okay," he said in a small voice.

"You have no right—" Aubrey began, but Oliver held up his hands.

"I know," he said, stepping toward him and holding out his hand. "Here's the key to the bakery."

"You could've left it somewhere," he said, pocketing it without meeting his eyes.

"There's one more thing, and then I'm gone. I promise." He reached for the bag on the steps. He slid toward Aubrey the donor-information paperwork that basically said he had been awarded a heart, with the date, which was the night Lisa passed away. He wanted him to have it for later, in case it might help him see that she had done some good in the world. "From the hospital." Aubrey took the paper but refused to look down at it. "For whenever you have the strength to read it. Or you can throw it away. Your choice."

Then he pulled out a long black-rubber object. "I don't want either of us to have any regrets. Regardless of how angry or hurt you are, you've given me a gift. The gift of life. I'll always be grateful. So I thought you might want to listen before I go..."

"What the hell is that?" Aubrey asked in voice that nearly wrecked Oliver, it sounded so reedy and scared.

"It's a stethoscope," Oliver replied, holding it up, then taking the metal end shaped like a disc and placing it directly against his heart. Aubrey staggered back as if he'd been punched, and tears sprang to Oliver's eyes. His chest positively *ached* for the man.

## 12

## AUBREY

He couldn't tear his gaze away from Oliver. Tears streamed down his face, and he stood frozen, transfixed by the rise and fall of Oliver's chest, knowing a piece of his wife remained alive. It was one thing to sign a donor card; that was the easy part. He imagined hearing the beat and pulse of Lisa's heart inside Oliver.

*My God. Her heart...inside Oliver.*

"Her heart? You...have her heart?" Painfully choked-out words Aubrey never thought he'd say. They might've prepared *Oliver* for meeting him, but Aubrey had been knocked off his feet and his breath taken away by this moment. He wanted to know and yet he didn't. He couldn't stop staring at Oliver's chest, as if he could see right through the man's skin and bones to the beating organ.

"Yes. I...I was on the transplant list for months and getting to a critical point. The doctors were afraid I'd die before a donor became available."

"So you got lucky," Aubrey lashed out, and seeing Oliver whiten, immediately regretted the harshness of his words, but it was too late to take them back.

Oliver shook his head, sorrow clouding his eyes. "I got blessed. I can't imagine what you went through, Aubrey. I don't pretend that we stand here in equal positions. I owe you everything. You and Lisa."

He wanted to pound the walls and scream out his pain like he had earlier when he'd raced across the fields to Lisa's grave. But it couldn't have been easy for Oliver and his family either, knowing someone had to die for him to live. "There's no winning side to this."

"No, there can't be. It's set up so that a horrible loss will always be another person's gain. But with the loss of her life, Lisa saved mine. She gave me a chance at seeing the glorious colors of an evening sunset streak across the sky, the ability to hear my little niece and nephew babble their first words. From the moment I heard her story, I wanted to come and talk to you, to tell you how much her selfless gift meant to me. I never intended to deceive you. It's not my way. It's not who I am."

"I don't know you. I don't really know who you are. I...I can't process this. My God..." Overwhelmed and frustrated by his disappointment in Oliver, Aubrey turned his back and strode into the house, heading for the large family room. He went straight to the liquor cabinet and pulled out a bottle of scotch. His hands trembled, and the neck of the bottle banged against the glass as he poured, but he managed to splash a healthy amount in the tumbler and down it straight. The liquid seared through him, but he welcomed its warming path. He'd been so cold.

"Aubrey?"

Still holding the stethoscope, Oliver stood in the doorway.

"Yeah." He set the glass down. "What?"

"I didn't want to leave without making sure you were okay. I didn't—"

"She was the most giving person. I didn't deserve someone as good as her." He walked to the large leather sofa and sat with a hard *thump*. "I always said her heart was as big and open as the sky. Every few days she'd gather up whatever didn't sell and give it to the shelter in the neighboring town. She'd bake bread and pies and pick up groceries for the elderly who were shut-ins and had no one to shop for them."

The sofa cushion dipped next to him as Oliver sat by his side. "Cassie and all the customers who've come by the bakery, everyone told me what a wonderful person she was. I wish I could've known her. I know it was a great loss."

Aubrey stretched out a hand, laid his palm on Oliver's chest, and felt the movement underneath his fingers.

*Thump, thump, thump. Alive. Alive.*

Tears burned his eyes, and he saw his own grief mirrored in Oliver's eyes. The man offered him the stethoscope. "Do you want to listen?"

His fingers curled into a fist on top of Oliver's shirt. "No. Yes...I don't know..." He wondered what Oliver would do if he laid his head on his chest, like he used to do with Lisa, and listen to the soothing rhythm play in his ear.

"Okay," Aubrey whispered and stuck the listening buds into his ears. Oliver sat silently, and Aubrey knew he was giving him the time he needed. His fingers fumbled trying to hold the disc, and Oliver placed his hand over Aubrey's and guided it to the place on his chest. Aubrey closed his eyes, his hand still in Oliver's.

The rhythmic beat played beneath his hand, and Aubrey swayed a bit, caught up in the thought that this was Lisa, there inside Oliver, giving him life. Oliver's cheek touched his hair and Aubrey leaned on his shoulder, the enormity of his emotions too heavy to bear. Tears streaked down his cheeks.

He lost track of time and had no idea how long they sat there with him listening, when he became aware of Oliver's breathing in the quiet of the room. At the touch of Oliver's hand to his cheek, Aubrey cast a glance upward into Oliver's eyes. Their faces were so close, he could see the freckles dotting Oliver's nose.

"Are you okay?"

"Yeah. Thank you."

"Don't. There's no need to. It's me who needs to give thanks for this incredible gift you've given me. I know I should've told you when we first met, and I'm sorry. I'm so sorry I waited and didn't speak up, and now I've ruined a potential friendship. But you have to know that not a day goes by where I don't thank you and Lisa for giving me back my life."

Aubrey listened again, every beat a comfort to the pieces of his healing soul. "Is it wrong for me to want to keep listening? I can stop if it makes you uncomfortable."

"No. Not at all. Take all the time you need."

Peace washed over him as he reclined on his sofa, Oliver's heart beating in his ears. Twilight deepened into the soft gray of early evening, and the crickets began their chirping in the long grass. To Aubrey, it seemed to be the most natural thing in the world to sit here with Oliver as the house settled in for the night.

Oliver's fingers stroked his cheek, and Aubrey's breath hitched as he felt the warmth of Oliver's face against his. The silence, only moments before comforting, now sizzled with tension. A beat began to pulse inside him, and without giving himself a chance to think, Aubrey tilted his head and brushed his lips against Oliver's. In contrast to the roughness of his cheeks, Oliver's lips were smooth under his, and for a second Aubrey's mouth clung to Oliver's, craving the warmth. Oliver stiffened, then molded his mouth to Aubrey's, kissing him back.

He fell back, breathing hard, the blood pounding in his head. Disoriented from the unaccustomed waves of desire rolling through him, Aubrey closed his eyes and took a deep breath, then expelled it in a great *whoosh* of air.

"I'm sorry. I didn't mean—"

"Don't apologize. I understand. You were emotional and weren't thinking. I get it." Oliver's strained voice sounded curiously detached, and Aubrey's swift glance took note of the flush across his cheeks and the tightness of his jaw and mouth. "I'd better go."

He stood, and Aubrey remained silent. He should tell him it was okay between them now. That he understood how hard it must've been to come here. God knows it took everything he had to put that stethoscope in his ears, knowing Lisa's heart lay beating in Oliver's chest. Instead, he said nothing.

Oliver walked away, the weight of their earlier anger and pain lying heavy between them. Not to mention that kiss. Aubrey's lips throbbed from it, and his body ached, pent-up and frustrated. It was dangerous now. Too dangerous to have Oliver around. Best that he leave. He could hire another baker who'd do a good job. Yet he followed Oliver out of the house and to his car, unwilling to make that final cut between them.

"So you'll be going back to New York now? Back to your old life?"

About to open the car door, Oliver faltered. "I hadn't thought that far ahead. I'll be fine. Thank you, Aubrey, for letting me help you get the bakery back on its feet and for giving me a glimpse into the remarkable woman Lisa was."

This time he opened the car door, got in, and started the engine, kicking up dust and gravel. Duke barked and sat at his feet, and Aubrey watched the car speed away, red taillights glowing in the dark. He didn't move even after the lights turned to pinpricks and then nothing.

"I'm a damn fool, aren't I?" He gazed down at the dog. Duke whined, then barked and ran down the driveway. Instead of going back inside, Aubrey tramped through the grass to the fields. Here was where he felt most comfortable, with the everlasting sky above him, the wind in his face, and the smell of damp earth.

"What do I do?" His words carried away in the breeze. "Do I let him go, or do I tell him to stay? He knew it was wrong." The long reeds bent before him as he pushed on, and stars sprinkled up above him in the midnight blue evening sky. From somewhere in the trees an owl hooted, and little creatures rustled in the grass.

He continued, now playing devil's advocate. "But what should he have done? Gotten out of his car that first day, walked up to me, a total stranger, and told me an incredible story? I'da probably kicked him out right then without ever getting to know him."

Aubrey had reached the strawberry fields now and surveyed the great flats of their spreading leaves. Soon there'd be a huge crop of the fruit, and they'd be making jam and jelly.

He dropped to the ground and sat, listening to the stirrings of the night. If he was being honest, he enjoyed Oliver's company and looked forward to their dinners together. They'd fallen into an easy camaraderie, and when Oliver said he planned on looking for a place to rent or potentially buy, that was one of the better days Aubrey could remember since Lisa died.

"It was the shock of it all. It's not his fault she died. Being an organ donor was important to her. She wanted to help save someone's life if she could."

But now that kiss. Aubrey touched his lips, still able to feel Oliver's heated breath. That kiss rekindled everything he'd thought dead and buried. Could he work with Oliver now that they'd kissed? Would Oliver even want to?

"Dammit." Aubrey stood and checked his watch. Past eight o'clock. It wouldn't take him long to get to the Clover Motel.

*Oliver, we got some talking to do.*

# 13

## OLIVER

Oliver was such a wreck, it was useless to swipe at the tears cascading down his cheeks as he pulled out of First Light Farm for the last time and drove toward the Clover Motel.

The emotions on Aubrey's face when he listened to his wife's heart—the grief, the agony, the absolute wonder that a part of his deceased spouse could still exist in someone else to sustain their life—were incredible to witness. Oliver's gut churned for the man, but he would never regret those last few minutes together. He somehow knew that despite Aubrey's initial confusion and outrage, he needed to wait him out to help him see the forest through the trees, so to speak, that were like roots holding him back.

No, he'd never regret making the offer, only the timing. The relief that flooded him when he finally got the words out was immense, even if it was mixed with despair.

And then there was the kiss. Aubrey's warm lips, his hungry mouth, the sounds wrenched from his throat—like a profound ache igniting a desperate spark of longing. It was something he wouldn't soon forget. The whole evening ranked up there as one of the most overwhelming moments in his life.

*Damn it.* He needed a fucking drink.

That was when he saw the familiar LAST CALL sign beckoning him inside. He'd always meant to stop here, and since this was sure to be one of his final nights in this town, there was no time like the present.

He parked in one of the remaining spots available in the lot in front of the charming bar that looked more like a large Victorian home. He slid out of his car and glanced toward the steps inviting him inside. His gaze moved upward to the second story, where Cassie had mentioned the three men lived.

It was a novel concept. One that made him pine for such a life. Every day he'd taken the train to work and stayed for long hours before commuting back home and falling into bed. He saw little of his expensive apartment or the city itself, unless it was the inside of a restaurant or the courthouse. He lived on a large body of water but rarely walked the High Line or took part in outdoor events. Yet in Heartsville he'd felt more part of nature in one month than he had during ten years of his old life.

As soon as he pushed through the door of the bar, he felt like he could breathe better.

He glanced at the occupied tables and then at the available barstools. When his gaze connected with Quinn, the man broke into a genuine smile and waved him over.

He made a beeline to an empty seat and sank down on the soft leather.

"Oliver. Good to see you again," Quinn remarked, wiping down the bar top in front of him with the towel he'd slid from his shoulder.

"You as well," he replied, glancing at their selection of beers on tap.

"Seems like you could use a drink," Quinn said, studying his face, and fuck, he hadn't even considered what he must've looked like. His eyes felt puffy, and his hair was probably standing on end from shoving his fingers through it.

"Definitely," he replied. "Can I have a shot of tequila and whatever beer is on special?"

"Oh, it's one of those kinds of nights," Quinn said with a wink before turning to prepare his beverages.

The shot burned going down, so he took a long sip of the dark draft Quinn had selected. He felt better already. The fog of his brain cleared a little, and it felt good to finally relax and tune in to whatever game was on the television above the bar or to the benign conversations happening around him.

Another attractive man with dark hair appeared from what must've been the kitchen, carrying food he served to a nearby table. When the scent of the fried food wafted over, he realized how famished he was. The guy, whose expression seemed cautious, stepped behind the bar, briefly clasping Quinn's waist as he stretched for a glass. It was a subtle intimate gesture that made Oliver shiver as a heaviness settled in his chest.

Not that he thought he'd ever have something like that with Aubrey, but he couldn't help licking his lips to chase the man's flavor nonetheless.

"Gray, this is Oliver," Quinn said after he poured a beer for a customer. "The man who runs the bakery at First Light Farm."

Before Oliver could even think of a rebuttal, Gray leaned over to shake his hand. "Ah, the guy who made a grown man weep over chocolate silk pie."

Quinn chuckled. "We needed to hide it from Emery so he wouldn't have it for dinner and breakfast too."

"No shame in that," Oliver responded with a laugh. "Glad he liked it so much."

"We'll be sure to send him your way next time he gets a midday craving for it," Quinn said, and Oliver turned away before they caught his expression.

"Speaking of which, you hungry?" Gray asked, reaching for a menu beneath the bar and laying it in front of him. "Emery will hook you up. His wings are amazing."

"Thanks." Oliver stared down at the offerings, his stomach growling. He'd better take advantage before his appetite betrayed him again. Along with the alcohol.

"Have you decided?" Quinn asked a couple of minutes later.

"The wings it is," he said, sliding the menu across to him.

He watched as Quinn rang up his order and then strode down the bar to serve a couple of ladies who'd sat down. He was glad for the alone time to get his thoughts in order. He supposed he had two choices in this scenario. Go home and figure out a new career, or find a new town to start over again. He thought of the quaint little house for rent from earlier that night. *Bad decision.*

Besides, it was too close to the farm. And suddenly he straightened in his chair. *The bakery.* Cassie would be expecting him in the morning. Not that she couldn't do it on her own for the rest of the week. They had a good system going. The pies for tomorrow were already in the cooler, and he'd prepped most of the muffin mixes. It definitely was more efficient with two people, but she could probably manage until Aubrey found someone else to fill his position. Unless he decided to shut down production again. The thought made Oliver sick to his stomach.

He desperately wished he could finish what he'd started. If only he hadn't messed everything up. *Fuck.*

"Can I get you another?" Quinn asked, startling him out of his thoughts. He hadn't even realized he'd already drained his glass.

"One more," he said, knowing that would be his limit. But his room at the motel felt too lonely to head back to just yet.

"Hard day at work?" Quinn asked in a hesitant tone as he set down a fresh beer in front of him.

What could he possibly divulge? Oliver didn't want to give too much away, but damn, he sure could use someone to talk to. It would be too late to call his sister, but he also didn't want to hear her lecture him about all his bad decisions.

"I guess I..." He sighed into his beer. "I majorly fucked things up."

"Why do I get the impression this has nothing to do with pies?" Quinn asked, concern etching his brow.

"Do you know Aubrey Hendricks well?" he asked tentatively. Fuck, this was a bad idea. Any information he'd glean from Quinn wouldn't help one way or another, but just bringing up the man filled his stomach with warmth.

"He's been in Last Call a handful of times," Quinn replied. "He's a quiet man, somewhat broody, which sort of reminds me of another guy I know."

He swung his gaze affectionately toward Gray, who was talking to a table of men in the back corner.

Oliver smiled for the first time in a couple of hours, and it felt foreign but good. "Yeah, those brooding types get me all the time."

"So then...you and Aubrey?" he asked with a raised eyebrow.

"No," he blurted out. *Shit.* "Sorry if I gave the wrong idea. I mean, *sure*, if he was into men, but pretty certain that's not the case."

*But the kiss.* Still, it wasn't his place to share any of that, especially if the man was only confusing grief with loneliness, if his need for a connection was misplaced.

"The way I heard it, his wife died and he's been grieving her pretty hard these last couple of years," Quinn said with sadness in his tone. "Seems like a good guy. So I hope you can resolve your differences."

"Thanks." He shook his head. "I should've never brought it up."

"S'okay," he replied, raising his hands. "Bartenders are sworn to secrecy just like therapists."

He blew out a breath and relaxed in his seat again. Besides, he'd be long gone, and Aubrey had lived here all his life. He certainly wouldn't want people to wonder anything more about the man.

Just then the third owner stepped out of the kitchen and

behind the bar, carrying what looked to be his basket of wings. Christ, he was just as handsome as the other men. His bronze hair and beard were scruffier, but Oliver would certainly never kick him out of bed.

"Gray said I should introduce myself to the man who might singlehandedly ruin my waistline," Emery said, placing his food in front of him. The wing sauce smelled delicious.

"After tonight, I might be saying the same about you," Oliver replied with a smile as he reached to shake his hand. "Pleased to meet you."

He noticed the brush of Quinn's fingers on Emery's arm as he turned away, and damned if that feeling of longing didn't return full force. He ruthlessly shoved the thought away so he could finish his beer and enjoy his wings. He'd be alone with his thoughts again soon enough.

After he paid the check and fished his keys out of his pocket to leave, Quinn lifted his hand in a wave. "Stop by again soon."

Oliver couldn't bear to tell him it was unlikely, so he forced a smile and headed out the door.

He drove to the Clover Motel, thankful he still had a little buzz going. He shucked off his clothes, sank down in bed, and fell into a restless sleep.

## 14

## AUBREY

"What? Is something wrong?" Cassie's brow puckered as she stared at Aubrey. "Oliver's never late."

Aubrey had spent a miserable, sleepless night. After Oliver took off, Aubrey had wandered through the fields, then jumped in his truck and raced to the Clover Motel, only to discover Oliver wasn't even there. Maybe he'd left the farm and kept driving. Aubrey knew that feeling of wanting to erase the past and leave everything behind.

And as hurt and angry as Aubrey was at Oliver's news, a pang of heartbreak resonated inside him at the thought of never seeing the man again.

"Uh." He took off his baseball cap and replaced it. "He 'n I had a few words last night. I'm not sure he's coming back."

"Words?" She shut the oven door after sliding in a tray of muffins. "About what?"

He paced back and forth, a feeling of helplessness running through him, but as Cassie was the most levelheaded person he knew, she would be the one to give him the best advice as to his next step.

"Come sit with me." He pulled out a chair for her at one of

the small tables and waited until she sat before taking the seat across from her. "It's a long story."

"Our customers don't start showing up for at least an hour, so we're good."

"Oliver didn't just happen to show up here."

"He meant to come? To First Light? Why?" Her eyes narrowed. "You don't look well. What's going on?"

"Remember Oliver said he gave up his stressful job to enjoy life? Well, it turns out he didn't choose to do it. He had to. Oliver was sick, Cassie."

"Oh, that poor man. And so young too."

"Yeah." Aubrey's hands clenched into fists in his lap. "He had a bad heart." The words tumbled out of him. "He needed an operation, and he'd been on the transplant list waiting, thinking he'd never get one. Thinking he might die. Then he got the call. A heart had become available." Pain lanced through him for both Oliver and Lisa. "Lisa's heart."

Cassie whitened and put a hand to her chest. "Oh, my. Oh, Aubrey." She stood and came over to put her arms around him.

"Yeah. Oliver has Lisa's heart, and he came here to tell me, but I thought he was here for the bakery job. It was a miscommunication that first day. And instead of clearing it up and talking to me right away, he continued the lie."

"I can understand that."

Aubrey needed this calm, practical side of Cassie to explain it to him.

"You can?"

"Yes. What should he have done, told you on the side of the road? Let's face it, Aubrey." She gave him a sad smile. "You're not the most approachable person, and it was probably the scariest thing he's ever had to do. So while I understand you were upset he didn't tell you right away, I can sympathize with his need to wait a bit and get your measure. Feel you out."

Recalling the softness of Oliver's lips on his, Aubrey's face heated. "I didn't see it that way. Not at first."

"I'm sure you didn't. But it wasn't a lie, exactly. More like an omission."

"You've been watching too many of those crime shows on television. You're talking lawyer speak now."

She snorted, her eyes crinkling with amusement. "It's no such thing." Her demeanor turned somber, and she touched his arm. "He was scared. Imagine coming to a stranger and telling them you have a part of their loved one inside your body." Her hand covered her mouth, and her eyes welled with tears. "Oh, Aubrey. Lisa's heart. It was so big, so giving and true. What a blessing to have it living in a man like Oliver, who's continuing her legacy by being kind and decent."

"I heard it," Aubrey whispered. "Her heart. Oliver let me listen to it through a stethoscope. At first I wanted to curl up in a ball, it hurt so bad. Then I couldn't stop listening."

"I'm sure." She rubbed his shoulders. "It's a gift Oliver gave you."

"I told him to leave." At the time he spoke the words he meant it, but now Aubrey wasn't so sure. He wasn't sure about much of anything. Not anymore. The past day had kicked the legs out from under him. "I tossed him out and told him to never come back."

"But you don't really mean it, do you? Whatever you said was in anger, in response to the lie you believed he told you." Practical Cassie knew him better than he knew himself, Aubrey realized.

"I've made such a mess of everything." He buried his head in his hands. "I don't know what to do."

"Sure you do. That's why you're so upset." Cassie gave his shoulder a squeeze and left him to go behind the counter to make the coffee. When it finished perking, she brought him a cup and a day-old muffin they sold for half-price. "What do you think you should do?"

The coffee warmed him but only to a point. Aubrey knew he needed to make it right between him and Oliver, no matter what the end result would be.

"I'll see you later. I'll be back."

"I'll be here waiting." Cassie hugged him.

Less than half an hour later, Aubrey stood outside room 214 of the Clover Motel, bouncing up and down on his toes. He'd been out there for almost five minutes, getting up the courage to knock.

"To hell with it," Aubrey muttered and rapped hard on the door.

"Hold your horses, I'm coming." Oliver's voice reached him through the door. "I thought I had until eleven a.m. to check out." The door opened, and he faced Oliver, who paled when their eyes met.

"Aubrey? What're you doing here?"

"Can I come in? I'd like to talk to you."

Pain flashed through Oliver's eyes. "Is there anything left to say? I thought we covered it all."

"I've been thinking." He gestured to the inside of the room. "May I come in?"

Saying nothing, Oliver opened the door wide and walked into the room to sit on the bed.

The tiny room fit only a double bed, a small chest of drawers, and a nightstand. Aubrey leaned a hip against the furniture. "I know I said some pretty rough things to you, but I spoke out of anger and shock."

"I understand. And I'm not sure I would've reacted any differently."

A bit taken aback, Aubrey rubbed his face. "I know I gave permission for the donor to contact me, but honestly? I never expected it to happen. All that time passed, and I'd grown accustomed to being alone. Then when Cassie convinced me to reopen the bakery, take that first step back to normalcy, you showed up and everything changed. I changed." He swallowed hard, past the lump in his throat. "Damn, this is the most I've talked in years."

Oliver joked, "Now there's a surprise."

A quick smile flitted over Aubrey's lips, and his voice quieted. "I'm serious. I'm not sure what's going to happen now, Oliver. But I don't think it's fair, after all you've done to bring the bakery back and better than ever, to kick you out and let it all go to waste. It's not going to be easy for me, but I understand now how hard it was for you to come here and speak to me."

A spark flared in Oliver's eyes. "Please believe me. I never, ever intended to hurt you. Every day I wanted to tell you, but I talked myself out of it, saying, 'Tomorrow. I'll tell him tomorrow.' Once we renovated the bakery and it became operational, I grew to love it. It wasn't a ploy. I wanted to stay here. Rent a house and put down some roots."

"And now?" Aubrey held his breath.

"I guess it's more up to you than me. What do you think?"

The enormity of having Oliver remain working for him wasn't lost on Aubrey. Before he'd found out about their curious connection, he'd enjoyed the man's company and was impressed with his business sense. Plus, one thing neither of them seemed willing to speak of was the kiss, but Aubrey was staying far away from that at the moment.

"I think you should stay."

## 15

## OLIVER

Oliver could hardly believe things had actually worked in his favor. After all the second-guessing he'd done, tossing and turning into the dawn hours, Aubrey had shown up at the Clover Motel and offered him his job back.

*"I think you should stay."*

Hearing those words had made him tremble. He felt them deep in his gut because he knew it wasn't easy for the man. Not wanting to waste one more minute or have Aubrey change his mind, he showered, paid for another week at the motel, and drove to the farm to help Cassie with the morning rush.

As soon as he stepped foot inside the door, he got an inkling that Cassie had something to do with Aubrey's change of heart. Throwing him a knowing grin, she didn't even ask where he'd been that morning, only pulled him into a hug. "Good to see you."

When she drew back, her gaze landed on his chest as if imagining what was beneath his shirt, and he knew Aubrey had confessed it all.

He almost thanked her, but he didn't want it to be awkward. Besides, Aubrey was pretty stubborn, so he wouldn't have approached Cassie in the first place if he wasn't conflicted and looking for solid advice.

The morning went by in a whirlwind of serving customers and reorganizing empty shelves. During the lunchtime rush, he glanced up to see Aubrey leaning against the doorframe just inside the bakery, taking in the crowd but also watching him intently. When their gazes connected he saw relief in his eyes, gratitude too. Not an ounce of the resentment from the previous night, and Oliver was grateful for that.

And when Aubrey's lips curved into a genuine smile, it was as if the sun decided to grace him with its presence after tense hours of storm clouds. He reassigned himself the mission of making the man's mouth split into a grin that magnificent every day.

Oliver had difficulty getting lost in the task in front of him without his gaze sliding to the man again and again. After Aubrey spoke briefly to a couple of customers who greeted him, he quietly slipped out the door, and Oliver was both relieved and disappointed. At least it gave his pulse a chance to slow to a steadier pace.

"I think someone's glad you're back," Cassie murmured in his ear as she passed by him to the kitchen, and he felt himself flush from his ears down to his chest.

She couldn't possibly know about the kiss, could she? Oliver didn't think Aubrey would go as far as telling her about that portion of the evening. He and Aubrey hadn't even mentioned it when he showed up at the motel. Not that it would be an easy topic to bring up. Besides, he didn't want to push his luck, so he chalked up the profound show of affection to the mixed bag of emotions that came with grief and laid it to rest.

*Mostly.*

At the day's end, he'd admit to lingering a bit, perhaps hoping for another glimpse of the boss man. Except after everything that happened, he didn't want to make any wrong moves. Prior to his confession, they'd shared a couple of friendly dinners and visits on the porch. But now...now it seemed like the reset button had been pushed, and he wasn't sure they could operate in a similar fashion.

It was as if everything felt more sensitive, more sacred—like any conversation between them from here on out would have to include or revolve around the heart ticking in his chest. And though he was glad they'd finally had it out and there were no more secrets between them—at least on his end—he also regretted the fact that it might become like a wedge between them. He was looking forward to getting to know Aubrey the man, more than Aubrey the grieving husband, though that was definitely part of who he was.

It was a double-edged sword, to say the least, because now every time they were in the same room, Aubrey might be thinking about the organ pumping blood through his veins. The best thing might be to throw himself into his new job in the bakery and forget he even knew how the man's lips tasted or felt against his own. Forget his smile, his deadpan sense of humor, or his empty cupboards, no matter how much the thought tempted him to extend a dinner invitation again.

He should thank his lucky stars he was doing something he enjoyed and could finally get settled in this town. It was like his life had been on pause, and now he could hit play again. Now that his secret was out.

As he made his way to his car, he caught a glimpse of Aubrey and one of the farmhands, Ross, on a couple of four-wheelers headed down the hill to the strawberry fields. He stood and watched a minute, wondering if there was another emergency frost warning. He considered waiting just to double-check everything was all right, but he knew that was irrational. Waiting around might give Aubrey the wrong impression.

Besides, he had other things to do. So he slid into the front seat of his car and pulled out his cell. His first call was to the real-estate agent, who agreed to meet him at the quaint rental property to sign a lease agreement within the hour. Instead of sitting in his drab motel room, he grabbed a sandwich at the new deli he'd spotted in town. He didn't realize how famished he was until he chowed it down on a park bench near the pretty pond he'd found the other day. Then he took a deep breath and dialed his sister.

"It's about time," Jennifer said as soon as she answered. "You've been avoiding me."

"No, I haven't," he griped, then changed his mind. Why fight it? "Yeah, guess I have."

"At least you admit it." She chuckled. "What's going on?"

"I *have* been busy with the grand opening," he explained. "But I also finally got up the nerve to tell Aubrey Hendricks about my transplant."

She gasped. "And?"

"He was stunned and then angry. So angry that he kicked me out." He could still feel that ghost of an ache in his chest from watching the man going through so much turmoil.

Fuck, it had been brutal.

She was quiet for a long moment before she sighed, her voice softening. "I guess I can understand why after you—"

"But then something incredible happened," he said suddenly, a shiver racing through him.

Her breath caught. "Your voice sounds different. Tell me everything."

Oliver was transported back to their childhood when they would sit on her bed with the door closed and tell each other secrets. She was the first person he told he was gay, and her acceptance made him feel like everything might be okay. He hated holding things back from her, so unpacking all his emotions now felt right.

"I...brought the stethoscope with me and offered for him to listen to my heart."

"Holy shit, Oliver, you're going to make me cry. Did he accept your offer?"

"He did." Oliver's voice wavered. "He broke down, and I did too. It was like nothing I'd ever experienced before."

"Now I've got chills," she said in a thick voice. "I hope in the end he'll be glad you stumbled onto his farm, no matter how long it took you to get your act together."

"Yeah, me too. Plus I get to keep my job and get settled for a while," he said. "I'll figure out what to do with my apartment later."

"I can keep checking on your place for you, make sure all is okay," she offered, and he breathed out in relief. "But why does it sound like there's something else you're not telling me?"

Damn, she was always so perceptive.

"There is something else that happened that same night..." Dare he say it out loud? But this was his sister, and it was an important detail he couldn't easily shake. "Aubrey...he, um...kissed me."

"Excuse me?" She sounded as confused as he'd been at the time. But despite his confusion, it still somehow felt right. Perfect in the moment.

"He just put his lips to mine and kissed me," Oliver explained. "And I think...he was just a jumble of exposed nerves mixed with grief. Know what I mean?"

"I don't even know what to say, Oliver." It was rare that she was speechless, and he might've poked fun if it wasn't still so emotional and raw for him. "Just...take care of yourself."

"I will," he replied as he pulled up to the quaint white house, the same feeling as last time coursing through him.

He signed a month-to-month lease without even going inside the property again. He just had a feeling he was supposed to be there. Like maybe it had been Lisa's doing or something.

He shook his head. *Ridiculous.*

Thankfully the place came completely furnished, but he still needed some staples, like sheets for the queen-sized bed and food for his cupboards. He spent his day off on Sunday getting most of it sorted. While he was checking out with a full cart at the general store, Carol told him about a Walmart fifteen minutes up the main road. He spent the afternoon stocking up on toiletries, towels, and a comforter set.

On Monday, he did something nearly as impulsive as showing up in this town in the first place. He drove to the nearest car dealership and traded in his Mercedes for a compact SUV.

Driving back to the motel to collect the last of his things, he thought maybe he finally...*finally* felt like he belonged in Heartsville.

# 16

# AUBREY

O liver stood before Aubrey, a smile as wide as the sky on his face.

"You did? That house?" The house Lisa had loved would now be inhabited by Oliver. "It would make sense for you to live closer to the farm." It had been a week since Oliver's big announcement, and Aubrey had wavered between spending time at the bakery and keeping his distance. The need to see Oliver won out in the end. Aubrey liked the man's carefree, friendly chatter, and there was no reason they couldn't continue to enjoy their morning ritual of drinking coffee together. Before heading out to the fields, he liked stopping by the bakery to see what the specials of the day were.

"Yeah. I thought...I don't know. It seemed right, you know?"

And Aubrey did. Everything about Oliver living in Heartsville seemed right. The people loved him, as evidenced by the growing lines outside the bakery every morning. And Aubrey had come to rely on him being at the farm early. When he sat on the porch, a warm feeling settled in his stomach, knowing Oliver was in the bakery, making it ready for customers. And yet there was more.

"I know. And, uh, if you need any help moving in, getting furniture and stuff, I'm happy to help."

Oliver's brows knitted a dark line over his forehead. "The house actually came furnished, and I think I'm all set." His cheeks flushed pink. "I'd love it if you'd stop by and take a look." He rubbed his chest in what Aubrey now recognized was an unconscious gesture. "If you want, of course. I still don't know many people aside from you, Cassie, and the guys at that bar, Last Call...so it gets kind of lonely in the evenings."

"I know that feeling, and yeah. Happy to come by and keep you company sometime. It'll be a nice change to get off the farm."

His gaze latched on to Oliver's. The memory of that kiss flared hot and bright between them, but Aubrey chose to ignore it.

"We can have dinner. I want to repay you for all the times I mooched off your hospitality. How's next Monday? The bakery is closed, so I have all day to get ready," Oliver said in a rush. "Nothing fancy, of course."

"Don't be silly, you never mooched. But I'd love to, thanks. And considering any meal touched by human hands and not a plastic tray is fancy to me, I'm looking forward to it."

"Chili and corn bread? Sound good?"

"Oliver, it sounds like heaven." They shared a smile, and Aubrey couldn't help the flutter in his chest and the blood beating hot in his veins.

---

On Monday evening, Aubrey stood on the wraparound porch, and before pushing the doorbell, surveyed the pretty garden. Roses, rhododendrons, and hydrangea bushes surrounded the small, wood-framed house, and Aubrey inhaled their sweet perfume. Birds chirped from tall, shade-casting oak trees, and Aubrey remembered Lisa asking him if he'd ever consider moving from the farm to buy this home. And now here he was, with Lisa gone, but Oliver ready to make a home.

*How strange is life?*

Aubrey rapped on the door and heard footsteps approach. His heart kicked up a beat, and he clutched the bottle of Johnnie Walker Black he brought as a housewarming gift.

The door opened, and Oliver's smiling face put him at ease. He glanced at Oliver standing at the door, and they both laughed. Each was dressed in a pale-blue T-shirt, jeans, and white sneakers.

"Hello, twin," Oliver said, swinging the door open wide. "Come on in."

Aubrey entered the house, its warmth and peace enveloping him. Wide-planked, knotty-pine floors stretched before him to the open kitchen, where Aubrey saw steaming pots on the stove. The front room was filled with light from the wide bay windows, and a comfortable-looking sectional sofa patterned in shades of beige curved around in front of the fireplace.

"Nice," Aubrey said. "Really nice place."

"Yeah," Oliver said with a hint of pride. "I'm loving it. I know it came furnished, but I want to put a few of my own things in to make it seem homey. I figured you could tell me of some places besides Walmart where I could buy stuff?"

Aubrey snorted, unable to keep the laughter inside. "I can ask Cassie. I'm not much for decorating."

Oliver joined him in laughter. "Yeah, who am I kidding."

"Here." Aubrey extended the bottle of scotch. "Happy house-warming, or whatever."

Their fingers brushed when Oliver took the bottle from him, and he jammed his hands into his jeans pockets and walked around the house. "It is nice here. And much closer to the farm."

Oliver had retreated to the kitchen and was at the stove, stirring something in a pot. A rich, mouthwatering aroma teased his nose, and his stomach growled.

"I heard that all the way over here. I hope you like the chili. I made that, and the corn bread has a little kick to it."

Sounded like heaven to him. "I love it. Like I said, it's a treat not to have to eat out of a plastic tray."

Oliver wrinkled his nose. "That's terrible. You're always welcome here, or I can make dinner at your place. There's no reason we should both eat alone."

But Aubrey didn't want to make the mistake of thinking Oliver would always be by himself. The man was good-looking, and if he put forth any effort, wouldn't have a hard time finding someone to be with. His lips tingled at the memory of their brief kiss, and he sighed. Maybe this dinner wasn't such a good idea after all. Being this close to Oliver again brought out unexpected desires Aubrey wasn't certain he could admit to or handle. It had been a long time since he'd felt another person's touch, and that one kiss had unleashed the emotions he'd managed to tuck away and forget about since Lisa's death.

"We'll see." And he left it at that.

"Well," Oliver said, joining him with a glass of scotch for each of them, "here's to new beginnings. I think that's a good way to put it, don't you? I promise no more secrets, Aubrey."

They clinked glasses, and Aubrey, unexpectedly nervous, took a hefty gulp of his drink, welcoming the fiery warmth. "Ah. That's good." He licked his lips and sat on the sofa.

Oliver waved at him. "Sorry you can't get more comfortable, but dinner is ready. Bring your drink and let's sit. I put a table out on the deck. It's nice and shady there."

He followed Oliver through the kitchen to the back deck where, as Oliver said, a table was set up with plates, glasses, a pitcher of iced tea, and a basket of corn bread.

"You went to a lot of trouble. That wasn't necessary, Oliver. It's just me."

"It made me happy to do it."

He held the door open for Oliver, whose hands were full with the pot of chili; then he sat and took the brimming bowl Oliver handed to him after ladling out the fragrant meal. He poured them each a glass of iced tea.

"Tell me what you think. I got this recipe from Emery, over at Last Call. He says people love it."

Aubrey dipped his spoon in the bowl and tasted the chili. It was chock-full of the flavors of tomato, cumin, and chili. "Absolutely delicious."

Oliver's eyes lit up, and at his genuinely happy smile, Aubrey's heart twisted in his chest. It was the knowledge that he was letting go of all the pain and anguish of the past years. Moving on. Never forgetting, because that would be impossible. But learning to live again without feeling like a traitor.

After dinner, they sat side by side on the deck for a while, listening to the owls hoot and the crickets chirping madly. A small, dark figure entered the backyard, and Oliver half stood.

"What is—"

"Shh." Aubrey put his hand on Oliver's arm. "It's a fox. We don't get to see them much around here anymore." Oliver sat back, and Aubrey grinned at his wide-eyed excitement.

They remained silent, Aubrey's gaze trained on the animal, who lifted his head to sniff the air, then took off into the bushes, disappearing as quickly as he came.

"I've never seen one before. I've never really seen any wild animals."

"You'll see plenty here. There's deer and possums and raccoons and of course groundhogs. But foxes are pretty rare nowadays. This was a treat for me as well."

"Thank you." Oliver's eyes glowed. "It was amazing to see."

At that moment Aubrey realized his hand was still on Oliver's arm. He withdrew it, but Oliver put his own on top to hold it in place.

"Aubrey," he breathed, his eyes focusing on his lips as if remembering the kiss from the other night.

His breath caught, and his heart pounded. He didn't know what made him do it, except it felt right to rest their foreheads together as their breaths mingled in the cool night air.

# 17

# OLIVER

Oliver could barely breathe as he and Aubrey shared some sort of overwhelming moment between them. It was strangely intimate without being...sexual. But there was definitely tension there, as well as something Oliver recognized as longing. Deep and earnest. It was as if they were acknowledging something profound was happening between them without having a name for it.

Aubrey pulled back, opened his eyes, and blinked at Oliver as if he'd just come to his senses. "I'm...*damn it*, Oliver. I have no idea what the hell I'm doing. I...my thoughts just get jumbled up sometimes, you know?"

"I get it," Oliver agreed.

"I mean, not only am I your boss, but you...*you're*..." When he glanced down at Oliver's chest, Oliver got the message.

He drew back as his shoulders slumped. "Probably a good idea to talk some things through."

"Yeah, okay," Aubrey said, wiping his brow with the back of his hand. It was hard to shake how close they'd gotten again, with scarcely a sliver of air between them.

Oliver stood up suddenly, trying to shake himself out of the moment. He began stacking dishes to give his hands something to do.

"I'll help you clean up," Aubrey said, grabbing their empty glasses and following Oliver to the kitchen, where they loaded the dishwasher.

Afterward, an uncomfortable silence descended as they walked into the furnished living room. Oliver didn't know what to say exactly or how to bring up the topic again, but he knew they needed to discuss it. He glanced at the large Thomas Kinkade style painting hanging above the fireplace and absently registered that he'd rather have some sort of black-and-white photography or abstract artwork there instead. He liked the decor for the most part—sort of shabby-chic, if he had to name it something. The couch was comfortable, as was the bed, but he definitely needed to make it his own. He supposed it would happen over time. For now, he was just happy to be out of that motel room.

"I still can't believe you rented this house," Aubrey remarked, glancing around the space. "Lisa would always...never mind..." He shook his head, apparently regretting the comment.

"Please, don't hold back," Oliver said, giving him his full attention. "I'd like to hear more about her."

Aubrey stared at him for a long moment, as if trying to read something in his eyes, before he finally conceded. "She used to ask me if I wanted to buy this house and give up the farm," he explained as he stared distractedly out the window. "She said she was only joking, but sometimes I didn't think so. I could see it in her eyes, you know? The idea of giving it all up and traveling the world or something."

Oliver swallowed thickly, feeling a heaviness in his chest. "Would you have...given it all up?"

"Dunno." He heaved a sigh. "The farm is all I have...all I've ever known, and I'm good at it, you know?"

Oliver nodded because he got it. He could never have imagined leaving his law practice to run a bakery, or needing a heart transplant, for that matter.

"But I guess it doesn't really matter...because we ran out of time."

"Fuck." Oliver sank down on the couch, feeling the full brunt of Aubrey's sorrow. He almost wished he could take it all back, rewind time and have Lisa here in his stead. It was probably the most unselfish thought he'd had in his life, but somehow this man brought it out in him. He didn't know what that meant except he'd sure been learning a whole hell of a lot about love and loss the last few weeks. And he'd decided that life was absolutely brutal and cruel yet profound and wondrous all at once.

"I've never been a believer in fate or whatever the hell you call it," he said, waving his hand at Aubrey. "But some of this stuff happening in the past month is really intense. Me showing up in this town, and this house I just happened to find..."

"Don't I know it," Aubrey replied, taking a load off beside him on the couch.

"And I have to wonder if that's why you..." Oliver stumbled through his confusing thoughts. "I figured the other night when you kissed me, it was likely just heartache muddled with loneliness or confusion. And that was something I could totally understand."

Oliver glanced at Aubrey, whose breathing escalated as he waited him out.

"And just now, when we got so close again, it felt different, like maybe..." He sighed. "I know I'm probably reading too much into it."

"I'm bisexual, Oliver," Aubrey said plainly, and quiet relief flooded Oliver. It hadn't been his imagination. "I had experiences with men before I married Lisa. She knew about my sexuality, and I was totally happy in our marriage. It's been a long time since I've felt desire for anyone else but her. Until *now*."

Oliver's mouth went dry. *Holy shit.* The idea of Aubrey being attracted to him was too overwhelming to consider. There almost seemed to be too much at stake between them.

"I'm attracted to you too," Oliver admitted, and he saw the pulse jump in Aubrey's throat. But this little voice inside Oliver's head kept asking him the same question about Aubrey's draw to him. Was it for the right reasons? It was the one thing giving him pause, and he needed to tread carefully. "But hey, we don't need to sort this all tonight, right?"

Aubrey shook his head, the wrinkles in his forehead evening out. "So what do you propose?"

"Maybe we could just enjoy each other's company, see where that leads us," Oliver replied with a shrug. "And if it only leads us to friendship, that's cool by me."

"Sounds like a plan," Aubrey said as he pushed back his bangs, and Oliver wondered if it was strange for him not to be wearing the baseball cap he seemed so fond of. Oliver decided he liked Aubrey both ways. Sweaty and dirty from a hard day's work and clean-shaven and showered like tonight.

Oliver picked up the remote before his thoughts betrayed him again along with his prick. "When was the last time you watched a movie?"

"On TV or in general?" Aubrey mused. "I can't even remember. Seems I always find something else to do with my time at the farm."

"Well, you're here now, and there's nothing that needs your attention," he said, flicking through the channels before pausing on one that caught his immediate attention. "Isn't that a blast from the past."

It was the first *Planet of the Apes* movie from the 1960s. He wasn't born until the seventies, but those movies were all the rage.

"Holy shit," Aubrey said, focusing on the screen. "My dad was a fanatic when I was growing up. He got me hooked too. I even had the action figures."

"Same. I had Dr. Zaius and General Ursus," Oliver replied with a laugh, remembering how much he'd played with those damn apes, pretending to have inhabited another planet with mounds of sand everywhere.

"Dr. Zira and Cornelius," Aubrey added with amusement, and they high-fived.

Soon enough they got sucked into the plot and settled back to watch even though the movie was nearing the end.

"This cinematic score was amazing for its time," Aubrey commented, and Oliver recalled how much he loved hearing the startling yet sweeping music, but that Jennifer always snubbed her nose at it all. Barbies and pop music were her thing.

"Right?" Oliver replied. "But the acting...not so much."

That got a belly laugh out of Aubrey, and Oliver loved seeing it, so he took some more jabs at some of the awful clichés used in the movie until the ending credits began rolling.

"That was fun." Aubrey stood and stretched. "Have you seen any of the newer prequels they made?"

Oliver sat up, noting the late hour. Not that he wanted the man to leave, but he knew Aubrey would beg off any invitation to stay longer. "Only one and it was pretty good."

"Yeah?" Aubrey asked as they inched their way to the door. "You thinking what I am?"

"A movie marathon?" Oliver replied as his heart quickened. "I'm all in."

# 18

# AUBREY

"You've been selling like wildfire today. Anything new?" Aubrey entered the bakery and surveyed the near-empty shelves. Oliver wiped his brow and gave him a smile, then came around from behind the counter. For the past three weeks, Aubrey had stopped by the bakery when he noticed there was a lull in customers. Seeing Oliver had begun to be a high point in his day.

"I was running a sale on my chocolate silk pies. With all the fresh fruit coming in, I figured now would be a good time to start moving toward that. I have the strawberry now."

Impressed with Oliver's business sense, Aubrey nodded. "Good thinking. And for that, you deserve this." He extended his hand. "Some of the first blueberries. Looks like there's going to be a bumper crop this year." A bunch of dusky blueberries lay nestled in his palm.

"Ooh." Oliver's eyes lit up, and he reached for them. Their hands brushed, and as always whenever Oliver touched him, he shivered. And there'd been some touching since that first dinner at Oliver's new place. Neither pressed the other, but when he'd come to watch their first *Planet of the Apes* movie marathon, Oliver had greeted him with a kiss. And when he left, Aubrey had kissed Oliver's cheek. They were learning each other. A slow dance, but their steps were more certain now.

Oliver trailed his fingers along Aubrey's palm as he gathered the berries, and Aubrey's cock hardened in his jeans. He curled his fingers into a fist, as if to keep Oliver's touch from drifting away. There was no doubt he was attracted to everything about Oliver. His smile, his eyes, the sweet taste of his mouth. He was a damn sexy man, and Aubrey didn't question his sudden yearning to be with him after years of being married to a woman. As he explained to Lisa when they got married, *"Being bisexual doesn't mean I chose a side because I married a woman or that I don't feel attraction for men anymore. It means I fell in love with what made you attractive to me. I chose you."*

"Uh, I was wondering if you'd want to come berry-picking tomorrow. It'd be nice for you to see the fruit on the vines, and you could get to know the farm a bit more than only my house and the bakery. Now that you're staying."

Oliver popped the last blueberry into his mouth and chewed it. "Mmm. Sweet." His eyes glowed. "Really sweet."

Aubrey took a step back. "We need to discuss something. Before any of this goes further. If it does."

Oliver leaned his hip against the counter. "Go on. I'm listening."

"I'm enjoying spending time with you. Really enjoying it. But I can't forget that technically I'm your boss here. I own the bakery, and you work for me."

Oliver rubbed his chin. "Yeah, that could get sticky. The appearance. How it would look to everyone else on the farm. That's what you're thinking, am I right?"

"Yeah. So..." Aubrey hesitated, hoping what he was about to say would come out right. "I think we should keep quiet about what's going on between us. I'm not ashamed of it and not trying to hide it for any other reason than it's no one else's business but our own. No one should have to out themselves for the purpose of a job or a friendship, and I'd like to think we're friends above anything else."

"Agreed. I don't want people thinking I'm sleeping with the boss to get what I want."

Feeling relieved, Aubrey smiled at Oliver. "Great. So tomorrow? Say after the bakery closes? Around four? It should be a bit cooler then."

"Sounds perfect. Looking forward to it."

"Me too."

Aubrey was beginning to realize he looked forward to spending any time with Oliver.

"READY?" AUBREY HELD OUT A BASKET TO OLIVER. "HERE'S A basket for you. Don't pick the green ones, and leave the squishy ones. Look for the fat ones with the dusky blue color. And check under all the leaves." It was four in the afternoon, but the sun remained a hot yellow disc in the endless blue sky and warmed his back. Oliver wore a jaunty straw hat and a pair of dark sunglasses.

"Yes, sir." Oliver gave him a salute. "Reporting for berry-picking duty, sir."

Aubrey's lips twitched. "Okay, okay, I don't know what experience you have in picking."

"No worries. You're cute when you get all bossy." He leaned over and breathed in Aubrey's ear. "Hot too. Turns me on."

Aubrey bit back a groan of frustration. When Oliver's lips touched his ear, an electric current shot straight to his cock, forcing him to shift away from the man. "Let's see how you feel afterward, hotshot."

Oliver snickered. "Yes, Aubrey."

Amused, Aubrey kneeled and began picking. Oliver wouldn't

be laughing long. The two of them worked in the blueberry bushes all afternoon, and by the time the sun had dipped below the horizon, they had collected several large baskets between them.

"Wow." Oliver removed his hat and wiped his brow. "You weren't kidding. Who knew a little fruit could be such hard work?"

"People forget how the food gets to their table. It doesn't magically pick itself."

Of course, Oliver had been eating some of the fruits of his labor and had blueberry stains on his lips and fingers.

"These are delicious," Oliver said while licking his fingers. "They'll make some awesome pies for sure."

Aubrey wondered if his lips would taste of the fruit. Oliver caught his stare, and their gazes locked for a moment before Aubrey broke it off.

"Let's go back to the house and clean up." Aubrey straightened and groaned at the crick in his back. "Damn. I'd forgotten what a chore it is to gather the fruit." The base of his spine gave another twinge, and he rubbed at it. "Plus, getting older sucks."

Oliver said nothing and picked up his two baskets, and they trudged back to the farmhouse. Duke met them halfway and ran back and forth between them, his tongue lolling and tail wagging. The sun sank lower, and the farm settled in around them for the night as they walked. It was Aubrey's favorite time, when the hustle and bustle of the day quieted down and he could take stock and breathe. Having Oliver there with him was a bonus.

They mounted the steps to the farmhouse, and Aubrey pulled open the door and held it for Oliver. "Let's go into the kitchen and put these down."

The energy that had flowed between them in the field while they picked the blueberries continued in the kitchen. Strangely quiet, Oliver stood waiting, as if he sensed Aubrey struggling internally. Aubrey set his baskets on the tile countertop and turned.

"Put yours up here by mine. We'll have to sort through them to clean and make sure they're all good, but that could take a little time."

"I've got nowhere else I'd rather be," Oliver said softly. He crossed the kitchen with his baskets and placed them next to Aubrey's.

The heat and smell of Oliver, his sweat mixed with the warmth of the day's sun and the fresh scent of the grass, proved irresistible for Aubrey. He slid an arm around Oliver's waist and drew him close.

"I'm glad you're here."

"Me too. Thanks for bringing me along today."

He couldn't hold back. Not that he wanted to. Not anymore. It was only the two of them. No secrets between them. No stethoscopes or devastating grief—at least he didn't think so. Just lonely people finding their way. Together.

He touched his lips to Oliver's, licking and tasting the fruit clinging to them. A pulse beat steadily in his blood, and he drew back to gaze at the handsome man before him. His pupils were wide and assessing—but also needy, definitely needy. Oliver leaned forward and brushed the soft curve of his lips against Aubrey's mouth.

When Aubrey responded with his own tentative pressure, Oliver sighed, sinking into the kiss, and Aubrey gripped Oliver's waist, pushing aside the turmoil in his head to give in to the moment. The faint noises in Oliver's throat made him want to pull the man more solidly against him so he could really feel him. Aubrey hadn't realized how desperate he'd been for this connection with another person until Oliver shifted and a moan escaped his throat. All doubts fled his mind that it wasn't right, that it was too soon. Desire didn't play by a calendar, and Aubrey wanted more of Oliver's mouth on his right then.

When Oliver nipped at his bottom lip, Aubrey trembled, his fingers tightening against Oliver's nape, then burrowing into the silky curls. Mouths resting firmly together, Aubrey groaned low in his throat and grazed his tongue over Oliver's lips, as if to chase the sweet flavor of the blueberries. His stomach flooded with a mix of warmth and longing.

The kiss turned urgent as the wet, velvety friction of Oliver's tongue delved deeply inside Aubrey's mouth, and they stayed that way, tongues leisurely sweeping and tangling. He ached to hold on to Oliver longer, wishing the kiss could last all night without reality finding a way to intrude. Aubrey pulled Oliver flush against him, splaying his hand across the span of his back. The lean, corded muscles shifted under the thin fabric of his T-shirt, but to Aubrey, it wasn't odd to be holding a man again. It was everything right and what he wanted.

When they recovered enough to breathe normally, Oliver backed away and gave him an uncertain smile. "You okay? That was..."

"Incredible? Yeah. It was. And don't go thinking I'm going to regret it. I see you looking at me funny. This happened because we wanted it to. I wanted it as much as you did."

A relieved smile curved Oliver's lips. "I'm glad. Very glad."

"But like I said, we need to keep this quiet, at least right now. I'd want to anyway. I'm not a person to parade around all lovey-dovey."

A twinkle lit Oliver's eyes. "Shocking, Aubrey. I'd have never guessed." He sobered. "I'm all for keeping this between us for now. Makes it more special."

A pleasurable languor swept through him, and Aubrey wondered how it would feel to lie next to Oliver and hold him all night long.

*Too soon. Don't think about that yet.*

"Okay. Let's get cleaned up and then sort these berries. I've been hearing enough about your blueberry pie. Time for you to put your money where your mouth is."

"I'm so ready."

They washed their hands and wiped themselves up as best they could. Side by side, they worked into the evening to clean and sort through the fruit. Aubrey kept some and gave the rest to Oliver to put in the bakery refrigerator and then take home.

"See you in the morning?" Oliver hesitated only a moment, then kissed him, and Aubrey's lips softened under his insistent mouth. He slid his tongue inside to touch Oliver's, and that heat simmering between them threatened to ignite once again. Reluctantly, he pulled away, and catching sight of Oliver's passion-clouded eyes and heaving chest, knew he felt the same.

"Yeah. You'd better go."

"Night, Aubrey."

He shut the door behind Oliver, and then with Duke at his side, walked into the family room and sat staring out the window as the night descended.

19

# OLIVER

"Where did all these blueberries come from?" Cassie asked in a confounded tone the following morning as she slid her handbag beneath the counter and reached for an apron on the hook in the kitchen.

"I'll have you know I picked these myself," Oliver said, patting them with a clean cloth to remove any residual moisture from the bowl. "With the help of the boss man."

*Boss man.* He couldn't shake Aubrey's request that their friendship—or whatever it was they were doing—remain under wraps. And though he definitely agreed for now, there was something about the idea of it that niggled at him. Maybe because he'd had one too many boyfriends over the years who wanted to remain in the closet and not claim him as their own, and he'd thought after a certain age it would be different. Easier.

He'd been out to his colleagues at the law firm and rarely minced words. Except he'd never been in the position of fucking the senior partner. That certainly would've raised a few eyebrows and rankled feathers.

But were the stakes as high on First Light Farm? Maybe they were for Aubrey. He had staff under him, several only seasonal, and he supposed it could be distracting to some, while others might disapprove. But Oliver suspected it had more to do with Aubrey being a private man and a grieving widower. He'd give him time to feel things out. Besides, he needed it as well. His life didn't seem real at the moment, and he needed to protect his heart in more ways than one.

He realized Cassie was still staring at him. "What?"

"Aubrey took you blueberry picking last night?" she asked in a skeptical voice.

"Uh-huh," he replied, lining up muffin tins for baking. "Why is that so hard to believe?"

"He doesn't do that with just anybody. He likes you, and that's a good thing," she admitted as she tied her apron. "Guess the man keeps surprising me, but I suppose with everything that happened with the transplant—" She clasped her hand over her mouth. "*Shit.*"

"No, it's okay. I figured you were the one who gave him advice after I finally found the courage to tell him." Oliver winced as he opened the oven. "I guess I should thank you for getting my job back."

"I didn't have to twist his arm all that hard." She chuckled, but then her features sobered. "I hope you know how brave you were to come here and seek him out. That's all I'll say on the matter, because you're probably tired of rehashing it."

"A bit," Oliver admitted and blew out a breath. Things had moved right along since then, and he didn't want to look back. Still, it all felt pretty overwhelming and too close to the surface.

After the noontime rush, he and Cassie spent the rest of her shift molding crusts for the blueberry pies. "These are going to be amazing."

"Even better with vanilla ice cream," he remarked, thinking of the bakery cooler, which held the dairy items they sold. "Ooh, that gives me an idea. I'll whip up a batch of fresh cream for the morning."

Once he'd locked up for the night, he headed to his vehicle. He'd only laid eyes on Aubrey once today, on his break earlier, speaking to some farmhands about spreading fertilizer. Seeing him made his stomach swoop, just like it did now with his view of him near the back of a delivery truck. As he opened the door, he caught part of the clipped conversation between the driver and his boss about the increased price of mulch per yard.

If Oliver didn't know Aubrey better, he might've looked as intimidated as the delivery driver. He thought back to that first day on the farm, when the grumpy owner had greeted him near the Help Wanted sign. It was one of the reasons Oliver wanted the job—the man challenged him as much as he intrigued him. And he suspected there were even more layers to unravel.

Shaking his head, Oliver slid into the front seat and headed straight home. Not only was he exhausted after a long day, but he also didn't want Aubrey to feel any sort of pressure about spending more time together, even though he greatly enjoyed the man's company. And he certainly had trouble shaking that first kiss between them. The way Aubrey's tongue flicked against his own...*hot damn*.

THE FOLLOWING MORNING, THE SCENT OF BLUEBERRY PIES BAKING IN the oven made Oliver salivate as he brewed a pot of coffee.

"I followed the scent," Aubrey's voice rumbled as he entered the bakery using the back entrance, and Oliver's stomach tumbled over itself.

"I'm just pulling the last pie out of the oven," he said, reaching for the oven mitts. "Want the first sample?"

"Mmmm, now you're talking," Aubrey replied around a yawn.

Oliver chuckled. "Have a seat and I'll serve you."

When Aubrey's gaze briefly turned heated, Oliver tried to control his fluttering pulse.

He poured his boss a cup and slid a sugar packet toward him, remembering how he liked his coffee. Then he cut a small sliver from one of the pies that had already cooled and set the plate in front of Aubrey.

"Wait, one more thing." He walked back to the fridge to grab the whipped cream he'd made last night, and using a spoon, placed a small dollop on the side of his plate.

"Damn," Aubrey said as he took a bite and chewed. "Not too tart or sweet. Just perfect."

Oliver grinned as his shoulders unwound. He'd take that compliment. He didn't know why approval from this man affected him so much.

He tried not to stare too long at Aubrey's mouth as he finished the last of the crust, imagining tasting his lips again. And other things. *Slow down.* By his calculation, it had to be nearly twenty years since Aubrey had been with anyone besides his wife, and he should feel lucky that the man was choosing to spend any time with him at all.

"Your line is going to be out the door today." Aubrey wiped his mouth with his forearm and stood up. "Better get to work. Harvest week. We'll probably send blueberries and strawberries your way."

"Sounds perfect. I'll take whatever you're offering."

Damn, that sounded like a double entendre even to his own ears.

Aubrey cleared his throat and headed toward the back entrance.

"And let me know when you want to watch the next prequel." Oliver hoped he disguised the longing in his voice. "Though I know it's a busy few days."

Aubrey turned and offered him one of those rare brilliant smiles that made his heart flutter. "You free tomorrow night? It might be later...depending..."

"I'll be waiting," he replied without a moment's hesitation.

OLIVER COULDN'T HELP COUNTING THE MINUTES THE FOLLOWING evening even though work had been busy and he was dead on his feet by the end of the day. But as soon as he saw Aubrey at his door, freshly showered, holding a bottle of wine, he felt instantly awake, his stomach a flurry of butterflies. He looked so good in jeans and a casual T-shirt that looked brand-new.

"Thanks," he said, taking the offering as he held open the door. "Hope it's okay—I only ordered a pizza."

"You don't have to cook for me," Aubrey said as he followed Oliver to the kitchen. "Your company is enough."

That sent a shiver down Oliver's spine.

They ate a couple of slices each, then sank down onto the couch to watch the second prequel to the *Planet of the Apes* movie franchise. Aubrey sat close enough that their thighs pressed together, and Oliver had trouble focusing on the opening credits, his warmth and scent infiltrating all his senses.

He sighed against the solid heat of Aubrey's skin, wondering what it might feel like being boxed in by the man. This close he could smell him—soap and cologne with a hint of citrus—and he didn't want to move or break contact. Instead, he became hyperaware of his every breath, gooseflesh lining his skin as Aubrey painted circles on his arm with the very tips of his fingernails.

Barely able to absorb the movie, he felt like he was in junior high all over again, his hormones raging from a newfound crush. His hand landed on Aubrey's thigh, and as the man tensed and shifted uncomfortably, that was when he felt it—Aubrey's cock was stiff as a fence post as it brushed against his forearm.

*Fuck.* It was just too enticing not to want to touch him again.

Fumbling for the remote, he paused the movie right before a big action sequence.

"You okay?" Aubrey murmured, and when Oliver glanced at him, his eyes were dark, probably as dark with need as his own.

But he didn't want to take any chances, not where Aubrey was concerned.

"Yeah," he replied in a shaky voice and stood up, heading to the kitchen for a glass of water. "I just need a minute."

Before he could even reach for the cupboard, Aubrey was beside him, grasping his jaw and his mouth crashing down on his. Oliver moaned into the bruising kiss as his hands framed Aubrey's face and Aubrey pushed him firmly against the counter.

"Aubrey," Oliver moaned and tipped his head back, giving Aubrey better access to his throat. "Fuck," he gasped. "I've been thinking about kissing you again all day."

"Shh." Aubrey pressed firmly against him, and Oliver could feel every thick inch of him as Aubrey nipped and sucked at Oliver's neck as if needing to claim every salty-sweet patch of Oliver's skin. Oliver slipped his hands around Aubrey's waist to cup his ass, and now it was Aubrey's breath that hitched. "Oh, God."

Oliver's cock throbbed inside his jeans, pushing up painfully against the confines of his zipper as they continued to devour each other's mouths. Oliver sucked greedily on Aubrey's tongue while keeping up a rhythmic squeezing of his ass. Lust blazed through him like wildfire, and everything he'd held in check for the past weeks exploded. Aubrey reached down, popped open the button of Oliver's jeans and unzipped him, and he felt his cock spring out through his damp briefs. Aubrey trailed his fingers over the thick head, and it twitched and jerked under his touch. *Holy fuck.* This man would be his undoing.

"Not fair," Oliver bit out while thrusting into his hand. "You too." His hands fumbled at Aubrey's jeans, and soon the two of them had their hands wrapped around each other's stiff cocks. Oliver thought he'd died and gone to heaven. They rutted against each other, the sounds of their moans echoing in the silent house.

Aubrey seemed to know instinctively where to touch him, the right place and time to rub him hard, then gently until he shivered and shook. He struggled to hold back, but Aubrey was insistent, rubbing him up and down, squeezing him, teasing at the head, and his orgasm hit him like a freight train, spreading from the balls of his feet through his groin and up his chest until it exploded and he came.

"Aubrey," Oliver choked out, his cock jerking endlessly. "Aubrey." He sighed against his cheek, which felt wonderfully rough from the early evening stubble.

Aubrey rubbed their cheeks together but didn't speak. For Oliver, having Aubrey there in his hands was the culmination of all the dreams he'd had of the man since their first kiss. He tightened his grip on Aubrey's heavy cock and played his thumb across the crown, using the friction of Aubrey's briefs to urge him on.

"Come on." He sucked at Aubrey's ear and felt him jerk beneath his hands. "That's it. I've got you."

With a harsh cry, Aubrey shuddered in his arms and came. Oliver felt his sticky warmth spread beneath his fingers. He held on to Aubrey until he softened. "Beautiful."

Aubrey kissed Oliver's shoulder and smiled lazily as he tightened his hold around Oliver's waist. They stayed like that, clinging to one another, each holding on as if the other was their anchor in a storm.

## 20

# AUBREY

I f Aubrey thought he'd feel guilty after that spectacular hand job from Oliver, the fact that he had the soundest sleep in over a year put that to rest. He woke up without that aching, empty space in his chest, and as he glanced over at the smooth expanse next to him in the king-sized bed and ran his hand over the top of the comforter, for the first time he didn't get that throb of pain from what he'd lost.

He swung his legs off the bed, and on his way to the bathroom passed by the window overlooking the front. Oliver drove up and hopped out of his SUV, and Aubrey's dick twitched.

"Down, boy. Time and place." As he showered and dressed, all Aubrey could think of was the absolute bliss of Oliver's mouth on him, his hands firm but gentle, yet a nagging thought remained, wondering how he and Oliver would manage to keep their hands off each other. The last thing Aubrey wanted was for the friendship between them to suffer.

With great reluctance, he refrained from visiting the bakery as had become more and more common these past weeks and forced himself to head straight to the fields and check on the crops. The corn was beginning to come in, and the vegetables promised to be a bumper crop. The seasonal workers he hired were already out in the fields, cutting the different types of lettuce they grew, plus the kale, spinach, and chard. The farm sustained itself by selling to the local grocers and stores as far away as Philadelphia, as well as to the local farmers' markets. The stand at the farm itself sold the extra produce and was open Tuesday through Saturday.

It was a hard, hot day, and by late afternoon, Aubrey was ready for a shower, a beer, and a meal. He watched as two women left the bakery, pie boxes in hand, and set his jaw. Hell, it was his damn bakery, and he could go in and say hi to Oliver if he wanted. And he wanted.

His step determined, Aubrey marched across the front yard and entered the bakery. It was quiet except for the music Oliver played, a combination of '70s and '80s bands like The Eagles, Fleetwood Mac, and Chicago. The shelves sat empty, Aubrey noticed with satisfaction, and he went looking for Oliver, whom he found in the back, washing blueberries. Aubrey flushed hot at the sight of him, and when Oliver glanced up from the sink and saw him, a smile broke out over his face.

"Hi. I missed you this morning."

"Been busy in the fields."

He itched to walk over and kiss him but held back, remembering his own words from a few nights before about them keeping their distance in public. Yet it gnawed at his gut not to be able to show even a little affection.

With deliberation, Oliver set down the bowl with the fruit and approached him. "You okay? You're looking at me funny." His face sagged. "It's last night. You're having regrets. I understand maybe it was too soon—"

"No," Aubrey cut him off, desperate to ease Oliver's mind. "Is...is Cassie here?"

"No, she's already left to pick up her kids. That's our sche—"

Aubrey grabbed Oliver to him and kissed him hard and deep,

pushing his tongue past the seam of Oliver's lips. He tasted like blueberries and sweet coffee, and Aubrey drank from his mouth, holding him close as he licked, nibbled, and tasted. Oliver sucked greedily at his tongue, pulling at it hard, making those soft, needy sounds that took Aubrey to the edge so quickly, he wanted nothing more than to bend Oliver over the counter and bury himself inside that round ass. He needed to rein himself in.

"Sorry. I had a long day, and seeing you here just made me lose a little self-control." He held on to Oliver, inhaling his sweet, warm scent, something he could easily become addicted to. Oliver rubbed his jaw against Aubrey's cheek and kissed it.

"I don't mind. I thought you were having second thoughts about last night."

"I had second, third, and fourth thoughts. I couldn't stop thinking about it." He palmed Oliver's ass and gave it a little squeeze. "But if you were thinking I was regretting what happened?" At Oliver's slight nod, he let him go so as to be able to speak to him eye-to-eye. "Not at all. One thing you're going to have to learn about me is that I stand by my actions. No one can force me into doing anything I don't want. And last night?" He cupped Oliver's jaw, rubbing the pad of his thumb over Oliver's reddened lips. "I wanted you. I want you now, which is why I'm wondering if you want to go grab a beer and a bite to eat. I could use the company."

His eyes sparkling, Oliver pushed back the little white hat he wore. "I'd love to. I could use a couple myself. When were you thinking?"

"I need to shower and change, obviously." His jeans were filthy, and even he could smell himself. Never a good sign. "Say in about an hour?"

Oliver returned to his blueberry mixture. "Perfect. I was going to make dough for crusts, but I'm thinking a crumb topping sounds better now." He gave Aubrey a wink, and the pleasure washed over him in waves. It had been a long time since he'd known this kind of happy, and with how fleeting life was, Aubrey intended to grab on to the feeling and hold it tight.

"Pick you up at your place, then?"

"That sounds like a plan."

AT A LITTLE PAST THE HOUR'S TIME, HE DROVE UP TO OLIVER'S house and found him already waiting on the porch.

Oliver hopped into the truck, and they took off down the gravel road. "Where did you want to go?"

He slowed down to make the turn onto the town's main road. "Well, we don't have much in the way of bars with a dinner menu, so I was figuring Last Call. The beer is good, the food is even better, and I haven't seen all the guys in a while."

"Good choice. I like that place. It's like a little bit of home, you know? I was only there once or twice, but I like it. Makes me feel comfortable."

"Yeah, they're all good guys."

"Do you, uh, know their living situation? Like are they really a threesome?"

Never one to gossip, Aubrey too had his suspicions but wouldn't dare ask the guys. It didn't matter much to him what they did in their bedroom. It was none of his or anyone else's business. He slowed for the red light ahead and came to a stop before answering.

"I don't know for sure. I believe so, but since it's none of my business, I don't intend on asking. All I know is, they were there for me when Lisa died and after. And I know what you mean about the bar. You can be yourself. You don't have to pretend."

Oliver took his hand and squeezed it as the light turned green. He drove the rest of the way with Oliver's hand on his. The parking lot at Last Call had several cars in it, but as it was nearing five o'clock, Aubrey knew happy hour was only starting.

"Let's go. I need a beer and burger like nobody's business."

"I'm on that. With fries."

They walked into Last Call, and Aubrey spotted a couple of folks he knew: Troy from the hardware store and Kenny from one of the big local supermarket chains that bought his produce. Aubrey hailed them from across the room, and he and Oliver took a seat at the bar where, as always, Quinn waited with a smile.

"Hey, guys. Good to see you two. What can I get you?"

"I'm good with whatever craft beer you have on tap. How about you, Oliver? First round's on me."

"Uh, sounds good. And a burger, medium, with Swiss cheese and fries."

"Same for me, but make mine Pepper Jack."

"Keeping it spicy, huh, Aubrey?" Quinn chuckled. "How about a bowl of Emery's homemade potato chips to nibble on while you wait? They go real good with the beer."

Gray, the tall, dark-haired owner, slid in behind Quinn and placed a hand on Quinn's neck that to Aubrey looked both possessive and protective. "Quinn's been dying for someone to order them so he can mooch a few himself." He slid his hand to Quinn's shoulder and gave it a squeeze before taking the tray of drinks and leaving.

There was no hiding how those two felt about each other. Quinn's gaze tracked Gray as he went about the room, serving the customers at their tables.

"I'll get this in to Emery and be right back. And don't listen to him about the chips." Quinn set their beers in front of them and disappeared to the back.

"It's okay with me. I don't mind sharing my food."

"No?" Oliver took a sip, and Aubrey couldn't help but stare as he licked the foam off his lips. "Good. Does that mean if I finish all my fries, I can have some of yours?"

Heat simmered in Oliver's eyes, and Aubrey held his gaze a

moment before grabbing the chilled mug and taking a hefty swallow.

"Dammit, Oliver. You gotta stop looking at me like that."

Something dark flashed in Oliver's eyes, and the silence between them thickened. Oliver pushed his mug away and faced him.

"Aubrey, look. I know you want to keep it quiet between us and all, but I've been down that road with other guys who were only into me as long as it was in the dark. I'm too old and been through too much in my life to hide."

"I'm not saying to hide. I'm saying to keep it between us for now. To see where it goes. The fact that we're here should tell you I'm not hiding." Studying Oliver's face, Aubrey could feel the man's tension and understood. "We're coming at it from two different angles. You see it as me being closeted and maybe ashamed of what's happening, but I've never been ashamed of who I am for one damn minute of my life. All I'm asking for is a little time to get to know each other. I haven't dated or been with anyone else in twenty years. It's not that you're a man. It's that it's me, sitting here with someone, *anyone* new. It's all strange to me. This really is a case of 'It's not you, it's me.' "

"Okay. When you explain it that way, I get it." The softness in Oliver's voice and the quick brush of his knee sent relief pouring through Aubrey.

"Good."

"Here you go, guys."

The smell of garlic and onions hit him as Quinn placed a big bowl of thin, fried, crispy chips in front of them. "Emery's special of the day. The burgers will be out in a moment."

"Thanks, Quinn." Aubrey crunched on a few. "Great. But then, everything I've ever had here is top-notch."

"Emery's the best. We're lucky to have him, in so many ways." Those big blue eyes of his focused on Oliver and him. "You know, sometimes things we never expected or looked for turn out to be the best thing that could ever happen to us. We have to be open for it and ready to accept it."

Unsure what Quinn meant, Aubrey sipped his beer and remained quiet.

"And as long as you're happy and not hurting anyone else, whatever you do is your own business." Quinn picked up a few chips and popped them in his mouth. "Okay, shoot me. Gray was right; I can't resist. But you know what I mean?"

"I agree," he said finally when it became apparent that Quinn expected an answer. "What brought this on?"

A slight flush tinged Quinn's cheeks, and looking a bit sheepish, he rubbed the back of his neck. "Well, I remember Oliver coming in one evening somewhat down, and then you guys looked so intense there for a moment when I came out with the chips. I don't know." He shrugged. "Just hoping everything between you all is good."

At that moment Emery came out of the kitchen, carrying the two burgers on plates heaped high with shoestring fries. "Here you go, guys. I gave you each some different sauces I've been trying out. Tell me which ones you like."

"How about me?" Quinn pretended to pout. "Don't I get to try?"

Emery rolled his eyes. "Like I don't already know what you like."

Quinn nudged Emery's shoulder and winked, and Aubrey watched them, fascinated by the dynamic. He darted a glance at Oliver, who was ignoring his food in favor of listening to Quinn and Emery.

From beneath lowered lashes, Aubrey caught the subtle touches between Quinn and Emery and admired the men even more. How would the small town feel about him and Oliver together, as a couple? Oliver had already started eating, but as if sensing Aubrey's eyes on him, gave a slow smile, then took a handful of fries.

"Catch you later, guys. Hope you enjoy the burgers."

"Always, Emery." He picked his up and took a bite. "Delicious."

"Mmm, yeah." Oliver stole a few fries off his plate.

"Hey, finish your own." He moved it away and curved his arm around the dish in a protective circle.

Quinn coughed. "Okay. So it kind of looks like I might be concerned over nothing. I'm glad to see you two are friends."

With that cryptic comment, he walked away to help the new customers who'd entered while they were talking and who were now waiting by the bar.

"What do you think that means?" Oliver stuffed a few more fries in his mouth while Aubrey chewed on his burger. "Do you think he suspects anything or is feeling us out?"

He swallowed. "Not sure. But what he said is true. It's our lives, and how we choose to live them is our business, no one else's. We'll see how it all works out, but all I know is that right now, there's no other place I'd rather be."

"Me either, Aubrey." He picked up his mug. "Cheers. To us and friendship."

He clinked his glass. "Cheers."

# 21

# OLIVER

For the next two weeks, farm life was busy with the harvest. According to Cassie, the harvest came in two waves, early and late summer, only to be outdone by the fall produce. Seasonal employees pulled up in droves to pick strawberries, blackberries, rhubarb, and corn. All hands seemed to be on deck, and by the end of the second week of long hours in the fields, Oliver noticed how weary Aubrey seemed. He imagined him falling into bed each night, dog-tired and having barely eaten, so he made a regular habit of dropping off leftover baked goods along with takeout for the man.

And outside of seeing him a handful of times here and there on the farm and once for a supreme after-hours make-out session in Aubrey's kitchen, like a couple of long-lost lovers, he didn't want to push too hard for more. Besides, he was enjoying the fruits of the labor. Blackberry pie and strawberry rhubarb were hits, along with freshly made shortcake with cream during the lunch rush.

Aubrey had been hard-pressed to even stop for what had become his usual morning coffee, so when Oliver saw him entering through the back door Thursday morning, it took him by surprise.

"You look dead on your feet," Oliver observed, handing him a steaming cup and noticing the bags beneath his eyes.

"It's the same every year, and we get through it," Aubrey replied, adjusting his baseball cap. It was a habit Oliver had become accustomed to when the man seemed on edge. "I'm sorry we haven't—"

"Nah, this is real life," he replied, reaching out to squeeze his shoulder. "Plus, I've been busy making use of everything that's come my way."

Aubrey cocked an eyebrow. "The blackberry pie might be my new favorite thing."

Oliver could feel the flush slashing across his cheeks because he knew Aubrey was referring to more than the slice he'd dropped off the other night. The moment began with Oliver unable to resist licking the remnants off his chin and ended with them hard and panting against the kitchen counter. They'd gotten off with their hands down each other's pants, and afterward, when Oliver noted his contented, relaxed grin, he had no regrets.

"We should finish by sundown today." Aubrey sipped from the liquid elixir that seemed to perk him up.

"That's good news," Oliver responded, feeling shy as the question he'd been dying to ask all week hung from his lips. He figured, why not? The worst he could do was turn him down. "So...there's this outdoor concert I heard about over in Fayetteville."

He had seen a couple of flyers in town about the performance. When he asked Carol at the general store, the way she described the laid-back, grassy venue, where you could bring food and beverages along with your own blanket, it sounded like a perfect way to unwind after a stressful few days.

"What sort of concert?" Aubrey asked after tipping back the rest of his coffee.

"This award-winning orchestra from Philly is going to be playing the score from the *Lord of the Rings* franchise."

Aubrey's eyebrow quirked with interest. During the last *Apes* movie, they had also geeked out on their mutual love of the Tolkien-based movies.

"So what are you suggesting?" Aubrey's voice was low and intimate as he caged Oliver against the display case. Unable to hold back a shiver, Oliver reveled in having his strong body near him.

"I wasn't sure if you'd have time to go with me?" Oliver asked in a hesitant voice. "It's tomorrow night."

"Hmm," Aubrey rumbled against his neck. "Sounds a lot like you're asking me out on a date."

"Could be," Oliver murmured. Why did this man unnerve him so much? "Or just two friends enjoying music."

"Friends who can't keep their hands off each other?" Aubrey sucked at a spot right below his ear that drove him mad. His hands clung to Aubrey's neck as he groaned. He liked this seductive, playful side of him. "I'd love to go with you."

Relief flooded Oliver. "Great. I'll pick you up at seven."

Aubrey drew back, his cheeks flushed in the morning light. "By chance, will you be wearing this apron?"

"Apron?" Oliver looked down at himself in the white-stained smock he'd slipped on with the bakery logo in the center of his chest.

"Let's just say I've had some fantasies revolving around you wearing this." He lowered his mouth to his ear as he reached around him to fiddle with the ties. "With nothing else on."

Oliver groaned, swaying into him. "You don't play fair. I've got a fantasy or two of my own, you know."

"Yeah?" he asked with a growl.

Oliver's neck grew hot. Maybe it wasn't such a good idea to share it, after all. The thought of Aubrey taking him when he was still dusty and sweaty from the field probably wouldn't appeal to everyone. But damn, did the notion of his rough hands on him as he fucked him hard and quick keep his imagination plenty entertained last night.

When Cassie's headlights suddenly gleamed through the window as she pulled into a space near the bakery, they broke apart.

By the time she got in the door, Aubrey had gone out the back, but not before making Oliver swear to tell him next time they were alone. Oliver only smirked and waved good-bye.

"Morning," he said in a rough voice as Cassie came bustling inside.

Thankfully Cassie was just as tired and oblivious as the rest of the staff, though for different reasons. Her daughter had caught a bad case of croup and had kept them up most of the night. She refused to take the morning off, however, insisting that her mother had come over to be with her child. She was as hard-working as the rest of the lot. They would give some of the lawyers from his firm a run for their money.

Unable to shake their conversation, he pulled out his phone and quickly texted Aubrey. *Thanks a lot. Now I'll be uncomfortable all morning.*

*At least you have the counter to hide behind.*

Oliver grinned. *Sorry not sorry.*

*Yeah. Just you wait.*

*Is that a threat?*

*Guess we'll see.*

Except the following night when Oliver met him in the driveway, Aubrey looked just as exhausted as the morning before. He considered giving him an out and asking if he wanted to stay in, but then he remembered the tickets he'd purchased in advance online along with the picnic basket he'd packed with wine and cheese and slices of pie.

The mood was quiet in the car on the way to the concert, but Aubrey took his hand and kissed his knuckles. He was freshly showered, his hair clean and wavy around his ears, and Oliver loved how his scent filled up the entire space of the car.

"Thank you for tonight. I'm not very good at this. I get too caught up in the farm."

"Of course. It's your livelihood," Oliver replied, remembering all his late nights at the firm. "Besides, no problem. I could use a night out too."

Once they arrived and walked in with the crowd, they spread out their blanket in the center of the large grassy knoll and set down the basket. They ate cheese and crackers and talked about any number of subjects, and it felt comfortable being with Aubrey. As the music began in the pavilion below, Oliver poured them wine in plastic glasses to sip throughout the performance.

They were surrounded on all sides by chattering families and couples, and Oliver had the urge to reach for Aubrey's hand but didn't dare in this setting. He didn't know how open Aubrey would be about public affection, but regardless, that same electric current that always seemed to be present between them had them scooting closer with their arms and thighs pressed together for the entirety of the show.

After the concert, they headed back to the farm, and though Aubrey yawned several times in a row, he still asked Oliver inside for a drink.

"I can see how tired you are," he said. "Plus, we both have work in the morning."

"Please," Aubrey replied, and when Oliver looked in his eyes, there was a plea there. "I'd like for you to stay a while longer."

Once inside, Aubrey poured them a couple of beers, and they sat on the couch, recounting their favorite parts of the concert before arms became entwined and they kissed lazily. It felt good to touch him freely after not being able to in public. And though it wasn't the heated exchange from their last couple of encounters, Oliver found he liked it all the same. The undercurrent of desire was still there but placed on the back burner by slow and gentle touches, affectionate kisses, and longing gazes that still lit a fire in his belly.

When he noticed Aubrey's stiff shaft beneath his zipper, he threw caution to the wind by nipping at his jaw, then lower at his throat. He curved his fingers beneath the hem of Aubrey's shirt to feel his warm skin. Aubrey's stomach contracted as Oliver slid his hand over the taut flesh, up to his hairy chest, and his thumb circled one pebbled nipple.

As Aubrey bit back a curse, Oliver lifted his shirt and sucked at the stiffened peak.

"Fuck," Aubrey groaned. "What are you doing to me, Oliver?"

Oliver smiled against his skin as he moved to the other nipple. "Just want to make you feel good. Is this all right?"

Aubrey arched his back and hissed. "Hell, yes."

He feathered kisses down his chest to his waistband, his abdomen trembling against his lips. "Can I make you feel good in other ways too? Want to put my mouth on you."

Aubrey shut his eyes tight as if trying to manage his breathing. "Damn, Oliver."

He licked, then nibbled at his hip bone. "It's okay if it's too soon."

"It's not that," he huffed out. "It's been so long, I don't know if I'll even last."

"It doesn't matter," Oliver replied, tugging Aubrey's shirt over his head and then trailing his fingers over his skin, marveling at how attractive the man was, how responsive to his touch. He leaned forward to kiss his jaw. "Just want to taste you."

He dropped to his knees, and before Aubrey had a chance to think too hard, Oliver tugged his jeans and underwear over his hips with little resistance. Aubrey's thick cock sprang free, red-tipped and leaking.

"Damn, you're gorgeous," he said in a tight voice. When

Aubrey moaned in response, Oliver's cock pushed at his zipper. But he ignored it as he leaned forward to lick along his smooth abdomen, then bury his nose in the wiry patch of hair at his groin, taking in his warm, spicy scent. His cock was silk over steel in his palm as he gripped him and stroked upward.

Aubrey shuddered as he watched him, his eyes glassy, his lips parted. "The way you look down there." His voice was thick, and as his fingers skimmed across his jaw, Oliver captured his hand and sucked his thumb into his mouth. "*Fuck.*"

Leaning forward, Oliver sucked a trail of openmouthed kisses down Aubrey's chest. Oliver's jaw grazed over the glistening head of his shaft, his precome leaving a wet trail across his chin.

When he gave the crown a tentative lick, Aubrey's fingers gripped his shoulder and his hips jutted forward, his eyes begging Oliver to take him in his mouth. He loved the way the man looked right then, so desperate and needy, and he couldn't wait to make him come undone.

His tongue circled the head before licking into his slit and tasting his salty-sweet precome. "Mmmmm..." he rumbled as Aubrey gasped and his fingers traveled upward to tug at his hair.

Oliver opened his mouth, and Aubrey's thick shaft stretched his lips as his tongue worked along the length. His hand low on Aubrey's cock, he stroked in unison with the soft caresses of his lips and got lost in the sensual noises he was able to draw from Aubrey. "Oh, *God.* Feels too good."

With Oliver's lips and tongue bathing his cock, and Aubrey's fingers urgently gripping his hair, it didn't take him long to bring Aubrey to the edge.

"Oliver. Oh, *damn.*" He began thrusting in shallow stabs, fucking into Oliver's mouth as his own cock lengthened and leaked. He'd take care of himself later. For now, all he wanted was to blow Aubrey's mind.

He redoubled his efforts, increasing pressure as he rubbed his tongue along a vein and sucked his cock in earnest, saliva dripping to his chin. When Oliver reached for Aubrey's sac and fondled his heavy balls, that seemed to be the catalyst that sent him over the edge.

"Holy fuck," Aubrey groaned, shuddering as his seed coated the roof of his mouth, and Oliver swallowed every last drop. He licked around the head, collecting the beads from the tiny aftershock that erupted when he squeezed his balls.

Pulling away from his softened shaft that had become too tender for his tongue, he helped tuck Aubrey back in. He trembled against the cushions, his forearm over his eyes, his chest heaving.

"Jesus, that was..." he mumbled, as he seemed to get his bearings.

"Yeah..." Oliver sighed, unable to keep the smile from his lips. "Yeah, it was."

Aubrey angled his legs up on the couch and motioned for Oliver to sit between them. Once his back rested against Aubrey's front, he wound his strong arms around Oliver and kissed his cheek. "Damn, this feels nice."

Before he knew it, they had both fallen asleep, and by the time Oliver blinked open his eyes, it was already dawn. *Shit.* How the hell had that happened?

He slipped out of Aubrey's embrace and whispered for him to wake up.

"It's already morning. I've got to open the bakery," he muttered groggily as Aubrey rubbed at his eyes and slowly came to. Oliver leaned over to offer him a chaste kiss. "See you in a few."

As he slipped out of the house, he noticed how rumpled his clothing was, and no doubt his hair was also a wreck. He needed to shower, change, take his heart meds, and brush his teeth. Just as he was considering his options, he stopped dead in his tracks as Cassie slid out of her car in front of the bakery. It was either later than he'd first thought or she had arrived early.

"Cassie, I—" He shook his head, unable to form any more words.

She held up her hands as her gaze darted away. "None of my business."

He stared at her over the hood of his car for one drawn-out moment until he finally nodded. He'd just have to trust her to keep his confidence.

"Okay to start without me?" he asked as he scratched the back of his neck.

"No problem at all," she replied, waving him on.

"Cool. I'll be back in thirty minutes."

And as he slid into his car and pulled out of the drive, he could still smell Aubrey's scent on him and feel the ghost of his breaths against his neck. He decided right then and there that he didn't regret sleeping in the man's arms all night. Not one bit.

Aubrey's mood matched the weather that day—sunny and bright. Waking up unexpectedly with Oliver put him in a better mood than he'd been in for months. He liked their easy friendship and the thrill of spending time with him alone. Plus, their little sexy meet-ups during the day were damned exciting. With a start he realized that where he'd once buried himself in the farm, staying out in the fields until it was almost too dark to see, now he looked forward to being with Oliver, whether it was watching movies, having a beer, or simply enjoying the sunset from the front porch of the farmhouse. Aubrey recognized that his soul had begun to heal.

"Okay, George, that's another good day." He slapped the hand of his farm manager. They'd finished a hard, back-breaking harvest of the crops, then packed them up to ship for sale.

"Yep. We got a ton of kale and asparagus. And the berries are out of control. Peaches look to be coming in nicely too."

"I'll make sure to tell Oliver. He'll want to make peach pie. Maybe we should make ice cream as well."

George's eyes lit up. "Heck, yeah. Growing up, we used to go to

Weaver's farm, and they had a peach festival every summer with the best homemade peach ice cream. Mmm."

The look on the man's face was almost orgasmic, and Aubrey laughed and patted him on the shoulder. "I'll talk to Oliver and see if he's interested." A quick check of his watch showed it to be getting on toward three o'clock. George and the guys had been up and working since six a.m., and after Oliver left at around seven, Aubrey had hurried through his shower to join them in the fields.

"Make sure these all get refrigerated before you leave. I'll call the distributors and tell them to come for their pickups. See you in the morning."

"Will do. See you tomorrow, Aubrey. Have a good night."

"You too." With a spring in his step, Aubrey headed to the bakery. He could use a little snack and a cup of coffee. Plus, seeing Oliver was the icing on the cake, so to speak. Chuckling to himself at his own joke, he didn't see Cassie until she waved her hands in his face.

"Aubrey, hello. Hello."

"Oh, sorry." He stopped and gave her a sheepish grin. "I was thinking of something and got all caught up in my head."

"Something or someone?"

Her plain words, coupled with her nod to the bakery, sent up warning signals to his brain. "Uh, what're you talking about?"

*Did she know? How did she find out?*

"Maybe we could sit for a minute? My mother's picking up the kids from school today, so I'm not in a rush."

"Come on inside. I've got iced tea if you'd like."

Her eyes met his. "Yeah. I think that would be nice."

His nerves showering sparks inside him, Aubrey walked with her up the steps and into the farmhouse. She sat at the kitchen table, and he poured them both the promised iced tea, although right now Aubrey could've used a shot of whiskey in his.

"How're the kids?" he asked. "Over the croup?"

"Yes, thanks. They're fine." She played with her glass, making wet rings on the old wooden table. "Okay. So I know this is none of my business, and you can tell me so and it won't matter at all, but I have to get it off my chest."

"O-kay," he managed, gripping his glass tight. "What is it?"

"This morning when I drove up, Oliver came out of the house, wearing the same clothes he wore yesterday. Did he..." She licked her lips. "I mean, last night...?"

His first instinct was to make light of it and blow it off like it was nothing, and he opened his mouth, ready to deny the ultimate question he saw in her eyes. But he couldn't. It wasn't fair to lie to Cassie, but more importantly, he didn't want to do that to Oliver. It would make their time together something shameful, something to be hidden, and their relationship was anything but that. Recalling their heated kisses and how Oliver's mouth on his dick made him come alive for the first time since Lisa died, Aubrey couldn't form the words to deny Oliver's place in his life.

"He stayed over, if that's what you're asking." He set his jaw. "He might do so again."

"Aubrey, you big idiot." Cassie's eyes flashed as she chastised him. "Do you think so little of me that I'd judge you?"

"Simmer down. That's not what it's about. It's not about someone judging me or us. I don't really give a damn what people think."

"Even me? We've known each other over fifteen years. I'd like to think we're friends and that you care about my opinions."

*Damn.* "That wasn't what I meant." Fumbling now, Aubrey tried to make it right. "It's not that I don't care about your opinion. You, more than anyone else, helped me through the worst times of my life. But." Here he paused to regroup and think about what he needed to say. "I'm not sure myself what's happening. It's not something I can put into words, at least not now. So Oliver and I decided to keep it quiet and between ourselves while we figure it out."

"Okay, I understand that. And you two have made peace, about the transplant, I mean?"

With a pang and almost a sense of incredulity, Aubrey realized he hadn't thought about that in a while. A very long while. He'd been too caught up in the day-to-day of simply being with Oliver and enjoying the present. The past had made him its prisoner for far too long.

"That's been settled between us. We're friends. Good friends. I like spending time with him."

"And he doesn't mind your grumpy self?" Her tone was teasing, and Aubrey heard the love behind it.

"No. He doesn't. Imagine that." They shared a smile, and Cassie clasped her hands together over the worn oak table.

"I only want you to be happy, Aubrey, and that includes the person who makes you feel that way. So if it's Oliver, then nothing more needs to be said. You deserve some joy."

His throat tight, Aubrey could do nothing more than nod.

"I'd better go before my mother kills me."

"I'll walk you to your car."

As they crossed the front yard, the door to the bakery opened and Oliver walked out with two big bags of garbage to put in the dumpster out back. Even from that distance, Aubrey caught the wariness in his eyes. He hurried inside without waving hello, even though there were no customers and it was near closing time.

"He's been on edge all day since I saw him this morning." The breeze ruffled Cassie's hair, and she pushed it off her face before sliding her sunglasses over her eyes.

"Guess I'd better speak to him." He adjusted his baseball cap and rubbed the back of his neck, which felt sticky. Dirt and grass clung to his clothes. He needed a shower before he talked to Oliver.

"I think that's good." She squeezed his arm. "Finding happiness is hard enough. Don't let anything stand in your way and steal your joy. You've been through the worst, Aubrey. It's your time now."

He bent and kissed her cheek. "Thanks."

She drove away, and he stood for a moment, then pulled out his phone and texted Oliver.

*I'm going to take a shower.*

Oliver answered immediately. *Come to the bakery afterward.*

*I spoke with Cassie. Don't worry. It's all good. Tell you when I see you.*

*Good. I'm relieved.*

With a determined stride, Aubrey ran to the farmhouse, hit the steps two at a time, and headed upstairs. Twenty minutes later, with his hair still wet but feeling a hundred times better, Aubrey walked into the bakery, now with the sign flipped to CLOSED, but Oliver wasn't in the front. He heard a noise in the kitchen and grinned to himself. Maybe he could get in a repeat performance of the last time they were together there.

Oliver stood with his back to him. Faded jeans hugged his firm butt, and he wore one of those long white bakers' aprons. Aubrey leaned against the door, watching Oliver stir something in a bowl while humming to himself.

"What're you doing?"

Oliver dropped the spoon. "Damn, you're quiet." He picked up the spoon again. "I'm macerating the fruit with sugar for the pies."

"Uh, okay." Aubrey had no idea what that meant. "Anyway. About Cassie. She's not judging either of us. She's protective and wanted to make sure that both of us had worked out the shock of the transplant."

Even in the bright overhead light, Aubrey could see Oliver pale. "And have you? Really? I know you said yes, but we need to be open and honest about it. Have you moved past the idea that I'm the recipient of Lisa's heart?"

"I hate this," Aubrey said, stepping farther into the room. "Not the telling you part, because that's something I can be honest with you about. We both know it was a shock. But I've gotten over that hurdle, and I'm not angry with you. Really."

A smile broke over Oliver's face, and his shoulders relaxed. "Thanks. Did she mention seeing me this morning?"

"Yeah. And like I said. No judgment. Only caring about us as a friend."

Oliver nodded. "That's good, then. I'm glad."

"I told her it might happen again." His smile matched Oliver's.

"You did?"

"Yeah. It was nice to wake up to you. Seeing you in the first light started my day off right."

"I thought so too."

Aubrey felt Oliver's hesitancy, as if he still wasn't certain of Aubrey's feelings, and that didn't sit right with him. His eyes narrowed in thought as Oliver moved about the kitchen, cleaning up and getting ready to shut down for the night. When he reached behind to untie his apron, Aubrey got an idea.

"Don't."

Brows knitted in confusion, Oliver paused with his hands on the tie. "Don't what?"

"Don't take that off. Just everything else."

"What?" Oliver snorted, but the laughter faded when Aubrey approached. "Aubrey, what's going on?"

"Nothing. It's what's coming off I'm interested in." Aubrey placed his hands on Oliver's hips and gazed at him with a slight smile. "Lose the clothes but keep the apron."

Without breaking eye contact, Oliver kicked off his sneakers, slid his jeans and briefs off, and after fumbling a bit with the apron, took off his shirt, then placed the clothes on the closest chair.

"Damn," Aubrey breathed. "I'm never going to be able to watch another cooking show without getting a hard-on, thinking of you standing here like this."

"Yeah? Well, I get a hard-on almost every time I see you, period. So fair's fair."

Aubrey gripped Oliver's shoulders and pulled him in for a deep, long kiss. Teeth clashed, tongues twisted, and lips sucked and nibbled as they fell on each other.

"Missed you today."

"Same," Oliver breathed, then licked a path of wet heat to his ear and sucked the lobe into his mouth. Wave after wave of a deep-seated need broke over Aubrey, and he held Oliver's face and plunged his tongue deep. Oliver rewarded him by sucking it, and Aubrey's heart slammed so hard, he was left breathless. Damn, he wanted Oliver. Now.

"I came in here for a little pick-me-up." He sank to his knees. "So I'm going to get down and get my fill." He glanced up to see Oliver's eyes bright with desire.

Aubrey reached around the apron to push it aside. Oliver's thick erection waited, the wide crown already pearled with precome. Aubrey breathed in the rich, musky scent of Oliver's warm skin and licked across the head of his cock, dipping his tongue into the slit.

"Please." Oliver hissed, but Aubrey was in no mood to rush. He buried his face in the springy dark curls at Oliver's groin and inhaled deeply, sucking and tonguing until the hair was soaking wet. "Aubrey." Shivering, Oliver moaned and slapped his hand against the marble top of the counter.

"Shh." He grasped the root of Oliver's cock and slowly took him into his mouth, swirling his tongue around the shaft. It might've been decades since he'd last given head, but Aubrey knew to go slow for pleasing his partner. And Aubrey wanted to give Oliver the ultimate in pleasure.

The taste of Oliver's salty precome burst over his tongue, and he drank it in while sliding fully down Oliver's engorged cock. He fondled Oliver's balls, squeezing one, then the other, loving the man's desperate, needy sounds. He bobbed his head, tightening his lips over the silky skin of Oliver's iron-hard cock, drawing up, then down, creating the friction he instinctively knew Oliver craved.

"Aubrey." Oliver flailed and tipped a bowl on its side, and it caught Aubrey's eye. It was filled with fresh whipped cream.

"Mmmm." Aubrey stopped for a moment, letting go of Oliver's cock long enough to reach up and scoop a few fingers full of cream, then coated Oliver's glistening erection with it.

"Aubrey, what the fuck?"

"Be quiet and let me have my dessert." Aubrey licked around the length of Oliver's whipped-cream-covered cock, sometimes scraping his teeth along the shaft, drawing a hiss from Oliver. His hips began to piston back and forth, and from the steady stream of precome mixing with the sweet cream, Aubrey knew Oliver's orgasm wasn't too far off. He gripped him around the thighs and took his cock deep again, his mouth and lips stretched wide to accommodate Oliver's thick, straining length.

"Aubrey. Oh God, oh..."

Oliver tensed and shuddered, his cock going rigid in Aubrey's mouth before shooting out streams of come. It filled Aubrey's mouth, and he greedily drank it all down until the pulsing ceased and Oliver softened and slipped from his mouth. Aubrey sat back on his heels, knowing his back and knees were going to hurt like a bitch but regretting nothing. This was the hottest and sexiest thing he'd ever done in his life.

Oliver touched his shoulder, and Aubrey met his gaze, happy to see a smile. "You owe me."

With a muffled curse at his cracking knees, Aubrey stood, placed his hands on Oliver's shoulders, and brushed their lips together. "Oh, yeah? I thought this was pretty damn good, if I say so myself."

"Oh, it was," Oliver said, his voice filled with laughter. "But you ruined my whipped cream. You need to make me a new batch."

Some of the cream had slid out of the bowl to the counter, and Aubrey dipped his fingers in it once again. "Well, not until we finish all of this batch." He licked the sweet, creamy concoction. "Got any ideas?"

Oliver kissed him, his tongue tracing the outside of his sticky lips. "I might have a few. Later. First, I need to get dressed." He pulled off the apron and began to dress. Aubrey couldn't help but admire his firm, round butt and long, lean legs, and hardly noticed the fading red line of the scar from the transplant.

"So we're okay now? I'm still for keeping this between us because I'm a private person. Nobody needs to know my business. But Cassie is special to both of us, and in a way, I'm glad she knows. She doesn't judge people, and she's only concerned for my ultimate happiness. And right now I'm happiest with you."

Fully dressed, Oliver stood before him, between his spread legs. "That's nice to hear. Because you make me happy too."

"Then let's stop worrying and enjoy ourselves." Aubrey grasped Oliver by the nape of his neck and drew him in for a kiss. " 'Cause we both deserve to be happy."

# 23

# OLIVER

"How large is this farm?" Oliver asked a couple of mornings later when Aubrey passed through the bakery for his morning coffee.

"Just under five hundred acres," he replied, tilting his head. "Why do you ask?"

"I was only curious how far it extends," Oliver remarked, glancing out the back window toward the orchard down below. "I've only ever been to the end of the strawberry fields. I'm a city boy, so these things are interesting to me."

"You certainly are a city slicker," he replied with a smirk.

"Watch it, you!" Oliver aimed a spatula in his direction.

Oliver didn't miss the spark of curiosity in Aubrey's gaze, and he wanted to tease that out. Clearing his throat, he asked, "Would you ever take a trip to the city with me?"

Aubrey's gaze turned wary. "It might be a bit hard to juggle... the, uh, schedule."

"Maybe just for a weekend?" Oliver persisted, wondering why it suddenly mattered so much, though he tried not to show it. "No worries either way."

Aubrey stared hard at him. Oliver couldn't help remembering

their conversation about how little traveling he'd done. He wondered if Aubrey had periods of wanderlust but felt too stuck to do anything about it.

"I'd definitely consider it," he replied with a sharp nod.

"Cool." Oliver let go of the breath he'd been holding as he filled more of the muffin tins. It felt like a small victory nonetheless. Maybe he'd get Aubrey off this farm someday.

"But since you asked, how about I show you around the farm a bit more?" Mug empty, Aubrey walked to the sink to rinse it. "We're closed Sunday, so if you don't have any pressing plans..."

"What do you have in mind?" Oliver asked, glad to ignore the pile of laundry waiting for him.

"If the weather holds, we can make a day of it. Ride around on four-wheelers and even do some swimming in the pond," he replied as he rubbed his thumb across Oliver's chin.

"Swimming?" Oliver glanced out the window again, amused that there was a body of water somewhere on the property. "I'm in."

Oliver thrummed the whole rest of the morning and well into his busy shift on Saturday. An entire day with Aubrey was not something he would take for granted. Every time their eyes met around a delivery truck, the secret smile they shared warmed him to his toes.

Sunday morning was sunny and humid, so he wore a pair of swim trunks, a T-shirt, and sneakers, prepared for anything that might come his way. As he drove up to the farm, he couldn't stop the grin that pulled at his lips or the happiness in his heart. Or should he say Lisa's heart? Would he ever start feeling like the organ ticking away in his chest wasn't on loan, that it belonged to him too? It was a sentiment he couldn't easily shake, and especially not since coming to the farm. But he supposed he'd had plenty to get used to the past few weeks.

"You ready?" Aubrey asked as he swung open the screen door

and beckoned him inside with a kiss on the cheek. This time Aubrey had packed the snacks as well as some towels in case they decided to cool off. Once they climbed on the four-wheelers, he followed Aubrey down the hill, past the strawberry fields toward the orchard, and then around a long bend. It felt amazing having the sun on his face, the wind at his back, and no real schedule. It surprised him to realize how hard he'd been working to make the bakery business a success but in a refreshingly different way than at the firm.

It felt like they drove for miles around the perimeter of the property, and it was the most fun he'd had in a good long while. He felt young and free and had he been more of a daredevil, he might've raced Aubrey through one of the dusty fields. But with his luck, he'd have to add a head injury to his list of ailments. They rode through several thickets of trees to the edge of a forest that extended into someone else's property, then circled back on a path through thick brush and finally parked beside a substantial-sized pond.

Once Aubrey laid their towels near the edge of the water, he kicked out of his sneakers and tugged off his sweat-soaked shirt. Glancing devilishly over his shoulder, he pushed his swim trunks down to reveal his firm, round ass, and Oliver nearly swallowed his tongue.

"It's only us today," he said as he dived into the water and emerged dead center, yelling out in exhilaration. Oliver felt rooted to the spot, still thinking about all that gorgeous skin on display and marveling at this playful side of Aubrey. A side he decided he liked quite a bit as Aubrey motioned from the water with a smirk.

He yanked off his clothes and dived under before he chickened out. He hadn't been naked in front of a man since his surgery, but hidden beneath the water, he could be frisky too. The water felt cool against his skin as he swam close enough to Aubrey to make a grab for his legs and try to kick them out from under him. He broke the water's surface with a mischievous grin, only to get immediately dunked by strong arms.

It turned into a splashing and soaking match until he was laughing so hard, he couldn't breathe. He was glad the man wasn't treating him with kid gloves just because he had a scar the length of his forearm up the center of his chest.

When Aubrey circled his waist with a meaty bicep and pulled him in for a steamy kiss, he moaned against his mouth. Beneath the water, Oliver grasped his hips as their groins aligned and their cocks perked up. "Fuck, Aubrey, the way you make me feel."

Aubrey hummed into another bruising lip-lock as he yanked Oliver flush against him. Oliver's legs circled his waist, and he kissed Aubrey with all he had.

They swam for a while longer and then emerged from the water and padded to their towels. Once Oliver was flat on his back with the sun beating down on him, he reached for Aubrey's hand and urged him to lie on top. They were skin to skin from shoulder to groin, and as they rutted against each other, he was out of his mind with lust. It didn't take long to ramp either of them up.

"Fuck, Oliver," Aubrey moaned and called out his name as he shuddered, their seed mixing between them on Oliver's stomach. As their chests heaved and they panted into each other's necks, Oliver decided it had been the most perfect of mornings.

After they cleaned up and let the sun dry them off, they ate lunch and talked more about First Light—the farm being in the family for three generations and how the produce had changed over the years based on what grew best and sold well.

Then Aubrey grew quiet, and Oliver tried catching his eye, wondering what had made him pensive. When he reached out and traced the scar down his chest with shaky fingers, Oliver sucked in a harsh breath. Fuck, he had no idea what Aubrey was thinking at that moment, and he almost wanted to cover himself.

"Tell me more about the surgery," Aubrey said in a hesitant voice.

"I..." He gulped in air, trying to tame his racing pulse.

"Sorry. It's okay if you don't want to talk about it." Aubrey's tone was soft as he brushed Oliver's wet bangs from his forehead.

"It's not that." Oliver captured Aubrey's hand against his skin, right above his heart. "I didn't think you'd..."

"I want to know." Aubrey squared his shoulders as if showing Oliver he could be brave. "I think we need to talk about it."

Oliver nodded as his chest heaved. He supposed it was as good a time as any with the soft breeze cooling their overheated skin in the middle of a deserted farm that was beginning to feel as familiar to him as the man sitting in front of him.

"For a while there, I pretty much thought, '*This is how I'm going to die.*' We'd only lost my mother a few years before, and it was hard to see the fear in my father's eyes," Oliver explained in a choked-up voice as he remembered the prognosis he'd been given. "But I'll never forget the night the nurse told me that a heart had been located. The elation and then the—" He glanced at Aubrey and saw the sorrow plain on his face. "The *pain*, knowing the organ was coming from someone who had recently passed. It's such a fucked-up mix of emotions."

He didn't know who moved first, him or Aubrey, but they became locked in an embrace, each leaning on the other. He and Lisa were two sides of a coin, he realized, and it was the most surreal thing he'd ever experienced.

"Can you...tell me more about the night of the accident?" he murmured into Aubrey's neck, his cheek rubbing against the scruff on Aubrey's jaw.

He could feel Aubrey's breathing change, and he nearly told him to forget it, but then Aubrey began speaking in a rush, as if he couldn't stop the words from flowing out. "She was coming home from a dinner with friends. The skies opened up, dumping buckets of rain, and her car skidded, went over the guardrail, and hit a tree. Flash floods happen pretty fast around here, and you need to heed the warnings because they're no joke."

Oliver thought about the rainstorm from the other night that deluged his backyard in a matter of minutes. The ground felt saturated the rest of the following day.

When Aubrey drew back from the embrace, his features wore as much shame as disappointment. "Her parents haven't come right out and admitted it, but...I can feel it in my gut. They blame me for that night."

Pain slashed through Oliver's chest. "No, they shouldn't....The weather and the roads must've been..."

Aubrey shook his head. "They would've expected me to pick her up. Of course, I called her, and she promised she'd stay put until the rain died down. She'd have been pissed if I'd tried to rescue her like some knight in shining armor. She was stubborn and fiercely independent."

"Aubrey, are you saying you have regrets that you didn't—"

"Of course I do," he replied in a hoarse voice. "What's a little argument with my wife when she could still be alive?"

Oliver's thoughts were swirling. "There's no way to predict any of that. The odds that you both could have been—"

"I know," Aubrey responded with a heavy sigh. "It's everything I've already told myself hundreds of times before." He reached over and dragged his thumb beneath Oliver's chin. "Besides, then you wouldn't have gotten your heart."

So many emotions bombarded Oliver at once. He felt like his skin was too tight. Like the air was so thick, it would choke him. The silence between them bordered on uncomfortable.

"I'd give it back...for her. For *you*..."

"No, don't say that. Please don't say that." Aubrey looked stricken as he pulled Oliver onto his lap, their clammy skin connecting along with their mouths and tongues in a frenzy of despairing kisses. Oliver poured all his regret into him, his sadness, his desolation, until his lips were swollen and his soul ached less.

Aubrey drew away, his chest heaving, his hands tunneled in Oliver's hair as he stared into his eyes. His gaze dropped to his chest, and he studied the scar before leaning forward and feathering kisses along its edges. Oliver shuddered. "Fuck, Aubrey."

It felt so intimate, so overwhelmingly profound, to be treated so tenderly by him after everything he'd suffered. Oliver realized in that instant that he was desperately falling for Aubrey, and he choked back his emotions. He felt the sting of tears behind his eyes, but he swallowed them down.

They sat with their arms and legs entwined for long minutes, lazy kisses on lips and jaws and throats as if they were in their own perfect bubble, the outside world never intruding. It was raw and emotional, and Oliver wouldn't have traded it for anything.

"I should've reached out to them already," Aubrey finally said. "She was born on the Fourth of July, and last year Lisa's sister drove their parents down to visit her grave. I invited them for lunch at the farm, but they never showed."

It was only a week before the holiday, he realized. The spring and summer had somehow meshed together in the whirlwind of his new life. "Would it upset you if I met them?"

The transplant coordinator from the hospital had only extended Aubrey's information as Lisa's next of kin. Now that he knew she had parents and a sister, he didn't know how to feel. Except sad. Sad for their loss and regret for their anger at such an honorable man.

" 'Course not." Aubrey winced. "If you ever did, we'd certainly have some explaining to do."

"Yeah, guess we would."

# 24

# AUBREY

"I'll be honest. I'm not sure how they'd take to seeing you." Pain flashed in Oliver's eyes, and Aubrey hated that his words might've hurt him, but he'd never been anything less than blunt. "On the one hand, they knew she was a donor, but there's a difference between knowing it could happen and then meeting the person who benefited. It's hard."

"Is—" Oliver swallowed hard. "Is that how you feel? That it's hard to be around me?"

"Fuck, no." Aubrey cursed harshly and pulled Oliver into his arms. "I didn't say it right, I guess." His hand splayed across Oliver's warm stomach. "Being with you has given me more happiness than I thought I deserved. You think it's hard to be around you?" He buried his lips in Oliver's hair. "It's becoming close to impossible to let you go."

The silence swelled around them, and they sat for a while with the sun warm on their backs, watching the birds skim over the surface of the water. Aubrey knew for certain Oliver had become much more to him than a friend to watch movies with and pass the time. He slid his palm up Oliver's torso until it lay flat against his chest and he could feel the strong, comforting *thump.* The scar, a smooth, hairless ridge of flesh, didn't feel like the rest of Oliver's chest, and under his hand, Lisa's heart beat. Aubrey closed his eyes and wondered how long it would take him to think of it as Oliver's heart.

The earlier light mood had been broken, and Aubrey wanted it back. He wanted the wind blowing in their hair and the laughter in their eyes. He wanted the carefree happiness of two people enjoying themselves and life. Vowing to put the thought of his inevitable phone call to Lisa's family out of his mind, he rolled Oliver over and began to tickle him, finding the spot that had made him squirm earlier in the water.

"Aubrey, what the fuck?" Oliver rolled up in a ball to get away from his teasing fingers, but Aubrey remained relentless. "Stop. I'm gonna kill you," Oliver gasped in between howls of laughter. "I give up, I give up." He lay flat on his back, chest heaving, eyes sparkling bright. "You're crazy." Their gazes locked, and Oliver's breathing slowed.

Aubrey had Oliver caged between his arms and had to bite back blurting out, *Yeah, crazy for you.* Given the heaviness of their earlier conversation, this didn't seem like the right time for him to say it out loud, but Aubrey knew it was true. He was falling so hard and deep for this man, he didn't have the words to explain it. Aubrey couldn't forget Oliver's ragged, painful declaration that he'd give up his own life to bring Lisa back, nor his own almost violent reaction at the thought of losing him. All his thoughts swirled around in his head as he leaned down to brush his lips to Oliver's.

"We should get going."

With a nod, Oliver scrambled to his feet, and after putting their clothes on, they collected their towels and walked to their vehicles. "You want steak for dinner? I can grill them up with some potatoes."

They'd only had some snacks all day, and Aubrey was starving. "Sounds good. If the weather holds, we can eat on the back deck." He climbed on the four-wheeler and turned it on. Clouds had filled the sky, but peeks of blue showed between the white puffs.

Already perched on top of his vehicle, Oliver grinned at him. "Race you back." He gunned the motor and took off.

"Cheater." Aubrey sped after him, and they jounced over the grassy road, the tires spinning up dirt and gravel. Together they roared up to the barn and parked, and Oliver jumped off first, fist-pumping.

"Winner. I declare myself the winner."

"Pffft," Aubrey huffed out, lips twitching as he climbed off the four-wheeler. "You cheated. But I'll let you have it since you're going to make me dinner."

"You only want me for my cooking. I knew it."

In the shadow of the barn, Aubrey pulled Oliver close. "I want you for much more. For everything." His mouth sought Oliver's, and they kissed hard and hungrily for a few moments before Aubrey pulled away. Their harsh breathing filled the silence of the barn.

Oliver reached for him. "Aubrey. What's happening?"

"Damned if I know," he said, pulling Oliver into his arms again. *Liar. You know.* But he couldn't say it. It was enough right now to have Oliver molded against him, the curves of their bodies perfectly aligned. Like they fit. Desire seeped through him, and he could feel Oliver harden, but they remained motionless, needing nothing but the comfort of each other's arms.

"I should let you go. And I've got a phone call to make." One he dreaded...but it had to be done.

"Okay. After I shower, I'll go pick up our steaks." Oliver's fingers brushed against his cheek. "See you in a little while?"

"Yeah."

They split up, Oliver going to his car and Aubrey trudging up to the farmhouse. Before anything, Aubrey took a shower. That would clear his mind. Dressed in jeans and a T-shirt, he picked up the phone and dialed a number that was once as familiar to him as his own.

"Aubrey."

The steel in Lisa's sister's voice hadn't softened over the year since they'd last spoken, and Aubrey paced the kitchen.

"Yes, how are you, Chelsea? And Morty and Donna?" Lisa's parents had barely spoken to him when they came to visit her grave. When Lisa was alive, there was always some tension during their visits to the farm, but she stood as the buffer between him and her family. In a lot of ways, he and his father-in-law were similar—quiet, simple, protective men. But despite that awareness, Aubrey could still never make a real break-through, and he'd come to accept it over the years. Then Lisa's death shut the door on any hope of a real connection between them, no matter how much of an effort he made.

"Good. Thank you. We're planning on coming over on the fourth to visit Lisa."

"I remember. I'd—I'd really like it if we could sit down at the table together and have lunch. It would be a nice way to honor her memory. And I have things I need to tell—"

"No. We're not ready for that."

Still, he persisted. "I know it's only been two years. But Lisa always wanted us to be closer. I always hoped for that as well."

"But she's gone. So it's too late for that now."

The floor reeled beneath his feet, and bile rose in his throat. "I —I loved her. I would've died for her. I wish it would've been me instead of her that night. But I can't bring her back, much as we all want her here. What am I supposed to do?"

Silence reigned, and his heart slammed in painful beats, forcing him to struggle for breath.

"I don't know. But you're living your life, free to marry again. My parents can't have another child. I won't ever have my sister back. So no, we aren't ready to sit across a table. Not yet, anyway. Good-bye, Aubrey."

The phone clicked in his ear, and Aubrey was left standing in the kitchen. Was he wrong to be happy now? To want to live? It was a question he'd wrestled with nightly, until Oliver came and swept away all the cobwebs he'd been tangled in. Despite the heat, he shivered. A knock sounded on the door, and he heard Oliver talking quietly to Duke.

His jaw hard, Aubrey strode to the front door and opened it. Duke bounded inside, but Oliver waited, gazing at him with concern.

"What's wrong? Did you talk to them?"

Without speaking, Aubrey pulled Oliver in close to hold him. He smelled of soap and his now-familiar cologne. The warmth from his body soaked into Aubrey, chasing away the chill of his conversation with Chelsea.

"Yeah."

Oliver stepped back and cupped his jaw. "It didn't go well, I gather." At his nod, Oliver took him by the hand and led him to the table. "Sit. I'll make you a drink and feed you."

"I don't need to be babied. I already knew how they felt. Just, hearing it…" Aubrey swallowed hard. "I understand their pain. I couldn't imagine losing a child or a sibling like that."

Compassion warmed Oliver's eyes. "You lost your partner. The person you loved most in the world. No one should ever have to go through that. I'm not dismissing their pain. People grieve in different ways, but to blame you isn't right." A tiny smile tipped up his lips. "And I don't mind paying you a little more attention. It's not such a hardship, you know." He winked, and leaving Aubrey, went to the living room and returned with the bottle of scotch. "Here." He set it down, got a glass, and poured Aubrey a splash. Aubrey grabbed his hand.

"Thank you. I know I don't always say things right, but I want you to know." His tongue felt thick. "Having you here is the best thing that's happened to me. Everything about it seems right. I wouldn't change anything about it for the world." It didn't adequately reflect his emotional state, but it was the best he could muster. And from the beaming smile on Oliver's face, it might've been enough.

Drawing in a shaky breath, Oliver slid his arms around Aubrey's neck. "I'm glad. I love being here too. And there's no place I'd rather be in the world right now." Oliver kissed the top of his head. "I'll start making dinner." He walked to the sink.

"Hey."

Oliver turned around but didn't speak, and goddamn if Aubrey didn't hate seeing that shred of doubt in Oliver's eyes. "That trip you mentioned, to the city?"

"Yeah?"

"That might be a great idea. Sooner rather than later. I haven't been off this farm in what seems like forever."

"Are you sure?"

He stood and joined Oliver at the sink. "I think we both need it. A few days away where no one really knows us." He ran the pad of his thumb over Oliver's lips, enjoying the audible hitch in his breath. "We can do what we want, be who we want to be. Together." Aubrey had no idea what it was about Oliver that brought out this unexpectedly soft and protective side of him. "Think about it. We can have more days like today. The two of us. All day and night."

A shaky laugh escaped Oliver. "I know. It was my idea, and I didn't change my mind. I think it would be wonderful to get away." Heat simmered between them. "When?" Oliver rubbed up against him.

Now that they'd spoken of it, Aubrey was anxious to make plans because more days like this one seemed like the best idea of all. "The weekend after the Fourth of July? Sunday to Monday would be good."

"Sounds like a plan."

# 25

# OLIVER

"What time do the fireworks go off?" Oliver asked as he pulled a second pie out of the oven.

"At dusk," Aubrey replied, fiddling with the window boxes near the front door, never one to sit still very long. He'd dug out the wilted flowers and replaced them with impatiens, zinnias, and begonias in bright colors that lent the bakery a homier feel and made the farm feel warm and welcoming. The customers always inquired about purchasing the rectangular planters, which told him that Aubrey not only had good business sense, but a decent eye for what drew customers in.

It was the Fourth of July, and he technically didn't have to be working, but the holiday had fallen in the middle of the week and he'd decided to show up at the farm this afternoon and do some prepping for the following morning. Later they would be meeting Cassie and her family and most likely all of Heartsville in the town square to view the fireworks display shot off from the community park.

It would be one of the only times that he and Aubrey would be seen in town together outside of their night at Last Call. By now most of the staff had figured out that some sort of friendship had developed between them, and though they got sidelong glances and questioning stares, for the most part the employees seemed unaffected.

Still, Oliver couldn't help feeling out of sorts, like he was keeping a secret. Not only about his progressively affectionate feelings for Aubrey, but the fact that he had inherited his deceased wife's heart. Much of the staff at First Light had known and loved Lisa, and he felt increasingly unsettled not being able to tell people more about himself and what drew him to the farm in the first place. He didn't know how people would respond, but at least he'd feel unburdened.

His text exchange with Jennifer last night only fed into his troubled thoughts.

*What's new?* his sister had asked, and he decided to keep it short and simple.

*Summer harvest. Lots of pies to bake.*

*Yum. I'd love to visit soon.*

*That would be great. Maybe before school starts or during a break.*

The idea of having his sister there was as much a comfort as a worry. Why did he continue to feel like he was in over his head?

*How about grumpy boss man?* she asked.

*He's not so grumpy anymore. Or maybe I notice it less now. LOL.*

*Hold on, there's something you're not saying. Are you DATING?!*

*I suppose we are.*

*Wow, Ollie. I can almost picture your smile. What do his employees think?*

*We're keeping it on the DL for now. I'll explain more later.*

A long pause before her final word of caution.

*Be careful with your heart—literally and figuratively.*

As he watched Aubrey fiddle with the last flower box, his face shadowed by worry, he also knew the man was trying to keep himself busy on Lisa's birthday.

Aubrey had gone to the cemetery on his own yesterday with a bouquet of irises to place on her grave, more than likely trying to avoid Lisa's family's visit at some point today. Oliver wished he could kiss his anxiety away, curl him up in his arms like he did last night on the couch, and tell him everything would be okay. But even he couldn't shake the restlessness between them, the sense of foreboding, that there was too much still standing in their way.

He looked forward to their weekend trip to the city. Maybe it would relieve some of the tension and give them a fresh perspective.

Done with the flowers, Aubrey washed his hands at the sink, then reached over Oliver's shoulder with a plastic spoon to dip into the bowl of whipped cream he'd made for the following day.

"Hands off," Oliver scolded, barely containing a chuckle as he felt Aubrey's breath huff across his neck.

"That's not what you said last night," Aubrey replied in a low, playful voice.

Just then the doorbell jangled, and Aubrey straightened immediately, his eyes going wide when he saw the woman standing at the entrance.

Instinctually Oliver knew who she was. She looked similar to the photo he'd seen of Lisa. Similar wheat hair color, same blue eyes.

"Chelsea," Aubrey said in a stunned voice. "Y...you came."

Her gaze swept across the bakery, taking in the wall color, the understated decorations on the shelves, finally landing on the glass cases that currently stood empty due to the holiday.

"I see you moved on rather quickly," she said in response, her jaw clenched.

"No," Aubrey said, moving around the counter toward her. "I...I didn't make a decision until this past spring when...it's been two years...and I just thought..."

"Hi, I'm Oliver," he said suddenly, unsure of why he'd decided to insert himself into this mess. Except he already was involved in a cursory way, and the tension had grown so thick in the room, it was difficult to even swallow. "I'm the new baker, and I hope I did your sister justice." Oliver's hand swept toward the shelf near the window. "I kept the milk jugs she loved so much; at least, that was what Cassie told me. I love them too."

Chelsea blinked rapidly, her eyebrows knitting together. "How did you know who I—"

"You look like her," Oliver replied even though he wasn't completely sure that was what she was about to ask. But he couldn't keep his mouth from moving and the words from tumbling out. "She was well loved and is definitely missed on the farm. I hear her name almost daily around here. I had some big shoes to fill, and I probably could never—"

"Oliver, you don't have to do this," Aubrey's voice rumbled in the empty space. There was resolve in his tone along with a bit of sadness.

The room grew quiet as Oliver's chest heaved and Chelsea looked between the two of them, so many questions lining her face. But she wouldn't have known—couldn't have. They hadn't been in a compromising position, thankfully, and it wasn't like his scar was visible beneath his clothes.

She couldn't tell her sister's heart was helping pump blood through his veins. To any outsider, it might've looked like he'd moved right into Lisa's life. The farm, the bakery, her man. Holy fuck, is that what people would think? Is that what Cassie thought? His own sister? Aubrey? But no, it wasn't like that at all. It was more complicated and too hard to explain by simply breaking down the facts. It had the additional complexities and nuances of feelings and sentiments and a sense of rightness he'd never experienced any other time in his life. But it also felt wrong and hollow too. Like he didn't belong here, would never belong here.

Oliver swallowed, his knees growing weak, but he continued on. He had to. For Lisa's family and for himself. "Would you like to bring your parents inside?" he asked, looking past her shoulder to the waiting car outside. "Take a seat by the window, and I'll serve you all some coffee and dessert?"

She looked behind her, then at Aubrey, who seemed to be holding his breath. "We weren't sure if we were going to stay—"

"I'd like it if you did," Aubrey replied, his voice quiet and reserved. As if bracing himself to be turned down. Again.

Chelsea bit her lip, studying him, then puffed out a breath. "Well, we did travel a long way, and Mom and Dad could probably stretch their legs again…"

Without waiting for her to second-guess herself, Oliver walked to the coffeepot he had prefilled for the morning and pressed the button. "Great! I just pulled one apple and one French silk from the oven."

Once he heard the door slam shut behind her, he tensed, knowing Aubrey was going to have some words for him. But the man stayed silent for a long moment, as if collecting the tornado of emotions roiling inside him. Once Oliver set the pies on the counter with the knife and plates beside them, he glanced in Aubrey's direction.

He was watching through the window, then suddenly snapped out of it long enough to push through the door and help Lisa's mother out of the back seat of the car. She bristled when she saw him, then offered him her hand so he could assist her to the entryway.

How could they fault this gentle, beautiful man who loved their daughter so much? He felt a sharp stitch in his chest, and he reached up to place a hand across his heart, trying to calm his racing pulse.

He put on his best smile as they came through the door, and introduced himself. They were as reserved and conflicted as Lisa's sister had been. But the mom seemed the least resistant of the three. In fact, as soon as Aubrey pulled out her seat and she spotted the milk jugs in the corner, her eyes softened a fraction.

They didn't know who the hell Oliver was, but somehow *he*

knew he was meant to be a buffer between them. It was a start, at least. But he couldn't stay. It wasn't his place to stay. Not unless it was requested of him. And even then, he didn't know if he could.

He suddenly wanted to get in his car and drive far away from it all. All the grief and sorrow and guilt and hollowness.

Fuck, this was so much. Maybe too damned much.

He pulled the apron over his head and hung it on the hook, then reached for his keys. As he walked past Aubrey, his mind was made up.

"I'm only a phone call away," he said as he swept out the door.

## 26

## AUBREY

Having Lisa's family across the table from him so unexpectedly, staring at him with varying degrees of pain and anger etched on their faces, left him weak. He waited until the furious pounding of his heart settled before speaking.

"Thanks for stopping by. It's really good to see you."

"Is it?" Chelsea cocked her head, her lips thin with anger. "It looks as though you've done a good job replacing the old with the new."

"You know, Chelsea, just because I hired someone to reopen the bakery a few months ago doesn't mean I've forgotten Lisa. I'll never forget her. For almost two years I sat in that house blaming myself, wishing it was me instead of her. But at some point, I had to start living again. It doesn't mean the past is erased."

"I miss her," Donna whispered, and Aubrey's attention swung to her. Sadness dimmed her once bright blue eyes, and her hair had gone completely gray. "All I think about is how scared she was and that she died alone."

Fighting back the tears, Aubrey swallowed hard against the tightness in his throat. "I do too. But..." His voice trailed off. Could he tell them—*should* he tell them now about Oliver and what had brought him to the farm? It could be the closure they might need, and Oliver deserved not to be hidden away. He'd done nothing wrong except wanting to live. "Sometimes life is funny, you know? It can be harsh and brutal. And yet out of that, impossible as it might seem, something good can actually happen."

The troubled expression on Morty's face deepened as he frowned. "You're talkin' in riddles. Nothin' good as I could see came outta Lisa's death."

"I've got something to tell you." Fear bubbled up in his chest, and his heart beat swiftly, but the courage Oliver had shown in coming to him and telling him the truth about his heart gave Aubrey the push he needed. "I'd put an ad in the paper for a baker to start up the bakery again, and one morning, this guy Oliver shows up. I hired him on the spot. I wasn't sure I should reopen it, but we needed the extra income and he seemed to know his stuff, so I did."

"Is there a point to this story? I don't see what this has to do with Lisa's death." Always blunt, Chelsea huffed her bangs out of her eyes.

"There is, but you need to know the background." He picked up the story thread. "Oliver redid the bakery, trying to keep some of Lisa's touches while still putting his own stamp on the place. People loved his pies and muffins, but he didn't seem happy. I could tell something wasn't right. And one evening Oliver came and said he had a confession." He paused, a bit freaked out at what he was about to tell them, because he couldn't imagine their response.

Caught up in his story, Donna set her coffee cup down. "What was it? Was he a criminal hiding out here?"

Recalling Lisa's and her mother's love for true-crime television shows, Aubrey almost smiled. "No. It seems Oliver had a heart problem, and if he didn't get a transplant, he was going to die."

"Oh, that's terrible. And he's so young too." Donna's brow furrowed. "He seems perfectly fine, though, from what I saw now."

"He is, thanks to a heart transplant." Sweat trickled down his forehead and stung his eyes. "Remember that Lisa was an organ donor?"

The searing memory of the hospital staff lining the hall, their heads bent as Lisa was transported by the donor team, was not something he'd easily forget. It was their way of paying their respects for her gift to the recipients, and it was as touching as it was agonizing.

Donna and Morty nodded while Chelsea stared at him, the realization of what he was about to say dawning in her eyes. "Oh, my God," she whispered. "He...that man has my sister's heart? He got Lisa's heart?" Her face crumpled as tears streamed down her face.

"Yeah. He did. Oliver never intended to come here and apply for the job. He planned to come and meet me and thank me for the gift of his life. He understands how precious Lisa was to all of us and wanted to find out a little bit more about her and tell me how grateful he was that she'd saved his life."

"I...I don't know how I feel about all this." Donna fumbled with her purse and drew out some tissues to wipe her streaming eyes.

"I heard it." Aubrey's hands lay flat against the tabletop as if to give him support from the world reeling around him. "Her heart. Oliver brought over his stethoscope he uses to check himself, and he let me listen." The memory of that night was emotional but bittersweet. Hearing Lisa's heart reminded him of everything he'd once had and lost, yet as it was the first kiss between him and Oliver, it remained unforgettable for that reason as well.

"I can't believe I'm sitting here hearing you talk about listening to her heart in someone else's body. I can't do this."

Chelsea buried her face in her hands but remained rooted to her chair.

Leaning forward, Aubrey spoke urgently, hoping he could break through to them. "I felt you had to know, that you'd want to. It's a lot to process...I understand. But Oliver didn't take anything from Lisa. She gave of herself in death the way she did in life. Over these past few months I've gotten to know him pretty well, and he's a good, kind man. The type of person who always has a smile, no matter how he's feeling. He's brought this bakery back to life and become a good friend to me."

At his words, Chelsea gave him an odd stare, then wiped her eyes with a napkin and stood. "We have to go. This is too much to take in at one time. And my parents are tired, right, Mom? Dad?"

They nodded, and Aubrey blew out a frustrated breath, knowing they wouldn't stand up to Chelsea. "You know you're welcome here anytime. You don't have to stand on ceremony and only come once a year."

"I think about her every day. I don't need to be here to mourn her," Donna said and dabbed at her eyes again. With Morty holding her elbow, they walked a few steps ahead of him and Chelsea.

"You and that man are pretty good friends, I can tell."

Aubrey tensed. Thanks to his poker face, he didn't react, but his heartbeat accelerated. "Like I said, he's a good man."

Her face remained expressionless. "Is he being good to you? Helping you get over Lisa's death? Just how good of a friend is he?"

Years ago, early in his marriage to Lisa and before things went south with her family, Chelsea and her then-fiancé would come to the farmhouse, where they'd drink beer and play games. One night he'd gotten a little drunk, and in a game of Truth or Dare, told everyone he'd been with a man. No one had mentioned it again, but Aubrey had always said he had nothing to hide. At the same time, no one needed to know about his sexuality unless he wanted to tell them. Obviously Chelsea remembered and now was insinuating something.

"He's the type of friend I can count on to be there if I needed help. Friends like him are often better than family, you know?" He held her gaze. "They don't have any connection except the one in their heart."

Without another word, Chelsea got inside the car, started the engine, and they drove away.

An overpowering need to see Oliver rose inside him, and after checking to see he had his keys, Aubrey got in the truck and drove to his house. It only took two knocks before Oliver, barefoot and with wet hair, answered the door.

"I was hoping you'd come." With his hand in Oliver's, Aubrey let himself be led to the sofa, where he collapsed with a grunt.

"There was no place else I wanted to be." He played with Oliver's fingers. "No other person I wanted to see. I told them about you. About how you have Lisa's heart and that I listened to it."

Oliver's mouth opened and closed a few times, and then he cracked a small smile.

"You look like one of those fish in the aquariums."

"How did it go? What did they say?" He gnawed on his lip. "They must really hate me now. I knew they weren't happy I took over the bakery. This is way worse."

"Hey," Aubrey said and grasped Oliver by the nape of his neck, bringing their lips close. "What matters is that we're okay. I'm happy you're here, and I'm looking forward to tonight and the fireworks."

At the vulnerability in Oliver's eyes, Aubrey could only kiss his fears away, hoping it would be enough for Oliver. He meant for the kiss to be soft and merely brushed their lips together, but somehow their arms wound around each other's necks, and Aubrey fell back onto the sofa, taking Oliver with him. They stayed like that for a while, their mouths exploring, tongues teasing and licking until Oliver pulled away with a shaky laugh.

"Well, we already know that if the fireworks are a bust, we can come back here and make our own."

"Oh, that was bad, Ollie." Chuckling, Aubrey struggled to an upright position. "We'd better get going."

"I have to put my sneakers on, and then I'm ready."

Aubrey waited by the front door, and when Oliver joined him, they left the house and headed to Aubrey's truck. Little by little they were going out more in public together. Baby steps but moving forward. Tonight at the fireworks would be another step.

They drove to the park with Oliver's hand resting comfortably on his thigh. When they pulled into a parking space and he cut the engine, Aubrey didn't get out. "I'm not here to hide, but it's not like I'm a man to hug and kiss in public."

"Aubrey, where's this coming from? I already know that, and I'm fine with it." Oliver's brows knitted in concern.

"I-I don't want you to think I don't care. Life's too damn short to worry about other people's opinions, especially when it's none of their damn business."

"You're hiding a whole lot of sense under that baseball cap," Oliver said, teasing him with a smile. "Who knew you were such a philosopher?"

His face warmed, and he opened the door. "Let's grab a good spot. They're gonna start in a few." He reached over and grabbed the blanket he'd thrown in the back.

They walked down to where a large crowd had gathered, Aubrey greeting people as they passed. Oliver too knew a good number of the townspeople, and Aubrey didn't miss the spark of interest in his lover from some of the women. They stopped by a spot where they could lean against a tree, and he spread out the blanket while Oliver surveyed the crowd.

"Looks like everyone is here tonight. Oh, there's Quinn, Emery, and Gray. Hey, guys." He waved to the three, and they walked over. Emery carried a large picnic basket, Quinn had a knapsack, and Gray held a six-pack in each hand.

"Hoping to see you two here. Care to share our picnic? Emery made those wings you love. And we have roast-beef sandwiches and cheese and fruit and a big bowl of the homemade chips." Quinn brandished two bottles of wine. "Chilled white and rosé. Or beer."

Touched by their offer, Aubrey patted their blanket. "Sure. Thanks. Come on and sit."

They spread themselves out, and soon the blanket was covered with food and drink. Quinn lay with his head in Gray's lap, and Emery sat on Gray's other side with his hand around the man's waist. No one paid them any attention except to stop by and say hello and chat about the weather.

The fireworks started, and everyone's attention was drawn to the sky and the exploding lights. As the crowd oohed and aahed, Aubrey sidled closer to Oliver until their thighs pressed together and their shoulders overlapped. "Are you okay with this?" he murmured to Oliver, his mouth dangerously close to Oliver's cheek.

"Yeah. I wish it didn't have to end." As gentle as a butterfly, Oliver's lips brushed Aubrey's ear, and Aubrey wondered if it had to, and if a future he'd never dared to imagine lay within his reach.

# 27

# OLIVER

The tension in the truck felt thick as Aubrey drove Oliver home after the fireworks. Though they hadn't shown any real PDA, Oliver figured some might put two and two together by how closely they were sitting, and Carol from the general store certainly smiled in their direction in a knowing way a time or two.

Oliver had met Aubrey's gaze at one point during the rather impressive pyrotechnics display while everyone else's attention was on the sky. For as cautious as they were being, Aubrey's emotions seemed right at surface level—Oliver could feel his affection as much as his melancholy, and even a quiet sort of hope that he wanted to grasp with both hands.

He had the immediate urge to crawl into Aubrey's lap, into the circle of his safe arms and connect their mouths, taste his tongue, inhale his scent. When his hand brushed against Oliver's on the blanket, it felt as intimate as if he'd stroked his cheek, and it was a struggle not to groan out loud. Instead, there'd been a slight catch of his breath, but Aubrey heard it. Had turned his full gaze on him and given him one of those rare genuine smiles that lit him as bright as the colors in the sky.

"Want to come inside?" Oliver asked even though he was certain he'd be turned down after the day the man had. "Maybe even...stay over?"

Aubrey gulped in a breath, looked out the driver's side window, seeming to avoid his gaze. "I'm not sure—"

"Yeah, I get it." Oliver blew out a breath, fighting to smooth out his brow and not let any disappointment show. "It's been a long, emotional day. Plus, today is your wife's birthday. *Fuck*, sorry. I should've been more sensitive to that."

"No, it's okay. And you're plenty sensitive." Aubrey turned to look at him, his gaze softening. "You didn't let me finish, by the way."

Oliver tried to keep his lips in a neat, straight line as his pulse jumped in his throat.

"It *is* Lisa's birthday, and it has been one hell of a day," he said, then trailed his fingers over to Oliver's hand, which was clenched in a fist. "But somehow you make me feel lighter and calmer. Closer to her somehow, which probably sounds crazy."

Oliver shook his head, unable to speak right then, the lump in his throat having grown to boulder size.

Aubrey's fingers trailed up his arm to his chin. "And I'm not sure I want to be alone tonight."

*Thank fuck.* Oliver shut his eyes, immense relief flooding him. "Me neither."

Before either of them could change their minds or talk themselves out if it, he pushed open the door and stepped onto the driveway. As Aubrey followed him inside the house, he was hit by a bout of nerves. Sure, the man had been inside Oliver's house a handful of times, but never with the purpose of sleeping in Oliver's bed. And given how overwhelmed and frayed around the edges the man looked, that was likely all that would be happening between them anyway, which suited Oliver fine. Honestly, he wasn't sure if they'd ever get to this step at all. This thing between them felt too precarious, too fleeting. Too fragile. Especially after today.

When he first set out on this journey of truth, he didn't realize how all the lives and delicate balances would be affected by his revelation, and that sat squarely on his shoulders. So for now, he'd take anything the man would offer, including resting his head beside him in soft sheets that were practically calling his name.

It had been so humid at the park that he'd poured them both tall glasses of ice water, which they downed at the kitchen sink, before he locked the front door and shut off the lights.

In his room, they stripped down to their boxers, but he could still see the wariness in Aubrey's gaze. "It's okay if you change your mind."

"I haven't," Aubrey replied. "I want to be here. With you."

Oliver shivered, then pulled back the comforter, inviting him as much into his bed as into his heart.

As soon as they slid beneath the cool covers, they became a tangle of arms and legs, lips and tongues, as Aubrey kissed him soundly into the mattress. It was exactly what he needed. What he'd been longing for all night. To be as close to him as humanly possible. To feel his pulse beating directly against his own.

"Mmmm, feels good holding you," Aubrey murmured drowsily against his lips.

Oliver ignored his stiff cock in favor of being wrapped tightly in the weary man's arms as Aubrey positioned them chest to back. And soon after, he fell into a deep, dreamless sleep.

---

"YOU SURE YOU'LL BE OKAY WITHOUT ME?" OLIVER ASKED AS HE helped Cassie make pies the following Saturday after the rush.

He could scarcely believe that he and Aubrey would be hitting the road in the morning and have two whole days to themselves. According to Jennifer, his apartment was just as he left it, his mail mostly junk, but he'd admit he was a bit nervous showing Aubrey his former life. It felt surreal, like he'd never lived in the city at all, but that was probably because he hadn't been back in nearly three months.

He had his biannual cardiologist appointment scheduled at the end of the month, but that was something he always did solo. His family worried enough, and he wouldn't want Aubrey to think something was wrong. It was just part of his life now, to take his immunosuppression and blood-pressure meds as well as keep up with regular checkups. It wasn't too much to ask for a second chance at life, but those things tended to worry the people closest to him, like it was too stark a reminder of what he'd nearly lost.

"Of course." Cassie chuckled as she rolled her eyes. "Now stop fussing and get that man off this farm. If anyone needs it, it's him."

"You noticed that too, huh?" Oliver asked, glancing out the window toward the farmhouse. Aubrey had kept himself busy well into the evenings to make up for being gone the weekend, and Oliver worried he might be working *and* worrying himself to the bone.

"We all notice it," she replied, sprinkling flour on the table before rolling out more dough. "He thinks he hides it well, but there have been whispers."

Oliver's back stiffened. "What do you mean?"

Cassie winced, like she was sorry she'd revealed anything at all.

"They see he's different...since you came to the farm," she said with a wink. "They'd never guess about your heart, of course. But other things aren't that hard to figure out."

Oliver thought about the morning coffee visits, the longing looks, the after-hours dinners.

*Our weekend trip.*

"And?" Oliver asked as he held his breath.

She shrugged. "It can be confusing for some. Not because he's the boss..."

"Because I'm a man?"

She nodded as she glanced at the clock. It was nearly time for her to pick up the kids. "But it's not my story to tell."

"Mine neither, at least not entirely," Oliver replied with a sigh. "I don't want to push him. He's been through a lot."

"You have too," she responded, and Oliver sagged against the counter.

He felt like he'd been holding so much tension in his shoulders; eventually, something had to give. "Can't help second-guessing everything," he admitted.

Cassie washed her hands at the sink, then wiped them on a clean towel.

"Well, if that smile on his face every time you're around is any indication..." she said, and Oliver could feel the blush staining his cheeks as she reached for her bag under the counter. "He's a stubborn guy, but he'll get there," Cassie said before heading toward the door. "Now go show that man how to live again. I expect lots of photos."

———

OLIVER PULLED UP TO WHAT LOOKED LIKE A TENSE AND SERIOUS conversation between Aubrey and his farm manager, George, near the hill. The sun was just beginning to peek over the horizon, creating a warm glow over the farm, once again making him feel grateful he'd found his way to this enchanting place on a whim.

As soon as Aubrey slid into the front seat, Oliver blew out a breath. He'd tossed and turned all night, dreaming up too many possibilities of the man backing out of their road trip.

"Hurry, pull out of here before I think of one more thing I

forgot to tell George," he said as the manager watched them back out of the driveway, then waved once they pulled onto the road.

"He'd probably run you off the property himself," Oliver replied with a laugh.

Aubrey had mentioned once that he needed to rely on George more, but he imagined it was a struggle for Aubrey to delegate his workload to anyone, regardless of competency level—and from what he'd heard, George was plenty capable.

"You okay?" Oliver asked when his handsome passenger grew quiet.

"Yeah, it was time." Aubrey absently made the motion to adjust his ball cap, except he wasn't wearing one, and Oliver loved seeing all that rich brown hair on display.

As they passed through the center of town and by Last Call, he noticed Aubrey relaxing by varying degrees. Maybe this really would be good for the man. "I bet the farm will look just the same when we return tomorrow night."

"Smartass," Aubrey replied with a chuckle, then cleared his throat. "Think George knows 'bout us."

"What do you mean?" Oliver asked, attempting to steady his voice along with his nerves. But Aubrey didn't seem put out or upset, so maybe he was only reading into it.

"He made a comment about us being pretty chummy lately, even going on a trip and all that," Aubrey explained, his eyebrow cocked.

Oliver winced. "And?"

"I told him we were good friends and I needed time away." Aubrey turned toward him in the seat. "Then he said, 'That were the case, how come you turned me down more times than not for fishing trips?' "

The air in the truck grew thick. Like Cassie had said, it wasn't that hard to line up all the dots. Oliver's pulse picked up speed.

"I told him he had a point."

"Then what happened?" Oliver asked as he pulled onto the

interstate. He wondered if that was the part of the conversation he'd observed between the two men when he'd pulled up. *Christ.*

"I told him, 'If you got a problem with how I spend my private time, I'd like you to be up-front.' " Oliver held his breath as Aubrey finally, *finally* reached out and touched him. Took Oliver's hand in his own. "And George said that he didn't have any problem whatsoever. That he respected me—that they all did. So I guess that's that."

Aubrey stared out the window as if processing it all. Oliver couldn't blame him. He'd done the same himself plenty of times.

"How do you feel?" he asked in a hesitant voice.

Aubrey turned his full gaze on him and cracked a smile. "Like I can't wait for you to show me the city."

Oliver couldn't help returning the grin. Truth was, he was excited on so many levels. Most of all to have the opportunity to spend time with Aubrey.

"First thing we'll do is go to my apartment and drop off our bags. Then the day is ours to spend however we want," Oliver said. "Of course, I'll need my fix of a couple of things. Because until you've been treated to New York pizza and bagels, you haven't lived."

Aubrey barked out a laugh. "That right?"

"Mmm-hmm," Oliver replied. "Then we can walk along the High Line and maybe even hit one of my favorite bars in Chelsea tonight."

Chelsea was the notoriously gay section of the city, and it was no coincidence that Oliver had chosen an apartment in that neighborhood. It was next to Greenwich Village, and he liked the vibe of downtown more than any other place he'd ever lived.

"Well, that would be a first for me," Aubrey said in a quiet, almost reverent voice.

"Which part?" Oliver asked, though he was pretty sure he meant the bar. Something Oliver hadn't even considered. Christ, what else had Aubrey never experienced? He hoped to do the trip justice for him. *No pressure.* Understatement of the year.

"All of it," Aubrey replied. "I read the other day that Central Park was once a useless swampland of rocks and soil that couldn't even grow trees. So they had to import the dirt from New Jersey and blow up all the rocks with gunpowder in order to clear the land and start from scratch."

"Well look at you." Oliver felt warm all over that Aubrey had apparently done his research. His focus, of course, had not been on the massive skyscrapers but on the trees.

"I have my moments," Aubrey replied, then grew quiet for a bit. "Do you wish you were back?"

"Sometimes, but maybe not in the way you'd think," Oliver explained. "In the city, you can blend in and be anonymous. I definitely wish for more of that when it comes to me and you."

Aubrey sighed. "Too true."

## 28

## AUBREY

"Damn, I don't know how people do this every day." They'd been stuck in a traffic jam heading into the city for close to twenty minutes, and all Aubrey could do was stare. Huge buildings, masses of people, loud noises...one of those things was bad enough. All three made him want to turn around and head right back for Heartsville and its simple peace. But with each passing mile as they approached the city, Oliver had grown more and more excited. As they inched across downtown toward his apartment, Oliver would point out favorite places and tell him stories.

"That's where we all used to go every Friday night to drink," he said, pointing out the window of some bar on the corner. "And that Italian place down the block makes the best pasta. We can go there for dinner tonight."

"Okay." Aubrey didn't say much else for the rest of the ride; none of it really meant anything to him. It was being here with Oliver, together as a couple, that meant the most, not the places. They could've stayed back at the farmhouse or at Oliver's cozy home. What really mattered to him was Oliver. They'd be with each other, day and night, and his pulse raced as a thrill ran through him. He felt as anxious as he did the first time he had sex.

They finally pulled into the apartment's parking garage, and with their overnight bags in hand, went to the elevators that would take them to his place on the twentieth floor. At home, Aubrey was in charge and in control. Here, he felt small and insignificant as men and women in suits hustled by him all busy and determined-looking. Dressed simply in his faded jeans and a T-shirt, for the first time in his life he felt out of place. Like he didn't belong.

"What's wrong?" Oliver stopped by one of the tall, potted ficus flanking the elevators. "You're so quiet."

"Nothing. Just taking it all in."

"It's a lot. I'd forgotten how crazy it actually is." He pushed the button. "You've really never been to the city? It's not that far. I figured maybe once you might've."

"Nope. Never any need to. When I was little, my parents were too busy running the farm, and in school we'd go to Philly for our class trips."

"Gotcha." One of the elevators came and whooshed them up to their floor, and he followed Oliver to his apartment. When Oliver unlocked the door, Aubrey had to chuckle. Oliver had explained that New York City apartments were small, but he hadn't believed him until now. The kitchen was less than ten feet long, and the two of them couldn't fit side-by-side in the narrow space. It wasn't a bad living space. The rectangular living room was nice and large, Aubrey had to admit, with a long window that let in lots of sunlight, and a comfortable leather sofa and club chair. A giant television was mounted on the wall, and floor-to-ceiling bookcases covered one of the walls. It looked sleek and modern and nothing like the warm and friendly house Oliver rented back in Heartsville.

"God, all this mail," Oliver said. He dropped his bag on the polished wooden floors and headed over to a small table off to the side. "Good thing Jennifer came by to pick it up for me, otherwise they'd have sent it back to the post office." He flipped through the mass of envelopes, pushing aside the obvious junk mail. Aubrey assumed this was where he'd eaten his meals. Everything had to fit into its own place because there wasn't any extra room. The ceilings might've been over ten feet high, but Aubrey felt closed in.

Which Oliver was the real one? The Oliver who lived here in this modern box or the Oliver who sang while he cooked and drove a four-wheeler with reckless abandon? Aubrey mulled that over as he circled around the apartment. He leaned against a doorjamb and rubbed the back of his neck.

"This space is smaller than my kitchen."

Oliver chuckled. "I'll have you know, this is a nice-sized one-bedroom for what I paid."

"Guess it's the location that makes it worth it, huh?" He walked over to the window, which had a view of downtown. "Sure is something, though. Look at all those people, going places and doing things."

Oliver's arms slid around his waist, and he nuzzled against Aubrey. "I'd rather look at you. I can't believe we're here. Together."

The now-familiar thrill of desire rose inside Aubrey, and he forgot about the view, preferring to concentrate on the man holding him. He turned from the window and slipped his arms around Oliver's neck.

"Me either. I'm glad you suggested it, 'cause I know I never would've."

"I have a lot of good suggestions," Oliver said with a twinkle in his eyes. "Wait and see."

"How about a hint? I'm impatient."

He brushed his lips over Oliver's, meaning to only give him a gentle kiss, but as had become habit lately anytime he touched Oliver, Aubrey found himself falling deeper into the sweetness of

Oliver's mouth. The more time he spent with this man, the more he wanted him. Their tongues teased, velvet against velvet, stoking his fire until he broke free from the kiss. Oliver stood panting, eyes dazed, mouth reddened, and Aubrey had to restrain himself from reaching for him again.

"Maybe we should unpack, and then you can show me around?" He licked his lips, tasting Oliver.

"Uh, yeah. Okay." Oliver flashed him a quick smile. "It's early enough that we can hit a bunch of the big tourist sites before dinner."

"Sounds good."

Oliver brought him into the bedroom, and Aubrey eyed the queen-sized bed but said nothing. It hit him hard that he didn't care what Oliver's apartment looked like. If Oliver had lived in one room, it wouldn't matter. Smiling to himself at his sappy thoughts, he opened his bag.

"Something funny?"

He shook his head. "Nope. Just thinking."

They quickly unpacked and headed out. One thing he did like about the city was how free everyone was to be themselves. There were people with hair every shade of the rainbow and with tattoos like body art. Aubrey heard no less than ten different languages as they walked the streets. There were biracial couples, multiethnic couples, and on almost every street he saw same-sex couples unafraid to show they belonged as much as anyone else. Oliver squeezed his hand.

"It's a little overwhelming, I'm sure."

"Yeah. But eye-opening."

Hand in hand they walked, Oliver taking him first to the 9/11 Memorial, and then they hopped on the subway to go uptown.

"I'm only taking you here so you can say you've been, otherwise I never go to Times Square. It's crowded and dirty, but it's a place you need to say you've seen."

They exited the train at 42nd Street to more people than

Aubrey had ever imagined in a lifetime. He held on to Oliver's hand tighter as they walked through the Theatre District, and after only about five blocks he stopped.

"I think I've seen enough already. Can we leave?"

Oliver laughed, but Aubrey leaned closer. "I don't care that much about this stuff. I really want to be alone with you, not a million other people. How about that pasta dinner you promised? Then an early night?"

Heat rose in Oliver's gaze, and a smile teased his lips. "Yeah. That sounds about perfect. Plenty of time for sightseeing later. I'll call for a car."

He pulled out his phone, and in less than ten minutes they were in the back of a sedan heading down Broadway. Their thighs pressed close, and Oliver toyed with his fingers.

"Are you okay with everything? Are you glad we're here?"

"It's definitely different for me, but yeah, I'm glad. How about you? Does it feel strange to be back?"

"Yes and no." Still holding on to his hand, Oliver leaned back. "It's almost as if I never left. Like I could walk right back into my office, sit at my desk, and start working again. And yet...I also feel as though I've been gone a hundred years." He huffed out a laugh. "Silly, right?"

Painful as it was, Aubrey needed to ask. "Do you ever miss it?"

"What, the job?"

He nodded. Aubrey could already see, without having to ask, that Oliver loved being in the city. His eyes glowed, and he hadn't stopped smiling. That was painful enough for Aubrey to acknowledge, and he held his breath, waiting for Oliver's answer.

"Yes and no. When you give yourself over so completely to something, it's hard to walk away from it without regrets. I didn't like the long hours and the endless research, but I liked the people I worked with."

"I understand."

More than Oliver thought. Not for the first time, Aubrey

wondered what a man like Oliver—well-educated and not worried about money, it seemed—was doing in a small town like Heartsville. Or with a man like him. It sent a painful jolt through him to think he might up and leave one day.

"Hey." Oliver squeezed his thigh. "What's wrong? Are you enjoying yourself?"

"Yeah. I really am. Just a little road-weary, but looking forward to that pasta dinner." Aubrey ran his hand down Oliver's jean-clad thigh and heard the audible hitch in his breath. "And afterward."

The car pulled up in front of a line of storefronts, and they got out. People bustled by, and once again, Aubrey had the sensation of being out of his element and out of touch. Were the streets always this crowded, night and day? He sidled closer to Oliver, who took his hand.

"When I lived here, I always thought this restaurant would be a wonderful place to bring someone I cared about. I'm glad I get to share it with you." Oliver gave him a kiss and tugged at his hand. "Let's go. I'm starving."

The smell of garlic and spices hit him when they entered, and his stomach growled. An older man with a thick head of salt-and-pepper hair came from behind the gleaming wooden bar to greet them.

"Oliver? I'll be damned. How the hell are you? And where the hell have you been?"

"Paul, it's good to see you again." They hugged briefly. "I moved to Pennsylvania. Left the firm and living the quiet life now."

"No shit?" Paul ran an assessing gaze over Aubrey, alighting on their entwined hands. "This man have anything to do with that decision? Hey, nice to meet you." He stuck out his hand, and Aubrey shook it, liking his firm, dry grip. "I'm Paul Calcagni."

"Aubrey Hendricks. Nice to meet you too."

"Aubrey runs a big farm, and I'm working in his bakery."

Dumbfounded didn't begin to explain Paul's expression. "You? A baker? But you're a lawyer."

"I left the partnership because I had a bit of a health scare. I needed a break. So I took a bunch of culinary classes, found out I liked baking most of all."

"No shit," Paul stated again. "I never heard of anyone doing that before. I hope it works out for you."

"It already has." Oliver laced their fingers together. "How about a table in the back, a nice bottle of red, and linguine with clams?" He turned to Aubrey. "Sound good?"

"Uh, sure, whatever you say. You know better than me."

"I can't wait until you taste the food. Nothing tastes better than this pasta."

He gave what he hoped was a believable smile. "Can't wait."

---

"ARE YOU SURE YOU'RE OKAY?" THEY WERE LYING IN BED, WATCHING something on Netflix, and Oliver posed the question to him for the third time since they'd gotten back to the apartment.

"I'm okay. I'm relaxed. I'm lying in this amazingly comfortable bed with you. What could be better?"

"Wasn't dinner good?"

"Mmm-hmm." He rolled on his side. "You're good. Better than good." The cocktails and wine at dinner made him a bit looser and more reckless than usual, but wasn't that what this trip was all about? Getting the chance to explore each other? He grasped Oliver around the nape of his neck and pulled him in for a kiss.

"So are you." Oliver met his kiss eagerly, pushing his tongue into Aubrey's mouth. Aubrey moaned and sucked on it, greedy to lose himself in Oliver.

They'd showered after dinner and now only wore their boxers. Oliver's heat enveloped him, and Aubrey slid his hands up and down the smooth skin of Oliver's back, kissing his shoulder as their straining cocks nestled against each other.

A rolling wave of desire beat hot and heavy through Aubrey's blood as he caressed Oliver. He continued to lick and suck at Oliver's skin, working his way down to flick and suck first one tight nipple, then the next. There was nothing holding them back now, and Aubrey wanted Oliver, wanted everything he could give and take from the man. He kissed a wet path down Oliver's stomach, inhaling his scent, sticking his tongue in Oliver's belly button, lapping at the trail of dark hair.

"Aubrey, please." Oliver lay flat on the bed, his boxers damp, the gleaming head of his cock peeking up from the waistband of his boxers. "Please."

"Oliver." Aubrey braced himself on either side of Oliver's hips. "I want you. Everything. I—I feel like it's time."

"God, yes." Oliver licked his lips, and a zing of lust sparked through Aubrey at that simple action. "Now, please. I've wanted you for a long time."

His heart twisted, and he bent to kiss Oliver, plunging his tongue into his mouth, sweeping through it, wanting to imprint the taste of Oliver on his tongue and lips. He sucked and nibbled until Oliver writhed beneath him, his dark head thrashing back and forth on the pillow.

"I'll be right back." Aubrey scrambled off the bed, pulled off his boxers, and grabbed the box of condoms and the lube from his bag. In his haste he ripped open the box and tore off a condom from the strip, letting the rest fall to the floor.

"It's been a good while for both of us, and I want us to be ready." He pushed Oliver's legs up and open, exposing his hole.

Though it had been over two decades since he'd been with a man, there was no hesitancy in his actions. Nothing held him back. He wanted Oliver. Needed him. And in that want and need was his desire to give pleasure to this man who'd brought him back to life.

"Beautiful." Without another word he licked around the rim, loving Oliver's soft whimpers and the trembling in his legs. He bent his head and slid his tongue inside, first soft and gentle, then increasing the push until he was tonguing Oliver with hard jabs. He gripped Oliver's thighs, holding them apart.

"Aubrey. Jesus, Aubrey," Oliver cried out, and he lifted his head to see Oliver, wild-eyed and panting. "Fuck me."

Breathing harshly, Aubrey nodded. He'd lost himself in the taste and scent of Oliver and struggled to regain control. He rolled the condom on, slicked himself up with lube, and pressed the head of his cock to Oliver's entrance.

"Are you ready?" he whispered.

At Oliver's nod, he pushed in slowly, working his way through the tight ring of muscle. He'd only ever been with Elliot. It was so many years ago, but Aubrey remembered, and it had never been like this. This was rightness. This was real. He sank into Oliver, deeper, feeling Oliver's body open and accept him, embracing his cock in the warmth of a lover's hold.

He grasped hold of Oliver's hips and rocked back and forth, increasing his pace, the friction of the sweet, hot clutch of Oliver's passage driving him mindless. Aubrey began to thrust, first slow and shallow, allowing Oliver a chance to get used to his size, then harder, driving into Oliver deeper. He wanted to fill Oliver with his cock, make him realize he belonged to Aubrey so he'd never want to leave.

Oliver dug his heels into the bed, rising up to meet him thrust for thrust. The friction against his cock felt unbearably sweet, and Aubrey could feel his orgasm building in the soles of his feet and buzzing up through his legs. His balls felt heavy and swollen, and sweat dropped down his face, stinging as it hit his eyes.

Oliver grabbed his reddened, leaking cock, and the slick noises of him jerking himself off, coupled with his broken cries, were enough to send Aubrey over the edge. Oliver came, shooting streams of milky liquid on his belly and chest, and Aubrey pumped harder and deeper inside Oliver until the ache burst within him, shattering him into a million tiny pieces.

"Oh God, oh yeah." Aubrey moaned and collapsed on top of Oliver, drenched in sweat, shivering and twitching. His cock continued to pulse, and all he could hear were the harsh and heavy sounds of their breathing.

Oliver held him, and Aubrey laid his head on Oliver's shoulder, loath to move. "See? I told you I was fine."

"If that's your definition of '*fine*,' I might be scared as to what *good* and *great* are."

29
_____

# OLIVER

On the ride home from their whirlwind trip, Oliver felt
some of the tension begin to drain, and he was more
easily able to swallow past the lump in his throat. A light drizzle
had begun, which provided a nice breeze through the cracked
windows, and as he flicked on the windshield wipers, he noticed
Aubrey's shoulders finally relax and his smile come a little more
effortlessly. "At least it'll cool down some."

Admittedly, Oliver was exhausted from the sheer determina-
tion of trying to show the man a decent time in the city. He had
never seen Aubrey less confident in himself, and it certainly
brought out the grouchiness as he stubbornly attempted to navi-
gate through the masses. It was a scowl Oliver had come to adore
—the two severe lines between his brows he longed to smooth
out—but not at the cost of his comfort or happiness.

No question that a crowded metropolis was not Aubrey's
favorite undertaking, and he supposed it was better to know now
—for future endeavors. If there were ever any more between
them. The only time he truly felt connected to the man all
weekend was when they were alone, and especially during the
mind-blowing sex. The way Aubrey sounded as he railed into

him with just the right amount of pressure, his gaze softening as he watched Oliver come apart beneath him, made hope bloom again. Made him want to say things to Aubrey that the man was likely not ready to hear.

And again this morning during their repeat performance, which was just as earth-shattering. Aubrey had woken him with his stiff cock jutting into his back and a soft kiss to his ear, fucked him so hard that his teeth rang, and then they'd fallen back asleep together. It was pure bliss. He wanted to pause time and live in those moments where the rest of the world faded away. The blaring of horns and jackhammers became a distant bleating to the sound of Aubrey's harsh breath against his throat as he whispered his name like a prayer.

With a bag of Murray's bagels and cream cheese, they'd headed uptown to walk through Central Park, a welcome pause in the commotion, where Aubrey seemed to breathe easier.

"Seems impossible to have so much green in the middle of all this concrete," he'd said around a bite, cream cheese remnants on his upper lip. Oliver couldn't help but swipe them away with his thumb before offering a quick kiss and then attacking his own breakfast, savoring every flavor.

Afterward, they took the A train straight down to the West 4th Street station in Greenwich Village and strolled at their own pace through the narrower streets, where it was less crowded. They stopped at Rocco's bakery, where the selection of Italian baked goods made Oliver's head swim at the possibilities, and then inside the Stonewall Tavern for a drink at the bar. Aubrey took in the plaque at the entrance that signaled the historical significance for the LGBT movement, and he seemed to square his shoulders when taking a seat on an empty stool. He could tell Aubrey was more relaxed in this part of town than the others. Possibly because it seemed more his speed, more like a small village, and for the first time he could picture Aubrey in the other boroughs that offered a neighborhood feel. But that was probably pushing it.

After slices of Ray's pizza for a late lunch, they were walking past street vendors selling their wares when Aubrey pointed and grabbed his hand. There was a table of vintage movie prints, and Oliver immediately recognized what he was zeroing in on. When he spotted the original *Planet of the Apes* posters, Oliver laughed. "Well, look at that." Stepping up to the table, he noticed several action figures as well, most likely dating back to the '70s.

"Whatever happened to your Dr. Zaius and General Ursus?" Aubrey asked.

"No clue," he replied, lifting a miniature Cornelius. "I guess I should ask my dad."

On a whim, Oliver handed two of the figurines to the man who ran the stand and added two rolled-up posters to the mix that would need to be framed later.

"You're crazy," Aubrey said with a laugh, and the way his eyes crinkled at the corners was all Oliver needed to know he'd made the right decision.

"Of course we need mementos from our trip," he replied as he handed the man some bills.

"Any way to frame that slice of pizza that was the size of my head?" Aubrey quipped as he reached for the bag the man was extending with their souvenirs inside.

Oliver snickered. "I had a feeling the pizza would make you fall in love with the city."

Aubrey rolled his eyes. "I wouldn't go that far."

Now, after changing lanes, Oliver glanced over at the gorgeous man napping with his head resting against the window. The city had probably worn him out in a completely new way than the farm. It took a different sort of energy to combat the people and traffic, the noises and scents.

Oliver asked himself if he missed the city, and the answer was undoubtedly yes. But he also longed for the serenity of the farm and the quaint coziness of his house. The simple comforts of Heartsville outweighed the hustle and bustle of the city—at least for now. Never in a million years would he have imagined meeting the man of his dreams on a fruit farm at the edge of the Pocono Mountains.

He reached for Aubrey's hand, then glided his thumb down his cheek. "Hey, sleepyhead, we're about thirty minutes out."

Aubrey yawned as he sat up and wiped the sleep from his eyes. He watched the passing landscape for a while as he got his bearings. Despite its shortcomings, Oliver didn't want their time to end.

"So, on a scale of one to ten, how likely are you to return to the city?" Oliver asked.

It took Aubrey about one second flat to consider the question. "A two?"

Oliver laughed, even though it sort of hurt. But he couldn't take it personally.

"Depends on if you're with me," Aubrey added. "I'd go anywhere to spend more time with you."

Oliver felt fluttering in his chest, like a bird taking his first solo flight.

"That how you really feel?" Oliver asked, stealing a glance.

" 'Course," he said, squeezing his shoulder. "I may not understand how all this happened—or even why—but I wouldn't take it back for anything."

Oliver's heart gave a hard thump, and for the first time, the foreign organ was beginning to feel all his own. Maybe they really could give this thing between them a go.

Aubrey straightened immediately as they pulled up to the farm and spotted George pacing back and forth at the crest of the hill with Duke at his heels. It was unusual for the farm manager to be here on his day off, let alone at the dinner hour. Unless something was up.

As soon as he threw the car in park, Aubrey jumped out, and Oliver followed on his heels. "What's wrong?"

George winced. "We're hoping there's not an infestation in our watermelon crop."

"Show me," Aubrey replied before twisting back to look at him. "Oliver, I..."

"Go." Oliver waved him off, then gave Duke a pat on the head. "See you tomorrow."

And just like that, real life intruded when he'd hoped to squeeze in one more night.

# 30

# AUBREY

Luckily, the infestation was segregated to only a small part of the crop, and they spent the better part of the following week watching and waiting to see if their hard work at combating the scourge paid off. By the sixth day, Aubrey thought they had it beaten. Or so he hoped. Sweat trickled down from beneath his baseball cap, and he removed it and wiped his forehead. It had been a long, exhausting week, but that night, as he tramped back to the farmhouse, more than ever he missed having Oliver with him. One weekend together wasn't enough. He didn't want to spend another night alone.

He trudged up the steps to the house and had a crazy thought that maybe Oliver was inside, waiting for him. His heart pounded, then just as quickly settled down when he realized that would be impossible, as the door was locked and he'd never given Oliver the key. Duke came in behind him and nosed around his heels. He bent to pet him, and Duke whined, gazing up at him with big brown eyes.

"Yeah, boy. I miss him too. Maybe it's time for me to do something about that, huh?" He gave Duke a final scratch and went to take a shower. He thought about calling Oliver to say good night but reasoned it was late, and he would be tired as well. Before getting into bed, he switched on the air conditioner, then slid under the covers. As exhausted as he was, Aubrey tossed and turned, flipping back and forth, unable to find a restful place in his bed. The past week he'd been too exhausted at night to think and had fallen asleep as his head hit the pillow. With the danger to the crops now likely over, he had time to think. Without Oliver next to him, the bed seemed way too big and lonely. And cold. Oliver was very warm, and in New York he'd slept like a baby with Oliver's arms wrapped around him. His eyes fluttered shut.

*Tomorrow.*

---

AT SEVEN A.M., AUBREY STRODE ACROSS THE FRONT YARD TO THE bakery. He knew Oliver had arrived, and Cassie had pulled up only ten minutes earlier. Hopefully he could grab a cup of coffee and a few minutes alone with Oliver to talk. He'd been up since dawn, and it seemed their efforts had finally worked and the infestation had been completely eradicated.

Sleep had eluded him for much of the night. At first Aubrey blamed the worry over the possible loss of income, but he could admit, if only to himself, that he missed Oliver. The house seemed too empty, his footsteps echoing in the silence. They might've only shared a few nights, but it emphasized how lonely he was. How alone. And Aubrey didn't want to be alone. Not anymore.

Figuring they'd be in the kitchen, preparing for the day, Aubrey circled around to the back and walked past the side window. It was open, and he could hear Cassie and Oliver talking. He knew better than to stop and eavesdrop but couldn't help it, especially when he heard his name mentioned.

"So tell me more about the trip. We got so busy during the

week I hardly had a chance to ask you. Did Aubrey enjoy the city?"

Aubrey peeked in through the window. Cassie and Oliver's backs were to him as they made the dough for piecrusts. He could see the tension through Oliver's bunched-up shoulders and heard his sigh all the way across the room to where he stood.

"I don't know. He said he did, but I could see he was overwhelmed. And I don't blame him. I tried to take him to my favorite places, but I'm not sure how he really felt."

"Well," Cassie said as she rolled out the crusts, "it'll take time. I'm sure he'll grow to like it, if not love it."

"I hope so."

"But you missed it, huh?"

Aubrey cursed himself for listening but couldn't walk away. He had to know if Oliver meant to stay or was merely here biding time until he found something else to spark his interest.

"I can't deny it. There's an energy there I've never found anyplace else. I'm hoping Aubrey might learn to love it too."

Cassie chuckled. "Don't count on it, but you never know. Stranger things have happened."

Passing his hand over his eyes for a moment, Aubrey gathered his racing emotions together. It was time for him to make sure that Oliver knew where he belonged, and that was here, on this farm, with Aubrey. With a smile plastered on his face, Aubrey pushed open the back door to the bakery.

"Hey, you two. Got some coffee for me by any chance? I'm dying here."

Cassie shot him an unreadable look, then gathered up the pie tins. "Oliver, I'll fill these. Why don't you and Aubrey go in the front and have a cup? Don't want the boss man to be a bear."

"Are you sure? I don't want to leave you to make everything. You've already covered for me enough."

Oliver barely glanced his way, and though Aubrey understood

he was respecting the boundaries they'd set, it didn't feel right anymore. After being so free in New York, it was hard to go back to keeping their relationship in the shadows, especially since Cassie did have an idea of what was happening between the two of them.

"It's only the front, Oliver. If Cassie needs you, I'm sure she'll let you know. I really need that coffee."

A smile tipped up the corners of Oliver's mouth. "God help me if I keep you from your coffee." He took off his apron and hung it on the peg by the door, then walked to the front of the shop. Aubrey followed and waited while Oliver busied himself with making the coffee.

Searching Oliver's face, Aubrey noticed he looked a bit worn, as if he hadn't slept well either. Coupled with his tentative smile and tense body language, Aubrey wanted to gather the man up and kiss him until they both couldn't breathe. But he couldn't. Not with Cassie only a few feet away in the kitchen. Instead, he took a cup and held it out.

"How're you doing this morning?"

"Okay. Everything work out with the crops? I've barely seen you all week, so I figured it must've been pretty bad. I'd hoped..." He shrugged, then took the cup from Aubrey's hand and filled it with coffee. "I mean...I thought maybe you'd call at some point and let me know how it turned out." Oliver handed the coffee back to him, and Aubrey could tell how hurt he was from the droop of his shoulders, and he regretted his silence. *Shit.* He'd been so wrapped up in farm business, he'd had his head up his butt when it came to his personal life. He needed to make things right.

"I'm sorry. I've been falling into bed every night barely awake enough to take a shower, but that's no excuse. You're right. I should've called." He sidled closer and lowered his voice. "But then funny enough, as wrung out as I was, I discovered I didn't like to sleep without you there. I was hoping that tonight, you'd maybe want to come for dinner, catch up on some movies, and stay the night?"

The beautiful smile Aubrey loved seeing lit up Oliver from within, erasing the darkness clouding his eyes. "Stay with you at your place?"

Aubrey nodded, his heart racing like a high-school kid asking a date to the prom. "Around six thirty? I figured that would give you enough time to close up here, go home and change, then come back." Taking a chance, he ran his hand up Oliver's arm and watched the desire rise in his eyes. "What do you say?"

"Yeah. I—I can bring something to put on the grill."

"Whatever you want."

"You. I want you." Oliver's breath tickled his cheek, and it took all of Aubrey's strength not to take his mouth and kiss him. He'd grown used to the soft, needy sounds Oliver made against his lips. It had become an addiction he willingly gave himself up to.

"Then we're in agreement." He downed his coffee. "Gotta run. We spent so much time on the watermelons, we need to check on the other crops to make sure it doesn't pop up there. Today it's all about the tomatoes, corn, and melons. We got a lot of places waiting for the crop, so I'll be in the field all day. I'll see you at six thirty, then."

"Yeah."

Oliver's smile kept Aubrey company all day while he hacked at the tough corn stalks and melon stems and during the back-breaking work of picking the tomatoes. He and his crew finished at six, and he sped across the field to make sure he got cleaned up before Oliver came. He'd just stepped out of the shower, dripping wet, when he heard the knock from downstairs and stuck his head out the window.

"Come on in. I'm just getting dressed."

He'd finished toweling off when he heard a noise behind him. Thinking it was the dog, he turned around to scold him. "Duke, you know you're not allowed in here..." Instead, Oliver stood in the doorway, his eyes wide and dark.

"Hey."

Aubrey dropped the towel and stood naked, his cock thickening to a painful hardness. "Hi."

"I figured..." Oliver said, advancing into the room but stopping within a foot of him. Their eyes devoured each other, and Aubrey found himself growing weak with the need to touch Oliver and be touched by him. He'd come out from the depths of a long, cold journey, and Oliver was his sunlight, warming him back to life. "You might want to relax a bit before eating. You've been going nonstop all day."

Oliver stepped closer, and Aubrey smelled his freshly washed skin and hot breath against his cheek. He felt no hesitation—being with Oliver was the right thing for him. The only thing. The past, while never forgotten, could no longer define him and run his life. Like the mists after an early morning rain, Aubrey saw with a clarity that stunned him where his heart belonged.

"That's nice of you. Maybe you'd like to help me with that." With a slightly shaking hand, Aubrey reached out and trailed his fingers down Oliver's face, swirling over the firm jut of his cheekbone, then cupping his jaw. His erection brushed against Oliver's abdomen, and he slid his hands over Oliver's chest, feeling the thump of his heart. *His* heart. Not Lisa's. Oliver's heart.

"I'll do whatever you want."

"You. I want you. Here, with me. In this bed."

Oliver, who'd been nuzzling into Aubrey's palm, stilled and raised his solemn gaze to meet Aubrey's. "I don't want to push you. When it's right, I'll be here."

*Will you?*

It was on the tip of Aubrey's tongue to ask Oliver, but the fear of hearing an answer he didn't want prevented him from asking. That, plus the flood of desire heating his blood, made him helpless to do anything but take Oliver's mouth in a desperate, claiming kiss. Their tongues tangled, and he poured into his lips everything he couldn't put into words. What his head couldn't come to grips with saying out loud, his heart would find a way.

"It's never been more right than it is now. With you. Be with me? Here?" He skimmed Oliver's jaw with his fingertips, then brushed their lips together, fighting the pull of his body to sink into Oliver's arms and hold him tight so he'd never leave. "I've never wanted anyone more than I want you right now."

At Oliver's nod, triumph soared through Aubrey, and he pulled Oliver's T-shirt off. He knew Oliver still didn't like to have his chest exposed, but tonight Aubrey would make sure to let him know he celebrated his scar. It was part of him. It was what brought them together.

After Oliver shucked off his shorts and briefs and kicked off his flip-flops, Aubrey took his hand and led him to the bed. Oliver hesitated a moment, and Aubrey sat first, gazing up into his eyes. He held out his hand, and they laced their fingers together.

"After a year or so, Cassie showed up here one night to have a talk with me. We were sitting on the porch, and she said it was time for me to make some changes. She knew I'd holed up here in the house and let everything go to hell, except for the running of the farm. So she took it upon herself to order me new sheets, comforters, and pillows. At first I was angry. I wanted to hold on to everything I'd lost, and I told her flat out she had no reason to poke her nose into my business. But she was right. I couldn't cling to a past that would never return. Then you came." New sheets or not, it would be odd to be in this bed with Oliver. But he couldn't say that. Not with things so tenuous and new between them.

At his words, Oliver sank down onto the bed, next to him. "I—I have to admit it was on my mind…to be in this bed."

"Now you're here, and it's like you've breathed life back into my body." Framing Oliver's face between the palms of his hands, Aubrey first touched their lips together. Softly. Reverently. He kissed the rapidly beating pulse in Oliver's neck and heard his sigh of pleasure. "I want you..." His mouth traveled down Oliver's throat, and then his lips and tongue traced along the jut of his collarbone. "And me..." He kissed the top of his scar and felt Oliver shiver. "Us." He placed tender, soft kisses down the pink ridge of flesh scoring Oliver's body. "Your heart beating fast for me." Oliver tensed, but Aubrey continued, his kisses growing insistent until the man lay pliant in his arms.

"I can't think straight when you kiss me."

He pushed Oliver down, caging him between his arms. Their erections bumped and slid against each other, and Aubrey shivered at the delicious friction. "That's the point. I don't want to think. I want to feel. What do you want, Oliver? Tell me."

# 31

# OLIVER

"*What do you want, Oliver? Tell me.*"

Oliver had so many things he wanted from this beautiful man, if only he were sure enough to voice them out loud. Instead, his brain was a menagerie of swirling thoughts.

The fact that he was currently in the bedroom where Aubrey had slept with his wife, Lisa, wasn't lost on him. And how gentle and reverent he'd been in kissing his scar...Oliver couldn't begin to wonder what the man was thinking.

Did it make him feel closer to her...to him as well?

He attempted to shake the thought that she was with them in this very space. And he felt so fucking guilty that he didn't want her to be. He wanted it to be only him and Aubrey.

Something only the two of them shared. And he felt so damned selfish even thinking it. He wanted the man like no one ever in his life, but if that meant always second-guessing how everything went down, he didn't know if it was worth it.

Except, when he glanced up into his sweet, soulful eyes, it absolutely was.

And right then, Aubrey looked like he wanted to devour him

whole, and it made Oliver's cock so stiff, he swallowed all his doubts. Though some must've registered on his face.

"Hey, you okay?" Aubrey murmured as his knuckles nudged his chin. "You look lost in your own head."

"I'm just...I want you to be sure..." Oliver replied, glancing away. "This...it's a big deal. This is the room you shared with—"

"I'm absolutely fucking sure, Oliver," Aubrey replied, clutching his jaw, making him look at him. "Let me show you how sure I am and how damned much I want you."

Suddenly his hands were gripping the underside of Oliver's thighs as he readjusted their position farther up the bed. With a growl that made the hair on Oliver's nape stand on end, Aubrey pressed him into the mattress with the heat and mass of his body. He loved being surrounded by the man, and he had a feeling Aubrey knew exactly what he was doing. That it made him feel safe and wanted. Their bodies connected shoulder to hip, their shafts realigned, and he could feel Aubrey's pulse battering against his own as Oliver moaned into his throat.

He felt the dampness of his cock leaking against his stomach as Aubrey's fingers dug into his shoulders and he rocked his hips, rutting against him.

"Please," Oliver begged as Aubrey sucked a spot on Oliver's throat, hard enough to leave a mark, but he couldn't find it in him to care—he just wanted him, all of him. He needed the man to fill him. To fuck him hard, make him feel the burn, to own him body and soul. "*Aubrey.*"

After one more tender kiss, Aubrey broke away and reached for a condom and lube in the nightstand drawer.

Oliver's breath hitched, his entire body thrumming in anticipation.

Aubrey's fingers fumbled to open the packet, a possible sign that he was just as eager or nervous, though the man was nothing if not determined. After suiting up, he slathered the condom with lube, his eyes seeking Oliver's once more.

Aubrey's fingers tangled in Oliver's hair, his eyes softening as they seemed to search for something in his gaze. Maybe the underpinning of truth or the raw evidence of his desperate longing that he tried to convey around his scratchy pleas. The more their gazes connected, the more the tendrils of Oliver's heart seemed to stretch and grow, bridging the gap between them.

Not a second later, Oliver's knees were lifted to his shoulders, and Aubrey was at his entrance, pressing inside. Oliver gasped from the sudden fullness, fisting the sheets, searching for his warm gaze.

"So fucking tight." Aubrey drove inside with shallow stabs as a moan tore from Oliver's throat. One more solid thrust and Aubrey stilled as he filled Oliver to the hilt. Aubrey groaned, his chest heaving, his eyes glassy, and then he sank down, his furry chest tickling Oliver's tender scar, their lips brushing. Oliver's hands clutched Aubrey's shoulders as he rolled his hips upward, seeking purchase, desperate for more.

"Oliver, look at me," Aubrey murmured as his hands burrowed in his hair. And Oliver realized how different this time felt—more intimate, more overwhelming, just *more*. There was a tenderness in Aubrey's eyes, a vulnerability he hadn't noticed before. "Love being inside you."

His chest ached so hard, he found he couldn't speak, so he just murmured his name.

Oliver's shaft pulsed between them as Aubrey started moving, rolling his hips in deep and satisfying thrusts, providing a sweet friction against his throbbing cock.

His spine arched and prickled, and just as he began seeing stars dancing along the edges of his vision, Aubrey kissed him like his life depended on it—slow and sweet, rough and wet—absorbing all his groans. And Oliver couldn't get enough of his lips and tongue, his taste and smell and sounds. He was in fucking heaven as his balls drew up tight and his climax barreled down on him.

Oliver cried out, his hole clenching around Aubrey's length, and he spurted his seed messily between them. He dragged his mouth away, trying to suck in air as Aubrey shuddered his release inside him. "Goddamn, Oliver."

Aubrey trembled in his arms as they breathed into each other's mouths, their tongues licking and sliding together until their lips felt swollen and the tendrils in Oliver's heart wove into a makeshift tapestry of hope and love.

After enough time had passed that Oliver began feeling sticky and cold, Aubrey pulled out, threw the condom in the trash can, and dampened a hand towel in the bathroom.

Swiping at the mess on Oliver's stomach, he looked him over, his fingers rounding his shoulder and grazing up to his jaw. "You'll stay the night?"

"Yes," Oliver said without hesitation, clasping his hand and kissing his knuckles.

That earned him a crooked grin. "Good. Then feed me."

Oliver barked out a laugh. "Oh okay, boss. That's how it is now? You giving me orders?"

Aubrey leaned down and took his mouth in a bruising kiss. "I think you like it when I take charge."

Oliver groaned. "I definitely do. Though you could stand to be a bit less grouchy."

"That so?" Aubrey replied with a wicked grin right before his fingers descended and tickled him in all the right vulnerable spots, like he knew how to push all of Oliver's buttons.

"I'm going to fucking kill you," Oliver replied, trying to move away and curl up in a ball, but when that didn't work, it turned into a wrestling match of epic proportions, both seeming to laugh so hard, they became winded and Oliver's ribs ached.

"Goddamn," Aubrey wheezed. "I'm an old man; you *are* going to kill me."

"Hey, you started it," Oliver mused as he rolled out of bed and slipped into his jeans. Once Aubrey was dressed, they padded down to the kitchen, hand in hand. Aubrey poured them glasses of water at the sink, and Oliver took in the contents of Aubrey's refrigerator.

Dinner decided, Oliver broiled a couple of medium-rare steaks and made up a simple side salad. Aubrey opened up a bottle of wine, and they took their plates outside to eat on the back deck.

Beneath the full moon, with Duke at his feet and Aubrey's fingers resting against his own, Oliver thought maybe he could get used to this.

# 32

# AUBREY

Aubrey awoke to the pale dawn brightening the bedroom and lay still, the glow of that first light making everything clear, enabling him to see how much Oliver meant to him. A warm, heavy weight snuggled up against him, and the rush of last night and making love to Oliver hummed through his blood. Joy swept through Aubrey along with a hefty dose of fear. Fear that what they had between them might be fleeting. That eventually Oliver would grow tired of the small-town life and leave, taking Aubrey's heart with him.

He pressed gentle, tiny kisses along Oliver's cheek, his nose nudging him awake.

"Good morning."

"Hey. How'd you sleep?"

Oliver's thick, dark lashes fluttered, and he opened his eyes, still dreamy with sleep. "Like a log. You?" His sweet, lazy smile warmed his face, and Aubrey couldn't resist grinning back, so damn happy, he almost couldn't believe this was him.

"Never better." The truth shocked him. "It's nice to wake up and have someone here."

Oliver blinked and lay back on the pillow. "What time is it?"

Oliver squinted at the clock on the nightstand. "Five thirty. You have to get up soon, don't you?"

Loath to let Oliver escape the bed, Aubrey rubbed their bristly cheeks together. His erection tented the thin sheet covering them. "I have time." He kissed along Oliver's jaw and heard him chuckle.

"I see you're already up, so to speak."

"I want you again."

"Yeah?" Oliver sounded breathless as they tangled their feet.

"Mmm-hmm. I got a long, busy day on the fields, and I need something to think about while I'm out there sweating and working my fingers to the bone."

"You poor baby." Oliver grabbed a condom and the lube from the nightstand and tossed them on the bed. "Guess I better make it memorable." He pulled the sheet aside to expose Aubrey, who'd slept naked.

"No worries there. I remember every moment we've been —*ahhh*, Ollie."

Aubrey had barely enough time to breathe before his dick was engulfed in the hot, wet suction of Oliver's mouth. *Damn.* Oliver's full, red lips sliding down his length would forever be a picture in his mind.

"Oliver, Ollie," he moaned. "Need to be inside you."

Oliver licked around Aubrey's dick a few more times, then let him slip from his mouth. He opened the condom, rolled it down Aubrey's aching shaft, and slicked on a copious amount of lube.

"I want to ride you."

Aubrey's dick swelled even further, and he grasped Oliver's hip. "Go on, then. Get on me."

The crown of his dick bumped Oliver's hole, then caught the rim, and Oliver slowly pushed himself down until he sat fully impaled.

"Oh God, you feel amazing."

Oliver's face revealed every emotion as he took him inside—

pain, wonder, mounting desire. He began to move, and Aubrey picked up on his rhythm, flexing and rolling his hips, sinking deep into the tight, silky clutch of Oliver's ass.

*So fucking perfect.* Using the slick of Oliver's precome dribbling from his cock, Aubrey began to stroke Oliver, earning a hiss. Nothing gave him more pleasure than seeing Oliver in full-on bliss mode: face slack, mouth open and panting, skin flushed a deep red.

"Aubrey." Oliver's eyes had slid shut, but they opened, his gaze smoldering. "P-please," he stuttered out.

Aubrey ran one calloused hand over and up and down Oliver's dick and was rewarded with a spurt of sticky wetness. His other hand fondled the smooth clench of Oliver's ass, loving how his touch caused Oliver to moan and twitch above him. Aubrey plunged in deep while simultaneously thumbing the head of Oliver's dick.

"Come on me. Let me taste it."

Oliver leaned forward and held his shoulders, then gave a final groan as his dick swelled and shot out streams of come, hitting Aubrey's chest and chin. Oliver's eyes rolled back, and he collapsed, burying his face in Aubrey's neck.

Holding on to Oliver, Aubrey turned over so he was now on top. He pushed Oliver's legs to his shoulders and sank in all the way until his balls rested on Oliver's ass, then pulled out only to push right back inside him. He lost himself in the velvety heat of Oliver, trying to hold on to him. Sweat dropped down his back and into his eyes as he continued to pump into Oliver, who'd come out of his orgasmic stupor to lock his ankles behind the small of Aubrey's back and meet his strong thrusts.

Like an electric shock, his orgasm hit, boiling through his blood in a trail of fire. He came, jerking hard, holding on to Oliver. Not wanting to let him go. Ever.

They held each other close, and Aubrey felt the pulsing of Oliver's heart against his cheek. The sound of its rhythmic beat filled him with incredible pleasure, knowing it meant Oliver was healthy and strong. He kissed Oliver's neck and throat, working his way down to the top ridge of the scar.

"That was amazing."

"Yeah. We'd better get up," Oliver said, twisting away from him. "We both need to shower, and I have to run back to my place before I open the bakery."

"All right." Aubrey wondered if he'd done something wrong. "Everything okay?"

"Yeah, of course. Wonderful." Oliver leaned back and gave him a toe-curling kiss that set his mind at ease. "Just back to reality, is all."

"Thanks for reminding me."

He got up and took off the condom, throwing it into the wastebasket before swatting Oliver's ass. "Share the shower and save my water."

Oliver smirked at him. "Who knew you were such an environmentalist?"

Aubrey took his hand and pulled him to the bathroom, where he turned on the shower, pushed him under the water, and kissed the smile right off his lips.

THE NEXT TWO DAYS TURNED OUT TO BE AS BACKBREAKING AS HE'D anticipated, and the overwhelming heat had Aubrey calling in the guys from the field to go home early. The relentless sun turned the fields into shimmering waves, and even the birds had fallen silent, perhaps saving their energy for song until the cool of the evening.

"Don't want you killing yourselves. Grab some cold waters from the fridge before you go."

The field hands all gave him exhausted smiles of gratitude, and he took off his soaked cap to wipe the sweat off his brow, knowing it was a futile effort. He was sunburned, grimy, drenched, and needed a shower and a cold beer like nobody's business. Oliver had texted him earlier that he was going into town to pick up some baking equipment he needed but would be back later.

*Dinner tonight?*

Aubrey couldn't text back quick enough. *Yeah. Maybe the new place in town?*

*Sounds perfect.*

Aubrey sent back a thumbs-up emoji, although he didn't need anything sweeter than Oliver's lips.

*Damn, I'm acting like a lovesick kid.*

But he whistled on the walk back to the farmhouse.

Maybe tonight he'd tell Oliver how he felt about him, Aubrey mused. If he told Oliver he loved him, maybe he'd want to stay and they could make a life together. It wasn't a question of *if* he loved Oliver; it was how to reassure Oliver that it was him he loved, not the fact that his heart had once been Lisa's.

A car with an out-of-state license plate sat in the drive, and he squinted in the waning sun. *New York.* At his approach, the car door opened, and a woman got out, her hand shielding her eyes.

"Hello, may I help you?" As he drew closer he saw she looked vaguely familiar, but he couldn't place where he might've seen her before.

"Um, yes. I'm looking for Oliver? Is this First Light Farm?"

"Yes. I'm Aubrey Hendricks, the owner. Oliver isn't here right now."

"Aubrey...oh, well, I'm Jennifer, Oliver's sister."

Now he could see why she looked familiar. She and Oliver shared the same wide brown eyes and angular facial structure. "Oh, um, hi. Nice to meet you."

"You too. Oliver doesn't know I'm coming. I thought I'd surprise him, especially since he decided to visit the city and didn't bother to call me. I don't live too far away."

Feeling at a disadvantage, all grimy and sweaty while Jennifer stood cool and fresh in her sleeveless white shirt and pressed tan shorts, Aubrey grew a bit defensive. "Well, it was kind of spur-of-the-moment. We didn't have any grand plans."

"I'm sure he was thrilled to get back there. No one loved the city more than my brother. Did he take you out to his favorite haunts?"

"Uh, not really. We just walked around and he showed me the sights."

Her mouth fell open. "You've never been? I can't believe it."

"Well, I had to run the farm, so no time for fun getaways."

"So"—she gestured to the expanse in front of her—"this is all yours?"

"Yeah, plus some. I have about five hundred acres."

"Wow." Impressed, she planted her hands on her slim hips and surveyed the house. "Is that your house?"

"Yes." It was time to act the gentleman. "Would you like to come inside and wait for Oliver? He shouldn't be long."

"Thanks. I could use a cold drink. The heat is brutal."

They walked together, and he couldn't help but be amused at her stopping every few steps to shake a bit of gravel from her open-toed sandals. He opened the door, allowing her entry first. The cool air of the house felt wonderful, but his nerves had started the sweat popping up again. "Have a seat in the living room. I have iced tea or water."

"Iced tea, if it isn't too much trouble."

"Not at all."

Opening the refrigerator, he gazed longingly at the beer but took a bottle of water for himself and poured a tall glass of iced tea for Jennifer. When he returned to the living room, he found Jennifer at the fireplace mantle, his wedding picture in her hand.

"Your wife was very beautiful." With care, she replaced the picture.

"Yes." He handed her the glass. "Inside and out."

"I'm sorry."

"Thank you."

"So I know Oliver told you he received her heart."

*Well, nothing like the direct approach.* "Yes, he did."

"How odd does it feel, having him here, knowing that? I can't imagine it's easy for you, considering how long you and Lisa were married, and from what Oliver's told me, she was an amazing woman."

"Thank you. She was. And as for Oliver, yeah, it was a shock." Aubrey pinched between his eyes to gather his thoughts. He knew he already seemed defensive to Oliver's sister, and wanted to make a good impression. Besides, she had every right to ask questions where her brother was concerned. So he made the effort to explain, for Oliver. "Guess time has let me heal. And I've adjusted but not forgotten. And life can sometimes give you wonderful surprises, like Oliver. His friendship saved my life, as much as Lisa's heart saved his."

Those big brown eyes of hers softened, yet assessed him with the precision of a surgeon with a scalpel. "I bet finding out he has your wife's heart, it's like a piece of her remains alive. As long as Oliver is here, she's here too."

Aubrey gripped the water bottle, his gut churning. *No. That's not what I mean. I'd care about Oliver no matter what.* "Oliver is a special man. I owe him so much more than I could ever tell him." He didn't...he *couldn't* put into words at the moment what he felt for Oliver. And he sure as hell wasn't about to say that to Oliver's sister.

"I'm sure he knows how much you appreciate him coming here. I'm still amazed he's stayed as long as he has. I don't think Oliver ever spent more than a weekend away from the city. He used to say he didn't ever need to leave. He could find whatever he needed within five city blocks."

What the hell was he supposed to say to that? He drank his water, feeling slightly nauseated.

"May I use your powder room?" Jennifer asked. "I've been on the road a couple of hours, and my extra-large iced coffee is doing a number on me."

Aubrey nearly laughed. "Down the hall, first door on your right."

"Thanks." She walked off, and he took several deep breaths to steady himself.

The door opened, and he heard Oliver's voice call out.

"Aubrey?"

"In the living room."

Swift footsteps sounded, and Oliver, breathing heavily, raced into the room, almost skidding to a stop. "That's my sister's car."

"I know." Aubrey stood.

"Is everything okay?" he asked, panic written on his face.

"She's fine," Aubrey reassured him. "Apparently just decided to pay you a surprise visit."

Oliver's shoulders relaxed. "Sneak attack. Wish she would've given me a heads-up."

"She and I have been talking, so I think I'll let you two have your own chat. I need to take a shower." He forced a smile.

Unable to leave fast enough, Aubrey strode out of the room and took to the stairs. Oliver called out after him, and he stopped on the steps and looked down at him waiting at the bottom.

"What happened? What did she say?"

"Nothing. I'm just filthy and smelly and need to get out of these clothes."

"Okay." Oliver's tight expression softened. "Are we still on for dinner?"

It almost killed Aubrey to say it, and his hand tightened on the banister until pain shot up his arm. "Um, well, maybe you want to spend some alone time with your sister? You can let me know later."

"Are you sure everything's all right?"

At those words, Aubrey's composure slipped for a moment,

and he wanted to crush Oliver in his arms and ask him not to leave, not to ever go away, but then he recalled Jennifer's words and drew in a deep breath. "Of course. I think you should talk, just the two of you. She's your sister, and you haven't seen her in a while."

"Even if that's true, the three of us can go out somewhere."

He'd rather eat nails than sit across the table from Jennifer and listen to the good old times Oliver enjoyed in New York City.

"Let's play it by ear." Without waiting for an answer, he bounded up the stairs two at a time and hurried into the bathroom, shutting the door behind him. Sure, he was being cowardly, but he couldn't think straight, imagining the emptiness of his life without Oliver.

# 33

# OLIVER

"Oliver?" Jennifer called from the hallway. "I thought I heard your voice."

What in the hell just happened? Had Jennifer said something to Aubrey? She wasn't the most subtle person.

Oliver turned toward his sister, whom he hadn't laid eyes on in months. She had the same wispy brown bangs and commanding presence, but she looked weary in a way that only parents did. Cassie displayed that same sort of fatigue in her eyes, and if he were to guess, she was as good a mom as Jennifer was.

"This is quite a surprise," he said through a clenched jaw. "How come you didn't call me from the road?"

"I wasn't exactly sure I was coming. I only needed to get away for a while—like I sometimes do—so I got in the car." In years past she had always alerted him from the road. Sometimes she'd come into the city from Westchester, sometimes she'd only drive around aimlessly and work out whatever was going on in her head. "I just started driving, and this is where I ended up. If I can't find you in the city anymore, guess I'll have to hunt you down here."

His irritation transformed into concern. "You let Kurt and the kids know—"

"Yes, of course," she reassured him. He understood needing a break from a hectic, overscheduled life, and she rarely got one as a mom. Her husband was very understanding when she got into these moods every few months. Normally dinner and some drinks in the city was the cure, and she happily returned home to the family she adored. Oliver felt a bit guilty that he lived farther away now. "If you let me stay on your couch, I'll be back on the road in the morning."

"You're more than welcome," he said, walking into the kitchen with his sister on his heels. "Had you called, I would've reminded you about my checkup on Monday."

In recovery, he'd had to wear a mask the first few weeks because his immune system was shot to hell. Once discharged from the hospital, he religiously attended weekly appointments until his sternum healed properly, and even then, it took a full six months post-surgery until he felt somewhat normal again.

Since then he'd tried not to read up on any of the mortality rate statistics for heart transplant recipients, and he certainly didn't want to worry Aubrey about any of it—the man had been through enough—which is why he still hadn't told him about the appointment. Besides, he'd planned to only be gone for a few hours on Monday.

"I'll remind you that you didn't tell me the last time you were in the city," she griped, glaring at him.

"That was different." He looked over her shoulder to see if Aubrey had come down from his shower yet, but he could still hear the water coursing through the pipes. "We didn't have a lot of time, and I wanted to show him as much of the city as I could."

"I'm only giving you a hard time," she said before pulling him into a brief hug. "Now, give me a tour of this place?"

"Let's go," Oliver replied as she followed him out to the porch and down the steps. The moment felt surreal. He'd left the city months ago, but as he sucked in the cool night air, he realized he could breathe better out here, and not just in a purely perfunctory sense. It was the town and the bakery and the people, but also the man he'd fallen in love with. He wondered if his sister could sense it too.

After pointing out the crops and orchard down the hill, which were difficult to see in the dusk hours, Oliver led her through the door of the bakery.

"This is unbelievably charming," she said, clapping her hands together. "I can understand the draw. And you mentioned a woman named Cassie. She assists you?"

"She's great," Oliver replied as he showed her the kitchen, as well as the pies they had prepped for the morning schedule. "You can meet her in the morning before you take off."

"What's that?" She eyed the French silk pie he'd removed from the middle shelf. "Mom's recipe?"

"Uh-huh." He moved the pie to a different part of the refrigerator. "I figure you'd want to take it home to share with Kurt and the kids."

"If you insist," she replied with a laugh. "Though don't fault me if I pull over on the side of the road and dig right in. Don't know how you stay fit with all this food around."

He chuckled as he cut the lights and they headed out the door. "Some days we're so busy, I forget to eat. Same with Aubrey. If he's been in the field all day..."

Jennifer tilted her head and threw him a strange look, which tripped him up a bit.

"I was only going to say that I sometimes cook for him. He hardly buys anything for himself." He stared off as he said the words, awareness dawning on him. It had been Oliver who'd first approached Aubrey and asked him to share a meal. It wasn't until he'd confessed about his scar that they had really connected.

Of course, Aubrey was a private person, hard to know at first, besides being his boss. But had he not pursued a friendship with the man, would Aubrey have ever made his attraction known? Or perhaps his attraction came after...after *what*?

He was startled out of his thoughts when the screen door slapped open and Aubrey stepped onto the porch, his arms filled with beer bottles and glasses that he placed on the wicker table. Without his ball cap and fresh from the shower, the man was so ruggedly handsome that Oliver's breath caught.

Jennifer cocked an eyebrow at him. "Someone is smitten, and I can see why."

"Thought you might want something to wet your whistle," Aubrey said as they joined him on the porch. "I also have an open bottle of wine."

"Beer sounds refreshing, actually," his sister replied, so he popped the cap and poured her a glass, topping off the foam before handing the drink to her.

Once they took their seats, Oliver watched as Aubrey took a long swig of his beer, seeming to savor it. His Adam's apple bobbed as he swallowed the cold drink, and Oliver wanted to lick the bead of water at his throat.

When Oliver glanced more closely, he noticed the shadows beneath his eyes. The long hours and sun had done the man in. He longed to reach for him, to wrap him in his arms, but something had shifted between them since Jennifer's arrival, and he wasn't sure what.

Besides, he definitely felt like he was under the microscope with his sister around. She was sure to notice any number of things and call him on it. Sometimes she was as hard to impress as Aubrey was. They had that in common, at least.

"You look dead on your feet," Oliver commented.

"Been a long week or so," he replied, wiping his brow.

Jennifer asked him some questions about the farm, and as he explained how they were about to prepare for the fall season, which Cassie had told Oliver was their busiest, he wondered if he could picture himself in Heartsville for the long haul. The thought of it excited him, but not if he didn't have Aubrey by his side. A stab of pain shot through him at the idea of a wedge growing between them, of them parting ways. Why was he suddenly feeling so unsettled?

"Feel like dinner?" he asked after another few minutes of small talk. "Figured we'd try that new Italian place in the square."

"You all right if I pass?" Aubrey replied after finishing the last of his beer. "Probably call it an early night."

"Yeah, sure," Oliver said, feeling like he was talking to a stranger rather than the man he'd shared a bed with. He vaguely wondered if another invite would have been extended after dinner, had Jennifer not rolled into town.

"It was nice to meet you," Aubrey said, stretching to shake his sister's hand.

She smiled warmly at him, and he could tell Jennifer was impressed with the man. "Thank you for giving my brother a chance with the bakery. He's nothing if not determined to make a good impression."

"I'd say we're the lucky ones," Aubrey replied with a smile. "Have you tried his pies?"

It was the first sign of fondness he'd noted in the man's eyes tonight, and his praise nearly made him blush.

"Why do you think I drove all the way out here?" she mused.

Oliver rolled his eyes. "I'll definitely be sending some home with her."

As he followed her down the steps, Oliver turned suddenly and planted a chaste kiss on Aubrey's lips. He just needed contact with him. "Get some sleep."

When he looked into his eyes, he saw affection but also a great deal of confusion. Maybe the man really was exhausted.

Once in the car, he drove Jennifer through the quaint town he called home, and he could tell she was pleased. The restaurant was beginning to fill, but thankfully, they were able to find a roomy booth to be seated in near the window. The late-blooming roses were sure to provide a pretty backdrop to the clock tower in the center of the square. And if he closed his eyes, he could almost picture a large Christmas tree dotted with snow.

After placing their order, he gave his sister the once-over. "Okay, spill. What's the real reason for your visit?"

"I told you I needed to get away for a few hours." When he quirked an eyebrow, she sighed. "And sure, I wanted to check up on you. You've been so...preoccupied with all this, and I was afraid you were going to lose yourself."

"In what exactly?" he scoffed as he reached for the bread basket.

"I don't know. I just needed to see with my own eyes..." She shook her head.

"Why?" Oliver's stomach rolled over on itself. "C'mon, Jennifer. You're never one to mince words."

"I don't want you to get your heart broken," she said in a strained whisper. "We almost lost you the first time."

Oliver scrubbed a hand over his face, feeling as much a pang of regret as frustration. "Why do you keep saying that? Nothing is going to—"

"Look at it from my perspective," she said, lifting a slice of bread to butter. "You left the city to meet your donor's widower. You found him, took a job in his bakery, and fell in love."

Oliver winced. "And?" He was waiting for the punch line. Or maybe to see if her doubts lined up with his own. He didn't know anymore; his thoughts felt all jumbled.

"Aubrey was a man grieving his wife, and you came out of nowhere offering him some measure of hope." She placed her knife down and looked pointedly at him. "A piece of his wife lives inside your chest. I'm not sure how I would react if it were me and Kurt, except I might want to keep that person close to feel some sense of comfort."

Oliver's mind was reeling as their food was served. Was that all this was between him and the man he was in love with? Some misplaced feelings? He cringed at the thought of sleeping in Lisa's bed the other night. No matter how much he tried to shove it out of his head, her presence was with them, and he didn't know if that sat well anymore. He didn't want to play second fiddle to anyone. He wanted Aubrey to think he hung the moon all on his own.

"I said as much to him tonight," Jennifer said around a bite of her pasta.

"What the hell, Jen? Why would you even—" He shook his head and set his fork down with care so she wouldn't see his hand shake. Jen had always been overprotective, even more so after his surgery, so he wasn't too surprised by her actions. Despite his frustration with his sister for being so forward, so pushy, Oliver couldn't help being curious. He desperately wanted to know where Aubrey stood. "Well?"

She shrugged. "He didn't deny it."

His face fell. Was that why he was being so distant?

Jennifer patted his hand. "Hey, look at me. You always want me to be straight with you, right?"

"Like I ever have a choice," he muttered, pushing his food around his plate. He suddenly felt like his whole world had tilted on its side. Again.

"I'm not saying he doesn't care for you. That much is obvious. I just want to make sure his feelings aren't misdirected," she explained as she dabbed her chin with a napkin. "Lay it all out with him, Oliver. It's the only way you'll know."

Was it? He wasn't sure if he could trust his own judgment anymore. Doubts were seeping through every nook and cranny in his soul.

Oliver was preoccupied for the rest of the meal as they discussed their holiday plans with their father and again as he made up the spare room for his sister to sleep in.

The next morning, she woke with him and met Cassie at the bakery as they prepped for the morning rush. As he'd predicted, they got along well, talking about their families and trading war stories like parents always seemed to do.

Aubrey stopped in briefly for his morning coffee, asked about their dinner out, then left to begin his long day in the fields. It was awkward and somewhat strained, and Oliver felt even worse than he had the night before.

"Make sure to call me straight after your doctor's appointment on Monday," Jennifer said over her shoulder as he walked her out to her car with three pies in tow.

"I will." Oliver had only planned to be gone for the day, but now he considered leaving for the city tonight and spending his two days off in his own apartment.

He needed to make some decisions about the place anyway, whether to sell it or find a tenant to rent the space while he was gone. Pushing the other grim possibility out of his head, he lifted his cell and phoned Aubrey. When he didn't answer, Oliver hung up, that same frustration coursing through him.

When he hadn't heard from Aubrey by the end of the day, his mind was made up, so he went home and packed a small bag.

As he left for the city, he pulled out his phone again and called Aubrey to make him aware of his plans. When he didn't answer, this time he left a message, trying to temper the disappointment in his voice. "I have some business to take care of in the city. Thought I'd go early and figure some things out."

He didn't know if putting distance between them would make him see things more clearly or not. But it was definitely worth a shot.

## 34

## AUBREY

For the third time that evening, Aubrey sat and listened to Oliver's message. He wished he'd heard his phone the first time he'd called. *"Things to take care of in the city."* Could the man be more vague? He took a hefty gulp of his beer. What things? Was he stocking up the pantry and preparing to move back? Did he have an old boyfriend he planned on meeting? A pang squeezed his heart, but realistically, Aubrey didn't think Oliver would see someone else.

The bell rang, and Duke gave a *woof*, then padded out of the living room. Aubrey heaved himself out of the chair, and when he opened the front door, he was greeted by an unsmiling Cassie.

"Aubrey, got a few minutes?"

"Hi, of course, come on in."

She refused his offer of a drink or something cool, and they sat in the living room. Cassie seemed on edge and not her usual calm self.

"Did you hear from Oliver?"

"Uh, yeah. He said he had to go back to the city to take care of things."

"Hmm. Yeah." Her sharp gaze probed him. "What did you think of Jennifer?"

To answer that question required Aubrey to first finish off the rest of his beer. "She seemed nice enough." It was the most noncommittal answer he could give without exposing how he really felt.

"Cut the BS. This is me you're talking to."

Of course Cassie saw right through him.

"What do you want me to say? She kind of intimidated me a little, asking me questions about Lisa."

Cassie's brows shot up. "She did? Like what?"

Damn, he wanted another beer. "Um, well, she asked if I thought having Oliver around was like being able to keep Lisa close. Something like that."

"She did not! What'd you say? If you don't mind me asking."

"Yeah...I kind of sidestepped the question because it really isn't her business. But she also went on and on about how much Oliver loves the city and how he'd always sworn he'd never leave..." He found he couldn't go on.

"I know Oliver loves it here. He wouldn't have rented that house if he didn't."

"But you know he went back to New York, right? To 'take care of some things'?" He repeated Oliver's words with emphasis.

"He told me that, yeah."

"Maybe since the summer is over, it's time for him to go back to reality. For all of us." At Duke's whine, he scratched the dog's floppy ears.

"Is that what you want?"

"No. I don't know. I can't keep someone here if they don't want to stay." Long, lonely, dark nights stretched out in front of him, the way it had been in the years since Lisa's death. Oliver had brought light back into his life and his heart.

"Have you given the man a reason to stay? Does he know how you feel?"

A thrill, both hot and cold, trickled through him, and Aubrey needed a moment to gather his wits before he could answer.

"Uh, meaning?"

"Okay. I'm going to say what I came here to, then go home, because I can only stick my nose in so far." Her warm eyes gazed at him with a frankness he'd come to trust and rely on the past few years.

"Cassie, I—"

"I think I know you pretty well. You're a proud man and a stubborn one too. But that's the outside Aubrey. I've seen who you really are. And this summer I watched you come out from under the shadow of death and learn to not only live again, but to love. I know how hard it was for you. And I also know that nothing lit up Oliver's life more than seeing you. Not me, not his sister. Was it strange how you two met? Absolutely. But don't cheat yourself out of a chance at happiness because of extraordinary circumstances. You have the beginning of something real here."

A person had to be lucky in friendship as well as love. "Thanks. I think I know what I need to do now."

"I'll watch over Duke for you. And I happen to know there's a seven a.m. bus that leaves from Stroudsburg to the city."

It felt good to laugh. "You thought of everything, huh?"

He walked her out to her car and leaned on the open window frame after she got behind the wheel.

"Thank you. I don't know what's gonna happen, but I'm glad we talked."

She reached out and squeezed his arm. "Some people never get a first chance at happiness. You've been given a second chance at love. The choice is yours whether to accept it." With that, she started the engine and drove off. Aubrey watched her taillights disappear.

For the rest of the evening, he grappled with himself. He desired Oliver. He wanted him. And, he realized with startling clarity, he loved Oliver. Was there a measure of guilt because of

Lisa? Perhaps. She was his first love. But humans had a wonderful capacity to love again. To pull themselves out of the blackest of nights to the clarity of the light. Falling in love again didn't mean forgetting the past. Who he was today had been shaped by all his yesterdays and allowed him to move forward. Create tomorrows. Before he closed his eyes, he set his alarm for five a.m. He had a bus to catch.

---

HE HAD NO DAMN IDEA WHERE HE WAS OR WHERE HE WAS GOING AS he held the paper with Oliver's address in a death grip. Aubrey stepped out of the Port Authority Bus Terminal and stopped. How the ever-loving hell was he supposed to find Oliver? People jostled him from both sides, and he quickly stepped out of the way, careful not to trip over the homeless man sprawled in the corner.

His heart pounded as he strode down the avenue. Tall buildings pushed skyward, and strange smells assailed him. He wrinkled his nose. Carts with big signs proclaiming HALAL sold all kinds of chicken and fish and rice. Some even had goat. He'd eaten the two peanut-butter sandwiches he'd thrown together that morning on the bus and had bought a cup of not-so-great coffee at the station. His stomach turned.

He knew he should get a taxi, but after all that time cramped on a bus, Aubrey decided it couldn't hurt to stretch his legs and walk. With a determined set to his jaw, he joined the teeming mass of people and walked down Ninth Avenue. After a few blocks, the crowd thinned out somewhat, and he took a deep breath.

"Looking for a show?" A young man handed him a card. "Live girls. Just down the block. Go on." He grinned, and Aubrey shook his head and tried to hand him back the card.

"Uh, no thanks."

"Keep it. They're there all day and night. You get special admission with it."

Aubrey folded the card and put it in his pocket. Half a block later, another man stepped in front of him. "Come inside. Beautiful dancers, all for you. Only ten dollars." Aubrey tried to walk past, but the man stuck into his shirt pocket a card with a woman naked from the waist up.

*What the hell?*

Aubrey almost laughed out loud, imagining the men's faces if he told them he was on his way to meet his male lover.

When after two more blocks, three additional people had stopped him, one for bus tours and two more for "gentleman's clubs," Aubrey had lost patience.

"Excuse me, sir. Can I talk to you a moment?"

"No, sorry. I'm not interested in seeing your naked women dancers."

"Uh, okay, but I wanted to know if you were willing to sign this petition to stop fracking upstate and save the fish and wildlife."

Now that he'd stopped and looked closer, he could see the Greenpeace T-shirt the man wore. His cheeks burned. "Um, yeah, sure," he mumbled, took the pen the young, wispy-bearded man handed him, and threw him an embarrassed smile. "Have a nice day." The light turned red, and Aubrey hustled across the street, anxious to get away.

He spotted a coffee shop and decided to sit for a moment and get his wits about him. He ordered and sat, his hands wrapped around the cup, debating whether to call Oliver. Happening to glance over at the man sitting next to him, he noticed there were at least half a dozen other people sitting around, staring at laptops. Back on the farm, at this time he and the others would be knee-deep in the fields. What did these people do all day?

The man caught his eye and smiled. Surprised, Aubrey

smiled back. "Good morning." He couldn't help it. If someone looked at him, he was taught to acknowledge them.

"Good morning." The man tapped a few keys, then stopped again. "Ughh, so frustrating." He threw his hands up in the air. "I've been working on this scene for hours, and I can't get it right."

Impressed, Aubrey had to ask. "You're a writer?"

The man nodded eagerly. "Yes. Well. I guess. I'm working on my first novel."

"What's it about?" Aubrey sipped his coffee, wondering how people could sit all day in coffee shops.

"It's a coming-of-age story of a young woman in the sixties."

Confused, Aubrey cocked his head. The man couldn't be any older than twenty-five. Aubrey had pants in his closet older than him. "Oh, uh, sounds interesting."

"Thanks. I know if I could just get this scene right, it'll make the whole book. I've written it five times already. I have to have it done today before I go to work."

"What do you do?"

"I'm a waiter. I mean, I'm an author, obviously, but I have to pay the bills. Once I'm published, I can give that up and write full-time."

Aubrey had a sneaking suspicion it wasn't as easy as the man made it seem, but what did he know? "Well, maybe you should leave it and come back to it."

The man shook his head. "Oh, no. I'm very linear. Plus, I had my cards done the other day, and she said I was about to have a breakthrough that would change my life."

"Cards?"

"My tarot cards."

Well, okay. Time to leave. He downed the contents of his cup, and giving the man a half-hearted smile, walked away. How the hell could all these people afford to drink five-dollar cups of coffee when they didn't have a job? He'd never understand it.

Fortified by the caffeine, Aubrey knew he had to get to Oliver's. He stepped outside, and like he'd seen people do on television, stuck out his hand. Within a few seconds, a yellow cab pulled up. He gave the driver Oliver's address, and they took off.

The scenery flashed by him, but he didn't stare out the window to see the sights. Oliver filled his head. Would he be happy to see him, or did he want to get away from the slow pace of the farm and come back to the electricity of the city? Aubrey chewed the inside of his cheek in frustration and not a little bit of fear.

The cab pulled up front, and Aubrey fumbled for a few moments, figuring out the credit-card machine. He got out and stood on the sidewalk, gathering his nerves, then set his jaw, walked inside, pressed the button next to Oliver's name, and waited.

"Yes?" The tinny voice sputtered, but Aubrey recognized Oliver.

"It's me. Aubrey. Can I come up?"

"What? Aubrey? Where are you? What the hell."

"Ollie, let me in. We need to talk."

"I fucking don't believe this."

The buzzer sounded, and Aubrey pushed open the glass front door and walked to where he remembered the elevators being. He took one up to the twentieth floor, where he found a very agitated Oliver waiting for him when the doors opened.

"Hey." He stepped out of the elevator car, and Oliver began to bombard him with questions.

"Hey? Is that all you have to say? Hey? What're you doing here? How did you get here? What—"

Aubrey couldn't think of any other way to shut Oliver up but kiss him. Peace stole over him when their lips met, and Aubrey sighed, content for the first time that day.

"I think I should be asking the questions. Why did you leave? Are you coming back?"

Oliver took his hand. "Let's go inside. I don't need to put on a show for the neighbors."

Once they entered Oliver's apartment, Aubrey sat straight-backed on the sofa. "I don't get it. Why'd you take off? If you're having second thoughts about us..." He shrugged, hoping his voice didn't give away his pain. "You can tell me. I'm a big boy."

"No, it's not that. I have my annual checkup with my doctor."

"You're okay, right? You feel good?"

"Yeah. I'm good."

At Oliver's reassurance, Aubrey smiled. "So why didn't you say that, though? You had dinner with your sister, and all I know is that the next day you disappear and come back here."

"I'm sorry." Oliver did seem genuinely regretful, but Aubrey sensed there was something else.

"There's more, am I right?"

"Yeah. I have to figure out what to do with this place. Whether I'm going to keep it, or rent it, or—"

"Or move back?" How Aubrey managed to say the words when his heart felt like exploding, he didn't know.

"I don't want to. But I guess it depends on if there's a reason for me to stay. I don't know how I fit in with your life. Am I staying for being Oliver? Or am I a stand-in for Lisa?"

The ball was in his court, and Aubrey knew he had to find the right words. But as he struggled, he discovered speaking from the heart was the only way he knew. "It was like the blackest of nights had settled on me, and I couldn't get out from under it. Losing Lisa like that with no warning almost killed me, and I never thought I'd fall in love again. I didn't want to. Then you came."

"With a part of Lisa inside me."

"Yes. I won't deny it was amazing to think she'd given you life. And it's equally horrifying to know that if she hadn't died, you wouldn't be sitting here. But." He captured Oliver's gaze with his own. "If for one moment you think I want you because of Lisa's heart, then I've made a mistake in not telling you sooner how I felt."

"How do you feel?"

"Alive. Happy." He swallowed down his fear and framed Oliver's face in his hands. "In love. I love you, Oliver. Not a piece of you. Not simply for your heart. I love all of you. Because of how you make *my* heart feel."

Aubrey brushed their lips together, and Oliver shivered.

"I left here not knowing what would happen if and when we met. I hadn't been so scared since my first day of law school."

"You? Afraid? Why?"

Oliver nuzzled into the palm of his hand. "I never expected to find a place that would bring me such peace from morning to night. I never expected to want to put down roots in a little town in the middle of nowhere. I never expected to meet someone I can't stop thinking about, someone who makes me happy every morning when I see him."

Aubrey wondered why Oliver remained so solemn; then he smiled, and hope, like a flower, unfurled through his chest.

"Tell me."

"I never expected to fall in love."

Joy spread through Aubrey, but he had to make sure. "You love me?" At Oliver's nod, Aubrey seized him around the neck and held him tight. "Then it's gonna be okay. Everything's going to be fine."

35
---

# OLIVER

Oliver was still flabbergasted when he woke up in Aubrey's arms in his apartment in the city. The man had come all the way to New York on a bus to profess his feelings, and Oliver had to admit it felt like some sort of dream. It was everything he'd wanted and needed, and now that it had happened, he probably should've pinched himself to make sure it was actually real.

Afterward, Aubrey had made love to him with a tenderness he'd never experienced before, and the pure emotions on his face had made Oliver shatter all too soon. They lay in bed naked and talked for hours, it seemed, about everything under the sun, before leaving the apartment to have dinner in a quiet corner booth at an Italian eatery.

Aubrey seemed more confident his second time in the city, no longer deer-in-headlights so much as open-but-still-guarded as they passed through crowded street corners with their fingers connected some of the time. Then, in lieu of a packed and noisy bar, they slipped inside a theater showing the latest action movie. Such a simple act, sitting together in the dark with popcorn between them, but it meant everything as well. By the time they got back to Oliver's apartment and tumbled into bed, they were wrung out, most likely from the combination of summer heat and their heightened emotions. Oliver had fallen asleep soundly, his head on Aubrey's chest.

"How about some breakfast?" he said against Aubrey's throat when he finally felt him stir.

"Bagels?" Aubrey replied in a croaky voice.

Oliver smiled into his skin. "Is someone starting to have favorites?"

"Maybe," he said, kissing his head. Then his fingers reached for his chin and their gazes connected. "I'm thinking you should keep this apartment."

Oliver's voice hitched. "You are?"

Aubrey nodded. "You love the city. It's in your blood. Plus, this place is paid for, and like you said earlier, it's an investment."

"All good points. But I'm still not sure..."

Aubrey readjusted his grip, his fingers sliding to Oliver's nape, his lips to his cheek. "As long as you promise not to use it to run away from me again."

"I promise," Oliver replied, his pulse pounding as Aubrey brushed their lips together. The man was surprising him at every turn.

He tangled their legs beneath the covers. "What would I use it for, exactly?"

"For us," Aubrey stated simply, and it made Oliver's heart soar. "The farm slows down after the New Year, and everyone takes a breather before the spring rush. There are things to maintain and plan for, of course, but..."

"I didn't realize, I guess," he mumbled, imagining the two of them hunkering down in the winter. He had so many questions, like what that meant for the bakery, but they had time.

"And, I've never seen the city at Christmastime." Aubrey's eyes crinkled at the corners as he gave him one of those rare, intimate smiles.

He thought about his recent conversation with his family about the holidays.

"Would you by chance be interested in spending a day with my dad and Jennifer's family for Thanksgiving?"

"I'd like that," Aubrey replied. "Though I'm not sure what your sister thinks of me."

Oliver sighed and rolled over to stare at the ceiling. "She was only looking out for me. She gets nervous...since the surgery."

"That's something I can understand," Aubrey replied as he sat up to stretch. Hooking his knee over Oliver's hip, he straddled him, eyes softening as he stared down at Oliver. "Would you like me to go to the appointment with you? I can wait outside or in the—"

"I would love that." Oliver's throat was thick as his fingers raked through the downy hair at Aubrey's stomach. His cock lay flaccid yet heavy on his abdomen, and the coarse hairs on his legs tickled Oliver's thighs. The man was stunning inside and out, and he loved feeling the weight of Aubrey pressed against him.

Oliver freely looked his fill; he might never get used to having the privilege.

"I haven't asked you. Guess I've been a bit scared," Aubrey said, seeming to swallow past a lump in his throat. "Are there complications from your surgery?"

"Always going to be some risks, especially with my immune system," Oliver admitted as Aubrey's fingers absently traced his scar. "But so far I've been pretty damned healthy. I'm not sure how long Lisa's heart will pump for me, but I also don't want to become a statistic. I want to enjoy life for as long as I'm able."

Suddenly Aubrey dipped his head to kiss the center of his scar, then lay on top of him, his head landing in the crook of his neck. Oliver's fingers tangled in his hair as a small sob tore from Aubrey's throat. It startled Oliver, and his fingers stilled. "Babe, what's wrong?"

"Fuck," Aubrey replied, sniffling into his neck. "I'm terrified of losing you, but I'm just as scared of having any regrets. Of never showing you how much you mean to me. How much I want to share my life with you."

"Then be with me," Oliver murmured in his ear. "Be all in. I want you, Aubrey, so fucking much."

Aubrey lifted his head, their watery gazes connecting as something solemn passed between them. Hope or maybe a promise of what was to come. Aubrey kissed him hard and bruising, teasing his lips open with needy flicks of his tongue.

He didn't know how long they stayed that way, mouths connected, arms and legs tangled, hearts beating as one. Oliver felt overwhelmed by his desperate, heady kisses. Like he was trying to seal their mouths, to get beneath his skin to his very bones.

Oliver fucking loved this man, so he gave back as good as he got, his fingers tugging at his scalp as he moaned into his mouth, their stiff cocks rutting until they came in near unison against Oliver's stomach.

"Damn, you're so sexy." Aubrey dragged his mouth away and stared down at Oliver with a sated sigh. "I am all in, Oliver. On one condition."

Oliver cocked an eyebrow. "What's that?"

He lifted his head and glanced around Oliver's apartment, his gaze seeming to land on the gray walls and modern fixtures. "Help me renovate the bedroom. Maybe a new paint color and furniture? Finally hang those movie posters?"

"I can do that," Oliver replied with a chuckle, wondering what had brought this on.

"I know you just rented a house and you love it there, but... stay over more?" Aubrey continued. "No pressure, only...I want to wake up with you as much as possible."

Oliver's eyes stung as he looked over the earnest man. He nodded, his throat thick.

After they showered and visited the nearby bagel shop, they

hopped on the subway for his doctor's appointment in Midtown. Aubrey sat in the waiting room with a magazine as he walked out with a clean bill of health. His meds didn't even need any adjustments this time. It felt fucking amazing to have Aubrey waiting there for him.

"You want a ride home, or you going to catch the bus?" Oliver quipped once they got to street level again.

"Ass." Aubrey barked out a laugh. "You *better* drive me home —but only after a slice of pepperoni?"

Oliver rolled his eyes. "I'll make a city boy out of you yet."

"Don't count on it," Aubrey grumbled as they began walking toward a place Oliver had in mind.

On the drive home, Oliver remembered promising his sister an update, so he dialed her cell.

"Well?" she asked after the first ring.

"All checked out okay," he replied, and he could hear her breathe out in relief. "You're on speaker by the way, and I have a passenger with me."

"You do?" she asked, and he could tell her curiosity was piqued. "Is it a tall and handsome man who happens to run a farm?"

In his side view, he could see the flush crawling across Aubrey's cheeks.

"Hey, Jennifer." Aubrey cleared his throat. "I...I think maybe we got off on the wrong foot."

"No, it's okay—"

"Please. I'd really like to get this out," he replied, and Jennifer grew quiet. "I didn't say things right the day you came to the farm." Aubrey reached for Oliver's hand and entwined their fingers. "Truth is, it wouldn't matter whose heart was inside Oliver's chest, I would've fallen in love with him regardless. He's meant to be in my life, and I...I wouldn't have it any other way."

Oliver choked back his emotions at Aubrey's beautiful declaration as silence descended on the other end of the line. "Jen?" he croaked, afraid she'd gotten disconnected or somehow took something the wrong way. Though he didn't see how.

"Sorry," she said after another moment. "I'm too busy swooning over here. I'm thrilled for both of you."

"Well, that's a first, Aubrey," Oliver mused as he grinned at the man beside him. "Rendering Jennifer speechless is not an easy feat."

"Hey, now!" she grumbled, and they all laughed.

When they pulled up to the property an hour later, Oliver's heart unfurled as he saw the farm with new eyes. The summer flowers were in full bloom, and the white gardenias' scent tickled his nose. The foreseeable future surrounded him on all sides, and it looked as bright and promising as that first light of dawn on the farm.

"Home sweet home," Aubrey whispered as he leaned over and kissed his temple.

Oliver sighed and felt the words tethering the last remnants of his heart together and embedding deeply—to his very soul.

# EPILOGUE

## Aubrey

THE SMELL OF APPLES GREETED AUBREY AS HE ENTERED THE bakery. "Delivery. Can I get a little help here?"

Taking care to wipe his floury hands off first, Oliver held the door while Aubrey carried in a basket of apples. "Oh, good. I was hoping you were coming with some more. We're almost out."

"I see the way it is now." He set the basket on the wide prep table. "You only want me for my apples."

"Well, it is a perk of sleeping with the boss."

Aubrey picked up an apple from the basket. "I meant to talk with you about that."

The smile on Oliver's face faded. "Uh-oh. Why don't I like the sound of that?"

"Oh, I think you'll like what I gotta say, but not here and now, when anyone can bust in on us. Dinner at six thirty?"

"Yeah," Oliver said, starting to sort the apples. "I put out a beef stew in the slow cooker this morning before I left."

"Good. And maybe a pie or an apple crisp for dessert?" Aubrey inhaled the delicious cinnamon-vanilla perfume in the air. "Or whatever you have baking. It smells amazing."

"Apple crisp. I have a small one for us, separate from the ones I'm making for the bakery." His warm gaze held Aubrey's. "I know it's your favorite."

"Second favorite." Giving a quick look over Oliver's shoulder to make sure no one was around, Aubrey kissed him, sliding his tongue into Oliver's mouth. He tasted of crisp apple and sugar. "You're my number one."

The dreamy expression he loved to see spread over Oliver's face. "You're such a romantic."

"Don't tell anyone. I'll deny everything." He kissed Oliver's lips one more time. "See you at six thirty."

He left the bakery through the back, whistling a made-up tune. It was a beautiful fall day. A hint of wind in the air nipped at his cheeks, but the sun still shone bright and strong. It seemed almost criminal to sit inside, so Aubrey took his laptop and stack of paperwork and sat on the porch with a pitcher of iced tea and caught up on the farm's business side. As he'd expected to see, the bakery was running at a profit.

The sun had begun to sink on the horizon when he closed the laptop, and the earlier pleasant coolness had sharpened to a chill. Fall had arrived, and the orange glow of the setting sun reminded him of the pumpkins they'd begun collecting for sale. Maybe, he mused, watching Oliver leave the bakery and lock the door behind him, maybe he should think about having a pick-your-own pumpkin patch for families. It could bring in more revenue, and it would be nice to have kids around the farm. He could even throw in a hayride or a tractor ride.

Oliver's lean, rangy form approached the house, and all thoughts of the farm fled his mind. Over the past several months since he and Oliver had returned from New York, they'd appeared together at the

Labor Day parade in town as well as at the Harvest Festival. They'd had dinner not only at Last Call, but at other restaurants around town, and had gone to the movies and outdoor concerts. They might not have made a public statement or engaged in outward displays of affection, but Aubrey assumed people suspected there was something deeper than friendship between them.

Not that he cared what other people thought, but the time had come to, as he liked to say, put his money where his mouth was.

"Hey, aren't you cold?" Oliver rubbed his arms. "I'm chilly and I've got a jacket on. You're in bare sleeves."

"I'm tough. I can take it."

Oliver rolled his eyes. "Okay, Mr. Tough Guy. Well, can we move it inside before I freeze *my* ass off? Besides," he said with a gleam in his eyes, "I need a beer and a kiss, neither of which I'm going to get out here on this porch."

The laptop went on the rickety wooden table next to him, and Aubrey stood, then slid his hand through the wavy hair at the nape of Oliver's neck to pull him close. Their lips hovered, and Aubrey could tell by Oliver's wide eyes that he'd shocked him into silence.

"Beer's inside, but I'm right here." He captured Oliver's mouth and kissed him softly at first, then with increasing fervor. His tongue slid inside and played with Oliver's, and Aubrey could feel him tremble beneath his hands. They pressed closer until Oliver's body molded into his.

"Aubrey, what's this about?" Oliver gazed up at him with confusion. "I thought we weren't doing this in public."

Keeping his hand on the back on Oliver's neck, Aubrey grabbed his laptop. "Let's go inside and have those beers. All I'm gonna say right now is, I'll be damned if anyone's gonna make me feel like I can't do what I want in my own house, on my own land."

"Okay," Oliver said, but Aubrey could tell he wasn't convinced.

They entered the house, and Aubrey switched on the lights. "Kitchen?" he said to Oliver, who nodded.

"Yeah. I need to check on the slow cooker."

The aroma from the beef stew made Aubrey's stomach growl. The house smelled like a home again, not of dead air with loneliness waiting in every dark corner. Oliver had brought warmth and light back into his life. And Aubrey loved him.

Once Oliver had made certain the food was ready, he turned off the slow cooker, went to the refrigerator, and took out two bottles. They sat at the wide, wooden farm table in the kitchen, and Oliver slid a beer across the table, twisted the top off his, and took a deep swallow. "So, that was nice...outside, I mean. That kiss."

"I know," Aubrey smirked, then sobered. "I want...I'm hoping...dammit, this is harder than I thought." He took a gulp of beer for courage.

"What is it? I'm not sure what you're trying to get at."

"Ever since we came back from New York, you've been staying over here most nights, aside from the occasional weekend when I stayed at yours. I don't know how you'd feel about it, or if you want your own place still, but I was thinking maybe..." He hesitated only a moment. "I'd love it if you'd move in here. With me. Live here with me."

The hitch of Oliver's indrawn breath was the only sound in the room.

"You're asking me to live with you. As your lover."

At his solemn nod, Oliver's eyes welled up. "Aubrey. How could you know that's all I wanted but was afraid to talk about?"

"Afraid? Why?"

Oliver focused on his beer bottle and made wet rings on the table with it. "I didn't want you to think I was pushing. It's still so new. But every time I go back home, I feel less and less like that's where I'm meant to be."

"That's because you were meant to be here. With me." Unable to keep his emotions in check, Aubrey's voice shook, but he didn't care. If he'd learned one thing, it was that life was too damned short not to live it and tell people how you feel. You never knew if you were going to have another chance. "Move in with me. Be with me. I can't imagine not having you in my life. Not anymore."

Oliver's eyes shone like twin lamps. "Me either. And yeah, I'd like that. At least I'll never be late to open the bakery."

"That's another thing I'd like to talk about. The bakery."

"Oh? What about it? It must be doing well—we sell out almost every day." Having finished his beer, Oliver stood, put the empty in the recycling basket, took a bottle of wine from the rack, and uncorked it. "I was thinking of maybe freezing some of the pies and selling them for people to take home to use at a later date."

"See? I love that about you. You're always thinking. Innovating. So." Aubrey set his bottle to the side. "I want to sell you the bakery. You and Cassie. Figure it out between you, how to split it up. I figure you two are the ones who deserve the profit, not me."

The silence between them was broken only by the jingling of Duke's tags as he padded into the room and lay down next to the table. Oliver stood frozen, his eyes wide as he stared at Aubrey.

"You want to sell me Lisa's bakery?"

"No. I'm selling you *your* bakery. Yours and Cassie's. You two are what made it come back from nothing. So what do you say?"

Oliver set the bottle back down without pouring a glass. "I'll have to talk to Cassie."

"I won't let her turn it down. If she needs a loan to buy her share, she can get it from me at a rate she can afford."

The happiness on Oliver's face matched his own. "Then for me, it's a yes. Yes to the bakery." He circled the table to stand by

Aubrey and wrap his arms around his shoulders and kiss his neck. "And yes to moving in here. Yes, yes, yes."

"I like when you're so agreeable. I want to hear that later on tonight."

Oliver's lips teased his ear. "The stew will keep. And I'm feeling very agreeable right now."

Aubrey stood abruptly, his chair teetering on its back legs before righting itself. "Let's go, then."

Hand in hand and laughing, they took the stairs two at a time.

THE HOLIDAY SEASON HAD BEGUN IN HEARTSVILLE, AND IT SEEMED like the mingled Thanksgiving and Christmas decorations had sprung up overnight. Oliver moved in at the end of October, after a deal for the bakery had been worked out. He and Cassie were co-owners, each owning a forty-eight percent share, with Aubrey owning the other four percent in lieu of them paying him rent. Aubrey had spoken to one of his supermarket distributors, and a plan was in the works to have Oliver and Cassie's pies in an exclusive deal with the chain.

The farm was running smoothly and heading into the Christmas season, and the acres of trees Aubrey had ready for customers were healthy and green as far as he could see. They had been invited to spend the upcoming holidays with Oliver's family in New York. Oliver wanted him to meet his father and his sister's family, and though he was nervous, Aubrey was looking forward to it. Professionally, Aubrey was in a good place. Personally, he couldn't be happier.

He and Oliver lugged the paint cans up the stairs. His old bedroom set had been disassembled and put back together in one of the guest rooms, and then they'd laid the new flooring down in their bedroom and let it set. They stood in the doorway, surveying the empty room.

"Looks good in here." Aubrey unwrapped the paint tarp and spread it out, then threw a roll of painter's tape at Oliver. "Let's get started. They said they were delivering the new furniture either tomorrow or Saturday, so we need to get this done today."

"Okay, boss."

He allowed himself a quick smile. "Sorry if I'm barking orders."

Oliver crossed the room and put his arms around his waist. "Are you okay with this? Really? I know you said you wanted to redo the bedroom, but tell me how you're feeling."

The comforting thump of Oliver's heart beat against Aubrey's chest, and his throat constricted. "I feel like I'm getting onto a roller coaster and I don't know where it's going to take me. But as long as I have you along for the ride, next to me, I'm okay. We're okay."

His phone rang, and he let go of Oliver to answer it.

*Lisa's sister.*

"Uh, Chelsea? Hello."

Oliver, who'd left his side to start painting, returned and put a hand on his arm.

"Yeah, Aubrey. I'm here with my parents."

"Everything okay? They aren't sick, are they?" Much as they hadn't been kind to him that last time, he'd never want anything bad to happen to them.

"No, nothing like that. I was visiting them today, and...well... dammit. Mom asked me to call."

"Okay." Bewildered, he gave Oliver a shrug. He had no idea what they wanted.

"I'm never going to stop missing my sister. But I can admit now that the accident wasn't your fault."

He expelled a harsh breath. "Thank you. You know I would've done anything for her. Anything."

"I know. Mom does too. Daddy's still struggling, though. Lisa was his baby. It's hard for him to let her go."

Oliver rubbed his back, and he grabbed him close, needing his stability and strength to keep him upright.

"I-I know. I'm not forgetting what was. But I can't live in darkness anymore. I did for two years, and it almost killed me too."

"Is that man, Oliver...is he helping you?"

It would be the first time admitting their relationship to anyone outside of their close circle, but if they ever did decide to visit, they needed to know. "Yes, he is. He's, uh, moved in with me."

"I see," she said, her voice slightly shaky. "Well, so...good luck. We wanted to call to wish you a happy holiday."

Nothing could've surprised him more than this exchange, but as he stood in his empty bedroom, it seemed appropriate that the tentative reconciliation had begun. There'd be no wiping the slate clean of their shared past, still filled with the pain of loss, but now maybe there was the hope of a future.

"Thank you," he whispered, not trusting himself to speak. "Thank you. And the same to you, Donna, and Morty. Please. Don't be strangers."

"Thanks, Aubrey. Bye."

The phone went dark, and Oliver took it from his hand and led him over to the window seat. "You okay? I caught a bit of the conversation. Do you feel like talking about it?"

"Yeah. It's good." And as he spoke, he realized it was. "It's going to be fine. Chelsea said they don't really blame me anymore. Her father still can't say it really, but it's understandable. He and Lisa were very close."

"That's wonderful. I'm thrilled for you and them. It's never good to carry so much hurt inside."

"I don't hurt anymore. You did that for me. Took away my hurt." He ran a hand down Oliver's arm and toyed with his fingers. "Gave me something to live for."

Oliver raised their entwined hands to his lips. "From the start you were familiar. Like I was coming home. I can't wait to get on that roller coaster with you. I have a feeling it's going to be a hell of a ride."

With the sunlight streaming in through the windows, Aubrey kissed Oliver, his lips warm and loving and tasting of forever. "Buckle up, then, and hold on tight."

# THANK YOU FOR READING FIRST LIGHT!

We hope you enjoyed it!
Reviews help other readers find books. So if you feel compelled
to leave a sentence or two on a retail site, we appreciate it!
Read on to view a short excerpt from LAST CALL, the first book
in the Heartsville series.

# ABOUT CHRISTINA LEE

Once upon a time, **Christina Lee** lived in New York City and was a wardrobe stylist. She spent her days getting in cabs, shopping for photo shoots, eating amazing food, and drinking coffee at her favorite hangouts.

Now she lives in the Midwest with her husband and son—her two favorite guys. She's been a clinical social worker and a special education teacher. But it wasn't until she wrote a weekly column for the local newspaper that she realized she could turn the fairy tales inside her head into the reality of writing fiction.

She's addicted to lip balm, coffee, and kissing. Because everything is better with kissing. She writes MM Contemporary as well as Adult and New Adult Romance. She believes in happily-ever-afters for all, so reading and writing romance for everybody under the rainbow helps quench her soul.

# OTHER TITLES BY CHRISTINA LEE

Co-written with Nyrae Dawn (AKA Riley Hart):

Free Fall series:
Touch the Sky
Chase the Sun
Paint the Stars

Spinoff from Free Fall series:
Living Out Loud

Standalones with Riley Hart:

Ever After: A Gay Fairy Tale
Of Sunlight and Stardust

M/F books that can all standalone:
All of You
Before You Break
Whisper to Me
Promise Me This
Two of Hearts
Three Sacred Words
Twelve Truths and a Lie
When We Met Anthology

## ABOUT FELICE STEVENS

Felice Stevens has always been a romantic at heart. She believes that while life is tough, there is always a happy ending just around the corner. Her characters have to work for it, however. Like life in NYC, nothing comes easy and that includes love. She lives in New York City with her husband and two children. Her day begins with a lot of caffeine and ends with a glass (or two) of red wine. She's retired from practicing law and now daydreams of a time when she can sit by a beach and write beautiful stories of men falling in love. Although there are bound to be a few bumps along the way, a Happily Ever After is always guaranteed.

You can join my reader group— Felice's Fun House to get all the scoop on what I'm up to, along with sneak peeks, giveaways and kisses...lots of kisses.

Subscribe to my Newsletter and get a FREE BOOK!

# OTHER TITLES BY FELICE STEVENS

Through Hell and Back Series:
*A Walk Through Fire*
*After the Fire*
*Embrace the Fire*

Memories Series:
*Memories of the Heart*
*One Step Further*
*The Greatest Gift*

Breakfast Club Series:
*Beyond the Surface*
*Betting on Forever*
*Second to None*
*What Lies Between Us*
*A Holiday to Remember: A Second to None Short Story*
*Hot Date: A Beyond the Surface Short Story*

Rescued Heart Series:
*Rescued*

*Reunited*

Together Series:
*Learning to Love*
*The Way to His Heart*
*All or Nothing*

Soulmates Series:
*The Arrangement*
*One Call Away*
*Perfect*
*Don't I Know You: An Arrangement Short Story*

The Man-Up Series:
*Austin*
*Rhoades—Undeniable*
*Frankie—Unforgettable*
*Cort—Unbreakable*
*James—Uncontrollable*

Other:
*Please Don't Go*
*The Shape of You*
*Under the Boardwalk*
*Last Call* (with Christina Lee)
*First Light* (with Christina Lee)

**BOOK #1 IN THE HEARTSVILLE SERIES**

Quinn Monahan and Grayson Page have been friends since high school. Despite their differences, they've been there for each other through thick and thin. Opening Last Call together, a bar tucked away in the small town of Heartsville, PA, seemed a natural progression—even if it makes it harder to live with the secret longing they've always had for each other.

Hoping to score an easy buck and a place to sleep, unemployed circus roadie Emery Woods chooses Last Call to run a few bets and enjoy a decent beer before moving on. When he finds himself stranded, the unexpected kindness Quinn and Gray show him leads to temporary work and a couch to lay his head. Sensing unresolved history between Quinn and Gray, he squashes his immediate draw to the men, opting to avoid trouble. But as days turn into weeks, denying the attraction is easier said than done.

When the men finally give in to the simmering sexual tension, it quickly develops into more than a way to pass the lonely nights. And as they begin to lean on each other for emotional support, it becomes nearly impossible to think of one man without the other two. But while Quinn and Gray are afraid to cross the line of friendship between them, Emery fears once they do, he'll quickly be cast aside. A real family is finally within their grasp, but unless the men can learn to trust each other, they just might miss their hearts' last call home.

# AN EXCERPT FROM LAST CALL

## CHAPTER ONE

## Quinn

I watched him enter Last Call, eyes darting side to side, and my antennae zinged to full alert. Not only because I'd never seen him before but because the wariness rolled off him in waves.

Keeping his head down, he made his way to the bar, found a seat, and raised his gaze to meet mine. I had to suck in a breath; the depth of loneliness and despair in those cat-green eyes hit me like a punch in the gut. It sent warning signals clanging through my brain, but my body shut them down in favor of my heart, which started beating faster. If he were here, Gray would be elbowing me in the ribs, already sensing my need to reach out and take care of the stranger.

*Yeah, he looks like trouble in a whole lot of sexy packaging, but damned if I know what to do about it.*

"What can I get you?" My voice huffed out, unexpectedly soft, leaving me a bit breathless with uncertainty. He looked skittish and weary, and I wanted to see him smile.

*Get a grip, Quinn.*

"I'll have a Bud." He smoothed out the bills laying under his palm.

I slid him a cold bottle across the bar but didn't walk away. Instead, I stood there and watched him take that first thirsty swallow, the strong cords of his neck standing out. This was nuts. I couldn't stand there watching him. Yet I did exactly that.

"Thanks." He gave me a faint smile that didn't reach his eyes. "Long drive."

"Oh? Where're you from?" The rag in my hand gave me the perfect opportunity to stay and talk to him while I pretended to clean the bar top.

"Here and there." His lips tightened, and I sensed a story but not the willingness to talk.

"Have a place to stay tonight?"

The guy stopped drinking and placed the bottle back on the bar, making wet rings with the bottom and not meeting my eyes. "Uh, yeah, sure. I found one down the road a bit."

*Sure, you did.* The nearest motel was over ten miles away. No way did he happen to wander in here for a beer with a few crumpled dollar bills I'd bet were his last.

"Yeah? What brings you here?"

"What are you, the CIA?" Green Eyes huffed out a nervous laugh. "What's with all the questions? I came in for a beer, is all, not to tell my life story."

Instead of getting angry at him, like Gray would, I wanted to know *why* he was so skittish. Was he running away from something? Or maybe someone? I doubted it was from the cops as he wasn't trying to hide his face. Maybe he split with his wife and was starting a whole new life.... I had to chuckle at the fantasy I'd built up around this stranger. I could hear Gray lecturing me to leave the guy alone and let him drink his beer in peace.

I scanned his long, rangy body, noticing his raggedy clothes and hair badly in need of a trim, yet...something about him was mighty appealing. Knowing further questions might get me into trouble, I put on my most charming smile, the one I had used to wheedle clients into signing with my advertising firm and not the competition, and tried a different approach.

"I don't mean to pry. We don't get many strangers here, so when someone new shows up, it's almost like a celebration of sorts. I'm sorry if I pushed."

Green Eyes weighed my words solemnly like he was trying to figure out if I was pulling his leg or had something to gain by him giving up any information.

"Uh, well, I'm not the partying type. All I wanted was to find a place to sit for a while and have a cold one."

"You got it. I didn't mean to get so personal." I withdrew to the other end of the bar to stack the glasses but still kept an eye on him. He never looked up once, just kept sipping his beer, making it last.

The door opened, and Gray walked in. I immediately knew he'd tell me I was being an idiot for spending my time thinking about some ragtag stranger who'd probably never come back after today, so I prepared myself.

"Hey, did you meet with the new distributor?"

A twinkle lit Gray's normally serious brown eyes. "I sure did. He thought he'd put one over on us by changing the price on the imported beer, but I pointed out the error of his ways."

That was why Gray handled the supplier side of the business. He trusted no one, and that made him the perfect one to hammer out the deals.

In addition to handling the books and paperwork, which Gray hated, I was the friendly face people opened up to behind the bar. I loved listening to their stories and offering advice. Too many years had been wasted with me listening to my father tell me the people didn't matter, only the bottom line.

Everyone wondered how Gray and I managed to stay friends all these years since high school. They didn't know how we helped each other, me leaning on Gray when I could no longer take my father's criticism and got myself fired from the family firm, and Gray confiding in me his fear of losing everything yet again when his company began laying off employees. Each of us holding on to the other when we came out to our families. People didn't understand how much he meant to me.

I loved him. He was as close to me as a brother. And sometimes I wondered if there could ever be anything more, but since I knew Gray only had the success of the business on his mind, I wasn't one to push him. Other guys were happy to share my bed, especially when I treated them to a nice dinner beforehand.

"Who's the guy?" Gray's nudge woke me from my musing.

"Hmm? Oh, he's passing through, he said. Couldn't get much more out of him. But I sense a sad story there."

With his typical caution, Gray cast a hard, assessing glance at Green Eyes, who remained hunched over his bottle of Bud, not paying attention to us.

"You would. All I see is a drifter who's probably gonna try and stiff us out of a beer. Make sure he pays and doesn't run up a tab, then sneak out without paying."

*Oh Gray, not everyone is out to give you the shaft or hurt you.*

But instead of voicing what was in my heart, I pretend-glared at my best friend. "I'm not an idiot. I've been keeping an eye on him, just so you know."

"Yeah?" Gray lazed against the bar, broad arms crossed while a devilish smile curved his lips. I loved seeing him so happy; it made my heart beat faster, and I couldn't help but smile back. "It wouldn't have to do with the fact that he has a nice ass, would it? I could see that as soon as I walked in. Don't do anything stupid, Quinn. That's all I'm saying."

He walked away, and my smile faded while my eyes darted over to Green Eyes. He *did* have a nice ass. And a handsome face to match, under his scruff. Damn Gray and his knowing eyes. To prove him wrong, I walked back over to the guy and kept my voice firm.

"Anything else?"

"Uh, no," he answered, jerked back into awareness that he'd been toying with the empty bottle. "How much?"

"Happy hour price is three dollars."

Green Eyes carefully smoothed out the wrinkled singles and pushed them over to me. "Thanks."

No tip, but I didn't expect one. "We run a happy hour every day from four to seven p.m. Three-dollar beers. You ought to stop by again. If you're still in town, that is."

"Huh? Oh, yeah. I'm not sure."

The spark of interest in his eyes for a moment caught me by surprise before he turned and walked out of the bar, and I once again admired his ass. I knew I'd promised Gray to be careful and not make any rash decisions, but there was something about this green-eyed man that made me think if we ever saw him again, things might never be the same.

57113569R00158

Made in the USA
Middletown, DE
27 July 2019